Praise for Whispers from the Dead

"Whispers from the Dead is my favorite book so far this year!" Unabridged Bookshelf

"I give Whispers from the Dead 5 out of 5! This installment explores how big city problems don't necessarily stay in the big city...it makes for a steamy and seductive read." Bewitched Bookworms

"LOVED this book! This book gives you everything..." kids buying illegal narcotics, revenge burnings, overdoses, secrets, lies, kidnapping and several shootings," and all in one northern touristy Amish community." Curling Up With a Good Book

"Whispers from the Dead is a success!" Her Book Thoughts

"Karen Ann Hopkins provides a realistic perceptive and her mysteries are unique and thrilling." Lose Time Reading

WHISPERS FROM THE DEAD

Karen Ann Hopkins

ISBN: 150774823X
ISBN 13: 9781507748237

Books by Karen Ann Hopkins

Serenity's Plain Secrets
in reading order
LAMB TO THE SLAUGHTER
WHISPERS FROM THE DEAD
SECRETS IN THE GRAVE
HIDDEN IN PLAIN SIGHT
PAPER ROSES
EVIL IN MY TOWN
UNHOLY GROUND
BLOODY TIES (coming in 2020)
FORBIDDEN WAYS (A romantic companion novel)
SWEET REGRETS (A romantic companion novel)

Wings of War
in reading order
EMBER
GAIA
TEMPEST
ETERNITY

The Temptation Novels
in reading order
TEMPTATION
BELONGING
FOREVER
DEPCEPTION

This one's for you, Opal! You've brought your enthusiasm and the unique perspective of a woman who's lived in both the Amish and English worlds to my writing. I'm always grateful to have you as a critique partner.

ACKNOWLEDGEMENTS

Many thanks go out to G. K. Bradford for once again putting her heart and soul into the edits, and Jenny Zemanek of Seedlings Design, for creating another amazing cover!

As always, much appreciation and love to my five children, Luke, Cole, Lily, Owen and Cora for all the everyday little things.

A huge shout of thanks goes out to my husband, Jay Detzel. If it wasn't for your support and encouragement, I wouldn't be able to follow my imagination…and my dreams. I love you always and forever!

PROLOGUE

November 11, 2010

Hedy walked slowly toward the door. The intensity of the banging on the wood grew with each step she took, grating on her nerves. She blew out a deep breath and shook her head to collect herself as her fingers clenched the old metal door knob.

"Who is it?" Hedy spoke the words calmly. She already knew who it was on the other side of the door. The day of reckoning had finally arrived.

There was a long, quiet pause, and Hedy took the opportunity to readjust her baby daughter, Cacey, on her hip. The pressure of Cacey's little hands twisting into her apron was the solid reality that Hedy needed to give her strength.

"Jotham, why are you banging on my door in the middle of the night?" Hedy scolded loudly. She pressed the side of her face to the narrow gap between the door and its frame, listening for a response.

"I'm sorry, Hedy. I didn't mean to startle you. But we need to talk."

Hedy considered Jotham's contrite tone and suddenly felt sorry for him. She had been waiting for this visit for eleven years and now that the time had finally arrived, she certainly wasn't going to turn the man away. Hedy believed that God had forgiven her sins from all those years ago, and maybe that was enough, but she doubted it. She had to tell Jotham the truth once and for all. The guilt had been chipping away at her soul for far too long. She only prayed that it didn't ruin her beautiful life with Rowan and their five children.

Hedy turned the knob and opened the door just wide enough to say, "Where's your horse?"

"He's tied in the barn. Don't worry, no one saw me. I rode through the back fields all the way here."

Hedy nodded with relief and opened the door wide enough for Jotham to pass through. She took a quick peek out into the darkness to appease her worries. The quarter moon cast just enough light to illuminate the gravel driveway down to the mailbox at the bottom of the hill. The night was especially silent and the puff of her breath on the cold, still air told her that the temperature had dropped considerably since she had waved goodbye to her husband and her four older children some six hours earlier.

Relaxing a little bit further, Hedy eased the door shut and turned to face Jotham. With her chin raised high, she said, "I had an inkling that you would come."

Jotham could only hold Hedy's gaze for a few seconds before he swallowed hard and looked away.

Clearing his throat and taking a whiff of air into his nostrils, he commented, "There's an awful strong smell of gas in here. Are your lines leaking?"

The drastic change of subject from where her thoughts had been startled her and Hedy couldn't help scrunching up her face and replying with irritation, "No more than usual. I don't think it's serious."

"Rowan needs to have the pipes and the furnace looked at straight away. You don't want to mess around with the gas, you know."

Hedy nodded impatiently. "Sure. I'll talk to him about it when he gets back from his trip."

Jotham began fidgeting with the black hat in his hands and said, "So your family got on their way all right today?"

Hedy had just about run out of patience and her raised voice caused Jotham to inadvertently take a step back.

"Why of course they did, and you already know it, or you wouldn't be standing here in my kitchen at this hour." Seeing his wide eyes and flushed skin, Hedy's voice softened a notch as she tried to smooth over her outburst. "I reckon they're all fast asleep at Rowan's sister's place by now. They'll be getting up early tomorrow for that horse sale."

Jotham took the nearest seat at the large oak dining room table. When he was settled, he admitted, "I overheard John and Rowan talking about the change of plans this morning at the mill. Is Cacey feeling any better?"

Instead of the small talk calming Hedy's nerves, it only rattled them even more. She had waited forever to have this conversation and now Jotham was beating around the bush as if he were a schoolboy again. Oh, how Hedy wished that she could be truly angry with the man seated before her. But it was no use. Whether it was her strong faith in the Lord or the fact that Jotham had only just buried his own wife a month earlier, she couldn't bring herself to have any real ill will toward him.

Realizing that this was the first time in many years that she and Jotham were pretty much alone—a suckling babe certainly didn't count—Hedy suddenly became bold. She finally looked at Jotham, really looked at the man who had been her very first beau.

He hadn't changed much from when they had courted as teenagers. Sure, his honey blond hair had darkened over the years and his beard was thick and long now, but he was still tall and proud. And his blue eyes still had the ability to mesmerize her.

Hedy cut short the shiver that began to spread through her belly by abruptly walking over to the cradle that was positioned beside the old potbelly stove in the corner of the room. She carefully lowered Cacey onto the quilt and handed her a felt doll.

Sighing, Hedy turned back to Jotham and asked, "Can we just talk straight, the same as we used to when we were young'uns?"

"We aren't kids any more, Hedy. We're grown people; you with a husband and five children, and me...well, me with a business and alone."

A tear slipped from Hedy's eye and she brought her apron up quickly to wipe it away before Jotham saw. She sniffed and said, "I am very sorry for your loss. Marybeth was a kind hearted woman. I really liked her. It's so unfair that she was taken away from you so young."

Jotham swallowed hard. "I wake up every morning thinking that when I roll over, she'll be there beside me. I must admit, I'm having a difficult time dealing with her passing. I'm filled with bitterness that all of my praying hasn't been able to heal me yet."

"Oh, please don't talk that way. The Lord has reasons for everything. You know that."

Jotham smoothed his hair away from his forehead and muttered, "Maybe if Marybeth had left me with a child, I wouldn't feel this empty pain right now."

Hedy stiffened as she braced for his next words. Here it comes, she thought, just what I've been waiting forever to hear.

When Jotham's gaze settled onto Hedy's wide-eyed stare, he looked more resolute than she had ever seen him. In that instant she was convinced that he had known all along.

"My love for Marybeth was different than what I felt for you. It was a quiet, peaceful sort of romance that never upset me once in ten years of marriage. It was a drop of sweet honey on my tongue, whereas you were the burning of hot cinnamon to all of my senses."

Hedy held up her hand and interrupted, "Please, please don't go down this road. I know we need to talk, but I'm married to another man and it just isn't right for us to let in old feelings."

Cacey's gurgle and crying squawk brought Hedy's and Jotham's attention back to her. Jotham stood and crossed the room to the cradle quickly. Hedy remained where she was and quietly watched Jotham reach into the cradle. He brushed a hand across Cacey's soft, wispy brown hair before he picked the baby up and held her close. He gazed at Hedy with a calm assurance.

"All these years, I never asked you about it. I was afraid of what your answer would be. I didn't want to ruin the life I'd made with Marybeth or the one you'd found with Rowan. Our love wasn't..." Jotham swallowed, "wasn't what the Lord intended, and even though it nearly killed me at the time, I moved on and found a different sort of happiness."

Hedy was holding her breath, unable to move a muscle as she listened to Jotham open up his heart to her. Hearing his simple testimony was painful. She had wronged him so badly and here he was speaking to her with the soft tone of a forgiving man. Deep down, she had always thought that Jotham had been too good for her, and now she was sure of it.

Jotham's expression suddenly changed into the fierce desperation of a man with nothing else to lose. He leaned in and whispered, "I have to know, Hedy. Is Gabe my son?"

Hedy had played this encounter over and over in her head with so many possible outcomes that she could hardly believe that it was really happening this time. The kitchen was almost too warm from the heat emitting from the stove and the scent of the leftover chicken casserole she had eaten for dinner was still lingering in the air. The soft light from the gas lamp over the sink left the kitchen in partial shadows and sudden foreboding flooded over her as she watched a strange tentacle of darkness dance across the wall.

Hedy shook the feeling away. Her mind was playing tricks on her, she convinced herself as she found the courage to stare back into Jotham's pleading gaze.

How would the truth affect all of their lives, Hedy wondered? While her grandmother had lain dying of cancer and old age a few years back, she had whispered to Hedy that the sins of the past always catch up on a person, and right now Hedy knew it to be true. She was only a teenager when she had fallen for Jotham's beautiful eyes and shy manner. She certainly never meant to hurt him, but when Rowan had favored her with a smile one day, her heart had melted and she knew that he was to be her husband, not Jotham.

The breakup had not only been difficult for the families, but for the entire community. And just when Hedy believed that she was free to follow her heart with Rowan, she had discovered that she was pregnant. Of course there had been whispers among Church members, and there was that one day shortly after her wedding ceremony to Rowan when Jotham had approached her at the stockyards. He had stumbled over his words, not able to build up the nerve to ask her about the baby that day.

Hedy couldn't lie any longer. She felt the presence of her granny beside her and the arms of God around her. She hoped the truth would finally set her free. Hedy had never stopped caring for Jotham and if knowing that he was a father to an eleven year old boy brought him some semblance of happiness once again, she had to do it.

Her mind made up, she said, "I should have told you this a long time ago. But here, let me light another lamp and heat some water for coffee. I believe we'll both be in need of a cup after you hear what I have to say."

Hedy walked swiftly to the counter, only sparing a quick glance at Jotham to see that he was content to wait a little longer for the truth. While she pulled the match from the box, Jotham carried her baby daughter to the window and looked out into the night. An odd, peaceful feeling spread through Hedy as she peeked over to watch Jotham holding Cacey's little hand between his thumb and forefinger.

The picture of Jotham and Cacey at the window was that last thing Hedy ever saw. She heard the *whissssp* of the flame rising from the match just as the world exploded into a million red and gold pieces around her.

At that final moment, Hedy wasn't afraid of dying. She

worried about Rowan and her other children, and she was sad that Cacey wouldn't grow up and have a family of her own. But her very last thought as she passed into the light was that she very much regretted not having told Jotham the truth.

1

January 1, 2015

It should have felt nice to leave the ten degree temperature and blowing snow behind when I entered Charlie's Pub, but I only had about ten seconds to enjoy the warmth before all hell broke loose.

The flying chair struck the wall a few feet to my right with a crash. Todd's sharp admiring whistle snapped my head in his direction.

Todd shrugged and said with a sheepish grin, "Happy New Year, boss."

I scoffed, rolling my eyes. It was bad enough to be working the beat on New Year's Eve, but having to ring in the New Year with my irritating partner, Todd, was a double insult. Quickly pushing my frustration aside, I grasped the baton at my hip and shouted over the myriad sounds of crashing, cussing and breaking glass.

"That's enough, folks! Everyone drop whatever object you're about to lob at someone and listen up."

The room did quiet somewhat, but I had to grudgingly admit that Todd's second, more threatening call-to-attention whistle, is what finally got everyone to face us.

I took in the scene at once. Normally, the combination of the beer stein collection on the far wall, the hardwood floors and the hunter green porcelain lamp shades gave Charlie's a quaint, northern European ambience. But tonight the place resembled a roadhouse instead. Besides several broken chairs, there was also a flipped over table and I couldn't help wrinkling my nose at the permeating smell of whisky and beer mixing together among the shattered glass in puddles on the floor. I was just glad that I didn't have to stick around to clean up the mess.

About two dozen patrons were standing and sitting in various positions around the room, some were amused and some wide eyed, but all were very alert. Charlie Dempsey was behind the bar, scratching his graying head of shaggy hair in dismay as he surveyed the damage to his establishment. I didn't have a lot of sympathy for the man, though. Bar fights were an occupational hazard in this business, and unfortunately, I'd made altogether too many runs in the middle of the night in crappy weather like this because of them.

The fact that the local boys had gotten riled up on the holiday didn't sour my mood nearly as much as having spotted my ex-boyfriend from high school, Denton McAllister, when I'd entered the building. At the moment, Denton was pointing a finger at Jory Goldblum who was holding what appeared to be an appetizer dish in his hand. But even all that wasn't as disturbing as catching a glimpse of the lone man who was sitting in the far corner of the room.

In the moment my eyes met his, he grinned and raised his beer bottle with a curt nod.

Daniel Bachman. This must be my lucky night, I thought sarcastically.

"This isn't your concern, Serenity," Ben said with an angry twist to his lips.

I rounded on him. I had had about enough of the town's people either treating me as if I was a complete stranger or with way too much familiarity. I was the sheriff now and I deserved a little more respect.

In a steady, but loud voice, I said, "Charlie's isn't your private playground, Mr. Goldblum." I paused to sweep the room with my gaze to make sure that I had everyone's full attention. "Or anyone else's for that matter. You are all dangerously close to ringing in the New Year in county lockup."

"I didn't come out looking for a fight," Ben shouted, wheeling again in Denton's direction. Todd was quick and got a hold of Ben's arm before he had a chance to let the dish fly. Ben quickly slouched in defeat as Todd secured both of his wrists behind his back.

"He's sleeping with Ruby. What was I supposed to do?" Ben choked out.

I never could stand a crying man, but I made an exception in this case. Back in high school, Ben and Denton had been inseparable, so by default, I had spent a lot of time hanging around with Ben. In those days, he was too shy to raise his hand in class and I could still vividly recall the time that he'd crossed a busy highway to hold a dying dog in his lap that had been hit by a car. It hadn't even been his dog, but you would never have known that from the tears he had shed that day. Ruby was also his high school sweetheart, wife and the mother of his three young daughters. It was bad enough to discover your wife cheating on you, but it was a double whammy for the other man to be your best friend, and way too much to expect any man to deal with calmly.

Now that I knew what was going on, I was just sorry that Todd had reached Ben before he'd hurled the dish at Denton's head.

Still holding out a shard of hope that it was all a huge misunderstanding, I turned to Denton and asked, "Is this true?"

The room was dead silent and all eyes turned to Denton. The thirty-two year old still looked every bit the high school football star, except that now he was even more ripped. Both of his arms bulged with muscles, and right below each sleeve of his t-shirt was an elaborate tattoo. One arm was decorated with a sun burst and the other with a pouting angel that looked kind of like a porn star with wings.

He didn't even have to answer for me to immediately know that what Ben had said was the truth. It was written all over Denton's unusually sagging face. I inwardly sighed in sadness for Ben's little girls.

Denton rubbed his hand vigorously through his blond hair before he finally said, "Yeah, but she's the one who came on to me." He glanced back at Ben and said, "Man, you have to believe me. I would never do that to you."

"That's enough," I said, waving him to silence with an irritated swipe of my hand.

Denton hadn't changed one bit since high school. He was still a self-centered, heart breaking dick, too arrogant to take any responsibility for it. And that made the sting even sharper when my body betrayed me with a racing heart and a dry mouth when I faced him.

"You're under arrest, Denton McAllister, for disorderly conduct and assault." He didn't resist when I cuffed him, but he didn't go silently either.

"What the hell, Serenity. Are you kidding me? He's the

one who attacked me and then Ruby's brother, Nathan, had to get involved. They're the ones you should be arresting!"

I turned him around and stared hard into his eyes. Once upon a time, those hazel eyes of his could make me do anything he wanted. I had been a lump of hormones and romantic dreams around him in high school. That is, until he cheated on me with my own best friend at the time. They say that high school memories stay with you for a lifetime. I had to agree, except those memories weren't always pleasant. In my case, they had turned me into a very jaded adult.

"For once in your life, keep your mouth shut or I'll find some other charges to tack on to the list. Now move." I pointed towards the door. He shook his head in disbelief, but started walking anyway.

"Todd, can you get Denton into the cruiser. I want to talk to Ben for a minute…and you can take the cuffs off of him." Then I addressed the crowd. "Everyone go home. Charlie's is closed for the night."

Quickly, people began dispersing, some with down cast eyes and others with smiling faces and Happy New Year wishes. I nodded curtly to get them moving on their way and told Charlie that I'd be with him in a minute to make a formal report. The old bar owner had already gotten to work with a mop and I moved my attention from him to look back at Ben. This wasn't going to be fun.

"I'm doing you a favor. I'm sure the last face that you want to be staring at all night through cell bars is Denton's, so I'm not going to haul you in. But I don't want you going home to Ruby and the kids tonight, either. You need to get a room at one of the hotels off the interstate and sleep this one off. When its morning and you're thinking clearer, you can go talk to her about it, but not tonight. Do you understand me?"

"Yeah, I do." I was satisfied with his answer and his demeanor, and was about to switch my attention back to Charlie when Ben reached out and touched my arm. I looked at him with a raised brow.

"Why would she do such a thing? We have a family...I thought we were happy. How could Ruby do this to us?"

Ben's eyes were wet and his face was pale. My heart went out to him, but I also wondered when his pain would turn to anger. In cases like this it was probably better to be totally pissed off rather than being lost in so much grief. And what could I say anyway? No amount of advice I could give him would make a difference. Ruby had cheated on him with his best friend, probably because Denton was a hot commodity and all the loving feelings were gone between her and Ben. She'd been nice enough when we were young, but she had always been a party girl. Some bad personality traits didn't disappear or change over time. They only morphed into something even worse. At this point, no words from me were going to make Ben feel any better, and really, I was the last person in the world who should be giving him advice on the subject.

But I was tired and wanted to go home, so I lied. "I don't know why...it was probably just a physical thing and not emotional at all. Try to get some sleep and maybe the light of day will bring you some answers."

Ben sighed and said, "Thanks, Serenity. I appreciate you overlooking my bad behavior. I won't do anything like this ever again. I promise."

"You better not. Next time I won't be nearly as understanding."

Twenty minutes later I was finally trudging back through the snow to the car. Luckily, Charlie had insurance for just such incidents. And he'd been so relieved that no one had been injured, he wasn't going to press charges either.

I was slipping my gloves on and almost to the car when I noticed Daniel standing beside his Jeep. Apparently, he was waiting for me. I was in the process of weighing the pros and cons of stopping to talk to the former Amish man when he pushed away from his vehicle and strode over, meeting me halfway to my cruiser.

"Happy New Year," he said sweetly.

I chuckled and my breath spread out into an icy mist between us. "Not much happiness going on around here."

"It could be worse."

I risked looking directly into his eyes and said briskly, "Oh, yeah, no one's dead this time, but Ben probably wishes he was." I shook my head. "Dammit, I don't understand why people do this to each other. If Ruby wanted out, why not just be up front with Ben. And then again, why would she even want out; three beautiful girls, a nice house in the suburbs, and a great guy. What's the matter with her anyway?"

Daniel smiled at my little tirade, looking down at his booted foot as he pushed snow around briefly before meeting my gaze once again.

"I'd really rather be talking about us."

"Us?"

"You know, you…me…us." His white teeth flashed in a brilliant smile and I was once again completely at a loss as to why this gorgeous guy was stalking me.

He was so tall and his shoulders were so broad that he actually provided a nice break from the wind that was gusting hard enough to catch the loose snow in the parking lot and spray it up into the air in wild sheets of bitter cold around us. I was even tempted to take another step closer and steal some of the heat that seemed to radiate off of him, but I controlled myself and stood still.

I had a sudden vision of Daniel, minus the Carhartt jacket and the flannel shirt. I knew that underneath all those winter clothes was a well-defined chest that connected to washboard abs. I definitely didn't want to think about his firm butt or his strong thighs so I quickly forced the image to evaporate, and squarely met his gaze. Unfortunately, looking at his wide spaced brownish-black eyes and the amused set to his jaw that was covered with a few days' worth of black stubble wasn't much safer. He was too damned handsome for his own good.

"We've already discussed this. It's not a good time for us to get involved."

His amusement quickly evaporated and he snorted. "What are you waiting for? We're both available and we're highly attracted to each other. We survived a harrowing experience together...what more do you need to simply go out for dinner and movie with me?"

Maybe I was being a complete idiot. I had issues—I knew it. But letting Daniel into my life was about the scariest thing I had ever faced. A gun pointed straight at my head was more welcome than the prospect of putting faith in any man, especially him.

"This is just a game to you, isn't it? The minute I agree and go out with you, you'll grow bored and move onto someone else. So why the hell should I even bother?"

His eyes widened for an instant in understanding and then he took a measured sigh. "Someone must have really betrayed your trust for you to be so paranoid."

I smiled and nodded, "Yep, I won't deny it. Just look at what went down in there tonight." I pointed at Charlie's with an angry thrust of my arm. "Ben and Ruby were supposed to be living the dream, with kids and a dog, the whole package. Now their lives are ruined. They'll probably be divorced and both sleeping with new partners by this time next year."

"I get what you're saying. I really do. But it doesn't have to be like that for everyone...or for us. I'm a patient guy, Serenity. And I have no problem waiting for you to figure out how unreasonable you're being. Besides, we'll have that long drive up north with only the two of us in the Jeep and then a whole week in a secluded Amish community together to discuss this. So I'm not overly concerned with your avoidance at the moment."

The return of his smug expression cut through the honey warm desire that had been spreading through me by simply standing too close to him. He thought he had it all figured out, but I was determined to show him that he didn't know anything at all.

The cold air once again sent a chill through me and I zipped my jacket up to my neck and said, "Actually, there's been a change of plans." The sudden arch of his eyebrows was priceless and I quickly hurried on, "I've decided to leave tomorrow after all."

"But you know that I have to finish the Mayor's guest suite. He has visitors arriving this week and I promised him," Daniel said carefully.

I shrugged. "Sorry, Daniel, I have a tight schedule also. Since I'm officially on vacation in six hours, I'd like to be on my way. Perhaps I'll get lucky and Bishop Esch and that Rowan fellow were overreacting about the mystery on their hands.

I might be able to wrap things up quickly and you won't need to make the trip at all."

Daniel took a step closer and looked down at me. I couldn't help but swallow hard at his close proximity.

"I thought you wanted my company on this one."

Seeing the resolute look on Daniel's face, a shiver of fear passed through me when I realized I could definitely push Daniel too far and then he *would* give up on me. As bitchy as I was being to him, I didn't want to completely run him off. Part of me wished desperately that he'd stick around.

"Sure, I'd like your help with the investigation. God only knows how bat-shit crazy this Poplar Springs community probably is. But I don't want to put you out, either."

Daniel took a long breath and stared at me for several more seconds before he finally said, "I'll join you as quickly as I can. I'm sure you can handle the locals on your own until I arrive." He suddenly had his arms around me in a tight, but quick squeeze. He whispered into my ear, "Happy New Year. I'll see you soon."

He turned and went to his Jeep without another glance in my direction. The infuriating emptiness that I had felt when he let go said plainly that I was already in way over my head with Daniel Bachman. We'd shared a lot of intense moments during Naomi Beiler's murder case. And Daniel was one of the few people who'd actually trusted my instincts about the Amish girl's death. But I reasoned to myself as I walked to the cruiser that we hadn't even had sex, so I was still in a good position. He did not have a hold of me—yet.

When I slipped into the passenger seat, I was glad that Todd had the heater cranked up inside the car.

"I need to give you some hugging lessons. You looked

about as responsive as a cinder block there," Todd scolded me with a wink.

"You were spying on me?" I growled the words out.

"I got better things to do than spy on you, boss, like text my fiancé," he held up his cellphone for good measure, "but it's hard not to notice you out there talking to Daniel when he's towering over you as if he's Superman and you're Lois Lane." He shrugged and put the car into drive.

I pointed the heater vent toward my face and took my gloves off. Gazing out the window and watching the soft spray of light from each of the lamp posts we passed by, I said absently, "We were only talking."

Todd chuckled and Denton, who I had almost forgotten about in the back seat, cleared his throat and said, "That guy wants you bad. Todd's right. You weren't being very friendly."

I thudded my head back onto the headrest at the irony of it all. It was as if I was trapped inside an eighties sitcom. Here I was in a police car with Todd Roftin and Denton McAlister on New Year's Eve. Either God was punishing me or he had a very sick sense of humor.

"It's none of your concern, Denton, so shut up," I said in a tired voice.

Todd had been flirting with me since middle school and even though he drove me crazy most of the time, he did know me pretty well and he must have sensed that I was indeed in a very angry state of mind. He lost the obnoxious expression and said with a less mocking tone, "Are you still making that insane trip up to the Amish settlement this week?"

"Yeah, as a matter of fact, I'm leaving tomorrow."

Todd was shaking his head as he pulled up to the sheriff's office and parked. "I would have thought that after Naomi

Weaver's murder investigation you would have had enough of those people and their crazy cult."

I ignored Denton's face pressed up against the glass that separated the back and the front seats and said, "That's the funny thing, I'm even more fascinated with their culture now. I'm no fool, though. I'll never forget that night in the barn. I know what the Amish are capable of, especially when they think they're protecting their own. But there was something about that minister, Rowan Schwartz, coming all the way down here to ask for my help that's pulled me in."

"Yeah, I get it, but don't you think someone in law enforcement or the fire department in Poplar Springs can handle it?"

"That's just it. I believe the man when he says that the local authorities aren't being much help. You know the way small towns are. Everyone's connected in some fashion and there can be long-held grudges." I sighed and went on, "I just get the uneasy feeling that there's a lot more going on up there in that northern community than I've been told so far. And I would like to figure it out."

"Can you talk personal on your own time and get me out of this damn car?" Denton asked with a tap on the window.

Todd turned and told Denton, "Shut up," and then he looked back at me. "I know that you have muscle-man as backup, but if you get into any kind of trouble, don't you hesitate to call me. I'll get up there right quick if you need me.

I had to smile. Todd was a good guy underneath it all and I was sure that he'd drop everything to save my ass in a heartbeat if needed, but the trouble was that he didn't have the ability to rescue me from the real danger ahead.

And that was Daniel Bachman.

2

It felt good to stretch my legs after the three hour long drive. I had passed the Poplar Springs township sign about a mile back and this was the first gas station that I had seen in a while. Besides filling the tank, I needed to pee and fill up my coffee mug. It was also the place that Mr. Schwartz had arranged to meet me. But at the moment, I felt pretty stupid that I had left Blood Rock at eleven o'clock at night on New Year's Day. I wasn't looking forward to sleeping in my car until day break, but I couldn't expect my host to come out at two in the morning to get me, either. Not only did the man not drive, but I'm fairly certain that he was just as into the whole early to bed and early to rise thing that all the Amish I had come to know were.

Stifling a yawn, I took note of the long, wooden hitching rail in front of the convenience store as I walked past it and entered the brightly lit building. I had already seen several Amish business signs along the roadway with their horse and buggy logos, so the fact that there was a hitching rail here didn't surprise me in the least. But the size of it did make me realize that the Poplar Springs settlement must be quite a bit larger than the Blood Rock Amish community.

After using the restroom, I asked the middle aged man at the counter a few questions about the area, and having a difficult time understanding his stilted English, I gave up. It was hard to imagine how someone from India ended up in the middle of nowhere Indiana and in an Amish community no less. I filled my canister with coffee and browsed the candy bars, considering whether it was a good idea to eat one if I wanted to get a few hours of sleep before morning.

When the four young people walked in, filling the small store with their lively chatter, I glanced up. It was a cop thing. Most people who were prowling around at this hour were up to no good. I quickly took in that all three boys were wearing the same royal blue sports jackets that had a soccer ball embroidered on the left front side and their names in cursive on the opposite. Since I had grown up playing soccer, I quickly relaxed, figuring that these kids probably weren't getting into too much trouble tonight. In my experience, the soccer kids weren't nearly as rowdy as the football players. Two of these boys had buzzed haircuts and the third, a taller one, wore his hair to his shoulders in the typical South American bohemian style that so many of the soccer professionals sported. The lone girl in the group was a pretty red head who was wearing heavy-duty farm coveralls, immediately garnering my respect. Any girl that puts personal comfort ahead of style in the wintertime was all right in my book.

But still, I couldn't help keeping one eye on the foursome as I plucked a chocolate bar from the shelf and moved over to the pretzels. I was craving salt, and since I was already going to be caffeined-up on the chocolate and coffee, I decided that I might as well fill up on my other favorite snack as well.

"Hey, Brandy, what do you want to drink?" the taller boy asked loudly.

"I don't know, whatever is fine with me," she said sulkily.

The dark haired boy in the group snapped, "I still can't believe that Gabe Schwartz had the nerve to flirt with Brandy that way."

The last name caught my attention and I paused at the bags of chips and tilted my head to listen more carefully.

"Don't talk like I'm not even here, Lyell. It was no big deal," Brandy said.

I caught the defensive shrug of Lyell's shoulders at the end of the aisle, but it was the tallest boy who spoke again. "He's got to be only fourteen or fifteen, and he's Amish. They act so prim and proper in front of the adults, but get them away from the establishment and anything goes."

"Oh, yeah," chuckled the brown haired boy, "we all know that they ain't perfect."

Lyell walked down the aisle I was standing in and muttered, "Excuse me," as he reached past me to grab a bag of chips from the shelf. I took a step back, but continued to pretend that I was deciding between the snacks.

When Lyell returned to the teens clustered beside the refrigerator doors, they began whispering. I couldn't make out what they were saying for a moment, but then Brandy spoke up, "You really should leave Mariah alone, Nathan. She's not interested in the likes of you and you're just going to get her into trouble."

"Why, is it a crime to be nice?" Nathan said forcefully. "She's going to get into trouble all on her own anyway."

"Still, no need to make it any worse. I sort of feel sorry for her having to live that way." Brandy turned to the tall boy and grasped his arm, shaking it. "Tell him what a jerk he's being, Cody."

Cody pointed a finger at Nathan and said in a mock tone, "Don't corrupt that good little Amish girl...and stop picking fights with Jacob and Jory. We should be ambassadors of good will for our people."

Brandy swiped Cody on the shoulder and abruptly headed towards the counter, saying, "You are so full of shit."

Cody and Lyell followed quickly behind Brandy, but Nathan lingered beside the packs of gum.

When Nathan finally moved to join his friends, I turned and grasped his left arm, quickly securing it against his back and pushing him forward against the shelf.

"What the hell," Nathan said in a suspiciously low voice for someone being suddenly accosted.

"There's a pack of gum in your back pocket that you didn't pay for. I suggest that you get it with your free hand and place it back on the shelf," I told him nicely.

Nathan's friends and the store owner were now gathered in the narrow aisle way with gaping mouths and wide eyes.

"Let him go!" Brandy demanded, but I ignored her.

I twisted Nathan's arm and said, "Please don't make me repeat myself."

Nathan's body relaxed at the same time he answered, "All right, all right."

Nathan plucked the pack from his pocket and quickly placed it back on the shelf. I released him and returned his stare as he rubbed his wrist vigorously.

Understanding struck the store owner and he rushed toward Nathan, pointing a finger in the boy's face and shrieking, "You hoodlum! I call cops on you!"

I stepped in front of Nathan and held up my hand at the swarthy man. "Hold on." I turned back to Nathan and asked, "I wonder what your coach will do if he finds out you were shoplifting. If he's anything like my high school soccer coach, he won't be happy and he'll probably be very much inclined to bench you for a few games."

Nathan's face paled, and he glanced nervously between me and the store owner. It only took a few seconds for the kid to resort to begging. "Please, please don't press charges. I promise I'll never steal anything again. I won't even come in here anymore."

I had always thought of myself as a pretty good judge of character, and right now, my gut was telling me that the incident had scared the crap out of the kid. He probably had done it before, but the chances of him taking the risk again over a dollar's worth of gum was not very likely.

"I think he's learned his lesson…and I wouldn't be surprised if his parents, aunts and uncles all stop by here for gas from time to time. I don't think that it would be worth the trouble of calling law enforcement on this one, if you know what I mean," I said coaxingly to the man.

The man frowned for several long seconds, silently deliberating before he finally sighed in annoyance. He wagged his finger in Nathan's face and said, "I be keeping eyes on you."

Nathan took that as his cue to leave and he swept past us. Cody and Lyell converged on Nathan and they hurried away together, but Brandy paused for a second to smile back at me and mouth the words, "Thank you."

But I only half acknowledged her. Rowan Schwartz was staring at me from behind her.

The Amish man's sudden appearance flustered me for a moment, and his unreadable expression put me immediately on guard, but I recovered enough to say, "Hello, Mr. Schwartz. I wasn't expecting you to actually come out at this hour."

"I'm the one who invited you here, so of course I'll bend my schedule to accommodate your needs. I would never allow you to wait in your car at a gas station the entire night when you could be sleeping in a soft bed instead."

"Well, thanks," I chirped out, still feeling extremely uncomfortable. "How long have you been standing there?"

The side of Rowan's mouth lifted into a small, lopsided smile, and he said, "Long enough to know that Bishop Aaron Esch wasn't kidding when he spoke about you."

Oh, brother. I already had a reputation and I only just arrived.

3

By the time I pulled into the long, gravel driveway, the weirdness of following the horse and buggy for the past five miles had worn off. I was actually more surprised at what good time we were making.

I was beginning to think this Rowan guy was quite the character. He still wasn't being overly friendly, but the fact that he'd made the effort to come and get me had scored him a few brownie points.

Now that he had slowed his horse to a walk, I crawled along behind the buggy at a snail's pace, taking the opportunity to look around. The horse's heavy breathing was creating large puffs of mist that floated back to my car, and the moon was nearly full. Its brightness illuminated the fields to my left and the scraggly hedge to my right with a soft glow that was enhanced further by the snow.

Even for the frigid temperatures, there was only about an inch of snow on the ground, which was a lot less than we had back home. When we crested the hill, a white farm house and several red barns came into view. The trees dropped away and wood board fencing began, creating large corrals on each side of the drive. Dozens of black cows were heartily eating from the round bales of hay that dotted each paddock.

I felt bad for the calves that were huddled up against their mothers. They looked miserable, but at least the morning was supposed to bring sunshine and warmer temperatures.

The two story house was dark and quiet except for the Border Collie that leaped off the porch and barked once at my car before Rowan leaned out of the buggy to call the dog to him.

I parked and zipped up my jacket. I also put my toboggan, scarf and gloves on. Rowan was already busily unhitching his horse and I guessed that my sleeping accommodations would have to wait until after the horse was cared for.

I certainly didn't mind the delay though. It might give me the opportunity to find out some more information about the arsons.

I walked closer to the side of the barn, hopeful that it would provide some protection from the brisk wind and said, "Do you need any help with that, Mr. Schwartz?"

Rowan paused from the strappings and looked at me with that same unreadable expression that he'd worn in my office a couple of weeks earlier. "You can call me Rowan and if you don't mind, I'll address you as Serenity." He continued to undo the straps while he talked. "I'm only a few years older than you at most. It feels a little awkward having you address me so formally."

I chewed the corner of my lip, trying to gage whether the Amish man was being sincere or sarcastic. I decided to take it at face value.

"All right then. Rowan, do you need any help?"

"Yes, actually, I'd appreciate it if you would brush Dakota

off for me." He handed me the lead rope that he had just clipped to the horse's halter and pointed to the barn door. "Go ahead and crosstie him in the aisle. The grooming box is in the tack room."

I led the horse into the barn and then paused to call over my shoulder. "Where's the light?"

Rowan was in the process of pulling the buggy towards the side of the barn where an open topped buggy was already parked in a covered bay.

He chuckled and replied, "Sorry, but we don't have lights in the barn. You should be able to feel your way around with the moonlight, I reckon."

Then he turned back to his job and forgot all about me.

Luckily, I wasn't totally ignorant around horses. Growing up, I had a horse-crazy friend named Missy who took me out for rides sometimes. Turning to the black horse that was standing patiently beside me, I said, "Being an Amish horse, you're probably very well behaved, so I think we can get this done without too much hoopla."

I squinted into the darkness and decided to tie the horse closer to the doorway even though the air blowing through it was icy cold. Better to have a little bit of light, I thought, as I found the rope that was already connected to the wall and latched it to the side of Dakota's halter. Since Rowan had mentioned 'cross ties,' I looked across the aisle and saw another matching rope. I pulled the rope to Dakota's head and was delighted to find that it reached perfectly.

It only took about a minute and a few bumps to get my hands on a wooden box full of horse brushes in the darkness of the tack room. I was hardly even aware of the fact that it was about three o'clock in the morning as I brushed the sweaty fur vigorously. The movement got my blood flowing again, warming me somewhat, and seeing that Dakota was stretching out in enjoyment to the attention made me happy to work even harder.

By the time Rowan reappeared beside me, Dakota was thoroughly brushed and there was only a little steam rising from his back. I looked at Rowan expecting him to admire my work, but instead, he pulled a small tool from his pocket and lifted each of the horse's hooves in turn to pick the debris out of them. He then placed a quilted blanket on Dakota, latched the straps beneath the horse's belly and led him into a stall.

I waited a few more minutes while the man filled a bucket of water from the heavily wrapped water spigot and placed some hay into Dakota's stall. When he closed the stall door behind him, he finally acknowledged me again, saying, "Now it's time to get you settled for the night."

Rowan insisted on carrying my heavy suitcase and I followed him across the frozen ground with my purse and a duffle bag over my shoulder. I had to stretch my legs to keep up with the tall man. As I walked in his moonlit shadow towards a small, square building to the side of the house, I once again noticed that Rowan's hat was larger and his coat longer than the Amish living in my jurisdiction. I didn't think it was possible, but Rowan looked even more outdated than the people of the Blood Rock community.

The kitchen was dimly illuminated by a shard of moonlight coming through the window. I found myself straining to watch my host as he fiddled with the matches and gas lamp above the table. He wasn't as tall or as broad shouldered as Daniel, but he was still a big guy. And although he didn't come close to the good looks that Daniel possessed, Rowan was a decent looking man. The arrogant confidence that oozed off of him made him even more attractive.

The room was suddenly filled with light, and I looked around the small interior of the box house, noting that although there weren't any pictures adorning the walls, there was a brightly colored quilt hanging on one of them. A round table with three high backed chairs, a trundle bed and a sleeper sofa completed the room. There was one doorway that led to a small bathroom and another that seemed to be a closet. The woodsy scent from the charred remains in the potbellied stove wafted on the air and I breathed in the pleasant aroma as memories of childhood campfires stirred in my mind.

"This is cozy," I said.

Again, Rowan chuckled and I knew this time it was at my own expense. He obviously thought that I was the one being facetious.

"No, really, I mean it," I told him.

Rowan smiled. "I built this for my parents to stay in when they come to help me with the children." He glanced around. "It serves its purpose well enough."

"How many kids do you have?" I hadn't really thought about Rowan's family and now I felt a little guilty for not doing so earlier.

"I have five."

"That must keep your wife busy," I said conversationally.

"My wife died four years ago. The children are my sole responsibility, except for when my parents are visiting."

Now I felt like complete dirt. "I'm sorry. I didn't mean to…"

"There is no reason for you to apologize. How could you have known? Besides, the reason I brought you here is because of your curious mind. I would be sorely disappointed if you didn't ask questions."

He had given me the perfect opening and I seized the opportunity. "When you were in my office a few weeks ago, you mentioned that a body had been found in the rubble of the latest fire. I pulled up the local newspaper articles and discovered that the remains weren't identifiable. Do you have any idea who it is?"

The sudden change of subject didn't seem to faze Rowan, but I could tell even before he spoke that he wasn't going to answer my question.

"It's awfully late. Let me take a few more minutes to show you how to light the lamps and to keep the fire going in the stove."

I bristled at the way he completely blew off my question, but I didn't have much time to stew over it when he quickly launched into an explanation of how to light the damp wick from the oil lamp above the sink. He also told me that instead of a refrigerator, I had the use of an icebox, and that because there wasn't any running water in the house, the toilet in the bathroom was not a real toilet at all, but a kind of indoor-outhouse. There was a small tank above the sink filled with water for both of my drinking and washing needs, and I found myself closely watching Rowan as he loaded up the wood burning stove for the night. He illustrated how to use the vent and advised me to put a few logs in when I woke up.

"I think you'll make it through the night," Rowan said, heading for the door.

I was a little worried about remembering all of his instructions, but a nagging question was forefront on my mind.

"Wait, Rowan. I won't keep you much longer, but I was wondering about something."

Rowan paused, letting go of the door knob. He looked back expectantly.

"How did your wife die?"

A fleeting shadow of surprise lit his eyes before he regained his composure and said, "She was killed in a house fire." As soon as the words left his mouth, he was through the door.

Finally alone, I sat down at the table and took a deep breath.

Any hopes of getting out of Poplar Springs before my two week vacation was up had just vanished with his words. And for the first time in many hours, I thought about Daniel, and how his familiarity with the Amish people would be very helpful at the moment. I was suddenly wistful, wishing I had waited a few days for him to join me.

4

ven with the foreign scents of the lamp oil and wood smoke, and the early morning crowing of several roosters, I still slept well. It was the bright sunshine slicing through the window at nine o'clock in the morning that finally got me moving.

Stoking up the fire in the stove, making a cup of coffee with a pot of water on the stove and even brushing my teeth with water from the tank had all been quite the adventure. I couldn't help glancing down at the dime size hole on the knee of my jeans where an ember had sparked out of the stove and landed on me while I had been stuffing the logs in. It had taken an unreasonable amount of time to just get the basics taken care of. And then there was the whole indoor-outhouse to deal with.

It was unfathomable to understand why anyone would put themselves through this kind of daily torture when it wasn't necessary. But as I peeked out the corner of the window and watched Rowan's children hooking up a devilish looking red pony to an open cart, I could kind of understand the culture's allure.

The kids had been busy little bees ever since the first time I pushed the sheer curtain aside to look outside. I caught glimpses of them throwing corn on the ground for a colorful flock of chickens, filling up water troughs with hoses dragged all throughout the barnyard and pouring feed into the long troughs for the cows that were patiently lined up waiting to be fed.

It was quite impressive really, how each child had specific jobs to do and that they did them without adult supervision. As I sipped the strong brew of coffee I'd made, I had the opportunity to watch Rowan going about his business, too. He hadn't stopped moving since the first moment I'd spotted him mending a fence with one of his sons.

The boy looked to be in his mid-teens and I wondered if he was the Gabe Schwartz that the teens at the gas station had been talking about. The group obviously had ties to the community and must have some opportunities to mingle or they wouldn't have been talking with such familiarity about the Amish kids. It was an interesting dynamic for sure and one that made me think about Naomi Beiler and her fateful relationship with my nephew, Will.

At the heart of it, teenagers were all very similar. Friendship, romance and fun were on everyone's mind—regardless of their culture. But I definitely thought that Amish teens had it worse off. Not only did they have to deal with the usual coming of age troubles, but they also had to adhere to a much stricter set of laws that forbid them from using any kind of technology, holding hands with their significant others or having much freedom at all. The lifestyle was definitely not Naomi's cup of tea and tragically, she ended up dead because of another troubled Amish teenager.

I turned away from the window and tried the internet on my phone once again. If I stood in the far corner of the room,

I managed to get intermittent service, but it was an irritating process, and so far I hadn't been able to remain still enough to pull up the information that I was looking for. Surely the house fire that had killed Rowan's wife had been mentioned in the local newspaper. Was there a connection between that fire and the more recent arsons? I had learned the hard way that true coincidences were rare, and if these events were indeed related, I worried about the implications for Rowan and his family.

The knock at the door startled me and I rolled my eyes at my own jumpiness. But as I took the few steps to cross the room, I couldn't help having a flashback to the darkened barn back in Blood Rock and the dozen or so Amish men with their long beards and black hats staring down at me as I lay on the floor, bleeding. That was really a bad night, and one that still gave me occasional nightmares.

When I opened the door, I was surprised to see one of the little girls who I had been spying on earlier standing on the steps. There were a few wisps of auburn hair free from her black bonnet and her cheeks and nose were pink from the cold, morning air. Her thick black coat was buttoned up to her chin and she wore muddy black boots.

Her bright blue eyes stared up at me unblinkingly and I realized that just as I'd been making observations about her appearance, she had also been studying me with rapt curiosity.

I held my hand out and said, "Hello, I'm Serenity. What's your name?"

I guessed that the girl was probably around nine years old and when she smiled, her face came alive.

"Lucinda." She pointed back at the open buggy that was now attached to the pony and went on, "Mareena got Toby hitched up. Do you want to go for a ride with us?"

A sudden jolt of excitement raced through me when I gazed at the large pony stomping his hoof with impatience. The sunshine had warmed the air and the rhythmic *drip, drip, drip* sound of melting snow from the roof tops filled my ears. The thaw also had created an icy sheen in the barnyard that glittered, making the scene look as if it was the cover of a Christmas card. I deliberated quickly, deciding that the invitation to go for a buggy ride through the winter wonderland was more than I could refuse. The investigation could wait a little longer I easily convinced myself. With an exhilarated rush, I said, "I would love to. Let me grab my coat and gloves."

My first impression of the spirited pony had been dead on. The buggy surged forward with a jolt that sent me thudding back onto the vinyl upholstered cushion. Mareena, Lucinda's older sister, held the reins tightly and I could see the strain on her face as she tried to keep the pony from an all-out gallop down the driveway. For a nervous moment, I mentally kicked myself in the butt for putting my life in the hands of a twelve year old, but when the girl jerked hard with the left rein and shouted out an indistinguishable German word, the pony finally slowed.

"Halt mal! Stop…!" The child's shout from behind us brought both Lucinda and I turning around. A small girl was running after us, shouting a confusing mixture of languages at the buggy.

"Ach…Cacey wants to come," Lucinda grumbled.

Mareena stood up to pull the high strung pony to a prancing stop. When Cacey reached us, she was breathing hard and looking up at us with pleading eyes. She said, "I want to come, Reena!"

"Oh, all right," Mareena responded, still fighting the pony to stand still.

Lucinda reached down and grabbed Cacey's hand as the little girl climbed the step into the cart. The three of us were already crammed onto the narrow seat as it was and I was wondering where the little girl would sit, when Lucinda pushed Cacey onto my lap and the buggy lurched forward once again.

As I clutched the child tightly, I caught a glimpse of Rowan standing beside the barn watching us. He wasn't smiling, but he wasn't frowning either. The man was impossible to read and that troubled me.

I had to put aside my anxieties about the investigation and focused on hanging on for dear life instead. Cacey leaned back against me rigidly and stared at the scenery flying by with a solemnness that made me wonder why she'd wanted to come along for the ride in the first place.

The cattle corrals swooshed by and soon we were turning out onto the main roadway with only a mild slow down to make the turn without flipping. My heart pounded against my ribcage as the outside wheels lifted off the ground a fraction. The buggy righted itself with a bounce and once again we were moving with speed across the wet pavement.

The bristling needle pricks of wind on my cheeks invigorated my senses and I gulped a deep breath of cold air as I watched fields, barns and farmhouses pass by.

Being in law enforcement, I still bristled at the fact that a mere child was allowed to careen around on the roadway without a license while everyone else had to wait until they were sixteen to drive legally. It was extraordinary what the Amish got away with.

"Mareena, do you have to go so fast?" I asked, still gripping Cacey's little body tightly.

"It takes a bit for Toby to calm down. He's awfully feisty," she told me, but she did begin tugging on the reins and amazingly the pony responded, slowing to a fast-paced walk.

"See, he's settled now," Lucinda chimed in.

"Don't you girls ever get scared when Toby runs off like that?" I said, releasing my hold of Cacey. Seeing the immaculate farmsteads of the Poplar Springs community at a slower speed was more like the wonderland buggy ride that I was envisioning a few minutes earlier.

"Naw, why would we?" Mareena asked. Her eyebrows were lifted and her mouth scrunched up to the side in honest confusion. I glanced at Lucinda to see her face holding a similar expression and it suddenly occurred to me that their brains worked differently than everyone else's. They honestly weren't afraid of something that would have made most grown men pee their pants. I wondered how such fearlessness would benefit a child as they grew up, but then I remembered that there were things that they were afraid of, such as getting punished by the Church elders for starters.

Daniel had cued me in that the teenagers were the ones to talk to when information was needed. He had said that they were usually rebellious and would say things that the adults wouldn't, or something to that affect. I wondered if it was even truer with the younger children.

"This is a very large Amish settlement, isn't it?" I spoke to both girls at once.

Mareena had the same auburn colored hair as Lucinda, but the locks poking out from beneath Cacey's cap were dark brown, similar to her father's. I imagined that their mother had probably been a red head and judging by her daughters' pretty faces, was an attractive woman as well.

As a cop, I was no stranger to broken families and kids in bad circumstances, but a knot still formed in my throat when I thought about these three vivacious girls growing up without their mother. It made me even more determined to find out the circumstances of the house fire that had killed her.

Mareena answered my question proudly, "This is one of the biggest Amish community in Indiana."

A slight hiccup of an accent was present in her speech making me feel a little bit as if I was traveling along the countryside in the Alps, instead of the American Midwest.

Lucinda tugged on my arm and pointed at a metal building on the hill to the left. "There's Jotham Hochstetler's store!" she exclaimed.

The building was white with a black roof and trim. The gravel parking lot in front was nearly full with a mixture of buggies and cars, along with a few of the large white vans that I'd become familiar with at Naomi's wake. It was obviously a busy place and as we turned up the road that led to the store, I was excited at the opportunities that might arise to dig for information about the arsons. I was also strangely anxious at the thought of being surrounded by a whole new group of Amish. I had learned firsthand they didn't like outsiders and they were all very good at keeping secrets.

As the beating of my heart increased, two buggies and a minivan approached us. Toby lifted his legs higher and arched his neck when we passed by the larger horses in their shiny leather harnesses.

"Hallo, Mareena. Hoe gatt het?" the woman driving the first buggy called out.

Mareena answered in English and I was once again puzzled at how they switched back and forth between English and their own form of German so effortlessly.

"I'm well, Mrs. Fisher. We're just bringing in a few pies for the bakery." And then, as if she had just remembered that I sat squeezed up against her, she added, "This is Serenity. She came to find out who is burning down the barns." Mareena pointed her chin toward the woman and said, "That's Joanna Fisher, the bishop's wife."

It took a lot of effort not to react to her words, but I somehow managed to keep my composure. "Nice to meet you," I said.

Joanna pulled her horse to a stop, even though there was a buggy and a minivan full of beards and caps waiting behind her.

"It's so very good to have you with us, Serenity. I do hope you'll be able to get to the bottom of these horrible fires so we can sleep better at night."

Joanna was younger than what I would have expected for a bishop's wife. She was slim and fair haired with the oval face of an aristocrat. Her overt friendliness was surprising considering my past encounters with the Blood Rock Amish people, but I was also getting the definite vibe that Joanna was a gossip and enjoyed the bad news the same as the good.

I would have to watch my guard around such a woman, but she also might be the perfect person to sponge information from, too.

"I can promise you, I'll give it my best." I hesitated only a second after seeing a few faces peering out from the buggy and said, "Can we meet sometime to talk?"

Joanna grinned, "Why of course. I'm butchering a hog this afternoon, but tomorrow afternoon would be a fine time for you to come to the house for a visit."

"Thank you. I'll see you then," I replied quickly, figuring the girls or Rowan could give me directions. Even if it was to my benefit, I still hated to keep everyone waiting in the road for us to finish our conversation.

"Until then, weltrusten!" Joanna clucked the chestnut horse and it surged forward.

Lucinda leaned in and said, "That means goodbye."

The inhabitants of the other buggy and the minivan stuck their hands out the windows to wave at us when they finally got on their way and I couldn't help but admire them all for their patience. In the city, such a delay would have had horns blowing and obscenities ringing in the air.

"So, does the entire community know about why I'm here?" I asked Mareena, already guessing the answer.

She shrugged. "Everyone's been talking about it."

I had to give the girl credit. She had a level head and wasn't going to willingly say too much on the matter. I guess Daniel had been right after all. The teens did seem to have the loosest lips in the Amish world.

Once we parked and Toby was tied to one of the many hitching rails provided for the Amish customers, I climbed down from the cart with Cacey in my arms and gently deposited her on the ground. The melting snow was splashing down in long, thin streams from the eaves of the building and I had to duck quickly to get to the walkway without getting wet. I unzipped my jacket and pulled off my gloves. The warm-up was a pleasant surprise.

"Here, let me carry one of those boxes for you," I offered Mareena.

She paused long enough for me to scoop the top two from the stack in her arms and then continued toward the doorway.

"Chores took longer than usual today, so we're running late. Jotham likes to have the pies on the shelves earlier than this," Mareena explained.

"And you slept past eight!" Lucinda added delightedly.

Mareena turned and frowned at her little sister. "I did not."

Lucinda giggled and half covered her mouth in my direction. "Yes she did," she whispered loudly.

I peeked into the corner of the top box that I carried and got a delicious whiff of baked apples, cinnamon and sugar.

"You made these, Mareena?"

"I helped," Lucinda exclaimed at the same time that Mareena nodded her head.

Mareena looked over her shoulder and said, "Jotham pays me four dollars a pie. I try to bake six fresh ones every Thursday morning."

As we stepped into the store, I couldn't help but think that Mareena had a pretty lucrative side business going. Cacey ran ahead of us and I fought the impulse to call the child back as I took in the sights and sounds of what I could only describe as the Amish equivalent to a mall.

One side of the building was a bakery, deli, and restaurant, and the other was filled with shelves brimming with every kind of grocery item. There was even a stairway leading to an open second story that boasted an array of wooden furniture and a wall crammed with bolts of colorful fabrics.

"This is a little more than just a store, Mareena," I commented, sniffing the wonderful smells of baking bread and frying chicken.

Mareena smiled proudly. "Have you ever had Amish cooking before?"

I caught sight of Cacey again as she darted around a cluster of Amish women who were chatting in front of a candle display. "I ate dinner at my community's schoolhouse dinner a couple months ago."

"Did you like it?" Lucinda looked up expectantly.

I smiled. "It was the best meal I think I've ever had."

Both Mareena and Lucinda beamed at my words. The girls were not only very well behaved, but they were both more mature than ordinary kids their age. I was impressed with the work ethic that they exhibited while they were doing their chores, and also that Mareena had her own little pie baking business. When I was twelve, I was still playing with stuffed animals and my mother had to chase me around with a broom just to get me to make my bed. Even though those times were all in good fun, I still had been a relatively lazy child.

With growing admiration for the Amish children, I said, "How would you girls like to have lunch here? It's my treat."

"Oh, yes!" Lucinda nearly shouted.

Mareena was more reserved, but there was a twinkle in her eyes when she said, "Thank you. That would be nice."

Every woman we passed by smiled and said hello in some fashion. Outwardly, the men ignored me for the most part, but I did catch a few of them glancing my way as we walked by. The same as the Blood Rock community, these men were careful not to show too much curiosity towards a new female. But they had definitely noticed me.

"Sorry we're running a little late, Jotham. We had a busy morning," Mareena rushed the words out.

Jotham was of medium height and would have been considered an attractive man, except that one entire side of his face was covered with leathery, red scarring. His hair line was receded with the scarring and he didn't have any eyebrows or lashes on that side either. The eye that stared out from the mangled tissue was glass, but his other was a piercing light blue that drew my attention even more than his fake one. He was also holding Cacey in his arms and the little girl who hadn't spoken a word after she'd gotten into the buggy was now chatting up a storm to him in her language. My initial appraisal of her as a shy child evaporated as I listened to her excited chatter to a man whose face would have scared most kids.

Jotham laughed heartily and said something to Cacey before he set her down on the floor. She squealed in delight and ran behind the counter where I watched her pick out a large, white iced donut from the display.

"Mareena and Lucinda, please take the pies to the table near the registers." When the girls lingered, he added, "Mach schnell!"

I gave my boxes to Lucinda and stepped back while they hurried away toward the front of the building. I recognized Jotham's intent to put the girls out of eavesdropping range and turned to the Amish man with pulsating curiosity.

He held out his hand. "I am Jotham Hochstetler. You must be the police officer."

I grasped his hand and said, "Serenity Adams. Do I look that much like a cop to you?"

Jotham smiled with his ruined face and glanced away. His unmarred cheek had turned almost as red as the scarred side and I decided that I liked the man in that instant.

"No. You look nothing like a cop to me. But I am at an advantage. Rowan described you on his return from Blood Rock."

I nodded. "Can we talk? I have a few questions for you."

"Of course," Jotham said. He guided me to the furthest table in the restaurant area, calling out orders to his employees on our way there. Even though I couldn't understand exactly what he was saying, I got the gist. To say that he was very involved in the goings-on in his establishment was putting it mildly.

As we sat down at a table, I took a quick look out the window beside us. My gaze immediately landed on a group of Amish teenage boys who were hanging out next to a barn. Several of the teens were smoking and I turned back to Jotham and thumbed towards the group.

"Are they supposed to be smoking?"

Jotham glanced out the window and took a measured sigh. "It is not against our Ordnung for the young men to use cigarettes, but it is certainly not something that I personally condone."

I was satisfied with his obvious distaste at seeing the youngsters smoking, but highly confused at the same time.

"I don't recall ever seeing any of the Amish in Blood Rock smoking."

Jotham shook his head vigorously and then held up his finger to me to wait while he spoke to the server who had suddenly appeared at the table. He addressed her as Mariah, and I forgot about the smoking boys for a moment to study her closely. She was definitely a pretty girl, the contrast between her pale skin and the small amount of dark hair that wasn't covered by her cap made her almost striking. Mariah's gray eyes darted nervously at me a couple of times before she graced Jotham with a tight smile and left us. Was this the same Mariah that the kids at the gas station had been talking about? I had the strong gut feeling that it was.

When Jotham returned his focus to me, I nodded my head towards the retreating girl and said, "She's a beautiful girl."

Jotham squirmed a little at my statement, but agreed, "Yes,

she's our bishop's only child. She's worked here at the sto for the past few years."

"Three years? She's seems awfully young."

Jotham shrugged dismissively, "I suppose Mariah's sixteen or seventeen now." He thought for a moment and then asked, "Do you understand what the Ordnung is?"

I nodded. "Yes, I do."

"A Church's Ordnung is very unique to it. Every community is different." He motioned to the boys by the barn and said, "Here in Poplar Springs, the young ones usually begin working at a paying job when they are right out of school, about fourteen years old. The boys are also allowed to smoke when they are in their time of Rumspringa. I believe that Blood Rock doesn't follow the practice."

"You mean when the kids are allowed to go out into the world and decide if they want to remain Amish?"

"Eh, that is making it simple, but yes. Personally, I think Blood Rock has it right. There is a lot of corruption here for our young people...and I would say that our leniency has something to do with it."

I turned my attention back to the Amish boys, watching them strut around outside as if they were puffed up roosters. The same as in the city, the warmer weather was already stirring up the teens. When I spotted Cody and Lyell walking up to the crowd, my eyes widened, and I thought, small world.

I glanced back at Jotham. He was sitting in the chair in a relaxed and confident way and I noted how friendly the Amish in Poplar Springs had been thus far. Compared to the Blood Rock Amish, this group had practically laid out a red carpet for me. But it also occurred to me that part of this community's openness might be because of their looser set of rules

fact that the area seemed to be a mecca for tour-
ly every seat in the restaurant was taken by middle
English folk. And by the look of their designer jackets
and high dollar purses, they'd probably driven here from as
far away as Chicago for an early weekend getaway.

These Amish had to do a balancing act between keeping
their culture separate and making a living off the romantic
ideals that their way of life inspired in the outside world. The
difficult dynamic had probably played a part in the way Poplar
Spring's leaders were handling the arsons and the unidenti-
fied body. The last thing these people needed for their quaint
and cozy image was a serial arsonist.

I looked back out the window at the intriguing sight of two
of the teenagers who I had encountered at the gas station the
night before, mingling with the Amish boys, and asked, "Are
the Amish kids pretty rowdy around here?"

Jotham weighed his words carefully before he answered.
"There are some serious problems among our young people
that need to be addressed."

I dove right in. "Like, setting barns on fire type of serious?"

Jotham's good eye widened and he abruptly leaned in
closer.

"Shhh, you must not say such a thing in a public place.
Anyone could be listening."

I took a moment to scan the restaurant. I wanted to make
a show of it and when I was finished, I said, "There's no one
around us at the moment except tourists. Why are you so
paranoid?"

Jotham lowered his voice and lifted his chin toward the
table to our right. The couple sitting there was older, probably in their sixties, and dressed more casually than the other

patrons. The man had a ragged beard and the woman's gray hair was pulled back in a loose ponytail. I mentally kicked myself in the butt for not noticing them before.

"They both drive the Amish and are very much the eyes and ears of the community." He paused and leaned back when Mariah returned with a tall glass of cola and a plate of food that she set in front of me. The sandwich appeared to be ham and Swiss and there was a pile of chips and a pickle spear on the side. I had to give the guy credit. He pegged my eating habits perfectly.

"Thank you," I told Jotham. As Mariah was turning to leave, I reached out and lightly grasped her arm. She stopped and looked down at my hand as if it was a rattle snake and I quickly let go. "Hello, I'm Serenity. I believe that I met your mother earlier as I was coming up the road to the store."

Mariah's eyes narrowed a little and in a what-do-I-care sort of way before her face became expressionless again. She replied, "Oh, that's nice," and then she smiled slightly and hurried away.

It was an awkward moment for sure, but I got what I wanted from it. Mariah was definitely the girl that Brandy had gone to bat for. I would bet money on it. The terse brunette didn't look at all like Naomi, but I still compared the two girls and wondered if Mariah had thoughts of running away from her roots, too.

"I apologize for that. Girls her age are moody and act funny sometimes."

"Is she quite a handful?" I asked with forced casualness.

His long hesitation answered my question, but he said, "Not really. Mariah has her moments, the same as the other teenagers who work for me. I'm sure it's difficult being the bishop's daughter." He paused and then changed the subject. "Your task here will not be an easy one, Ms. Adams. Many in our community don't want to even ponder the thought that our own youth may be involved."

"Please call me Serenity. Do you believe that the fires might have been set by Amish teens?"

Jotham shrugged and said, "I don't really know, but I think it would be silly to overlook them completely."

"All right, I'm going to need a list of names of interest from you. I've already created a timeline of the arsons, but I need a lot more clarification than the little information that I was able to piece together online."

"I can do that...but not right now. I have to get back to work." He began to rise, but before I could stop him to arrange our next meeting, he paused and abruptly sat back down again.

"How far back did you go when you did your research on the computer?" he asked.

The slow and precise way that he asked the question made me shudder.

"Rowan told me the first fire happened on October fifteenth of last year...so that's where I began." Reluctantly, I added, "Why?"

Jotham looked around for eavesdroppers once again and then leaned in even closer. The fact that he was risking such close contact with a woman who was basically a stranger to him impressed onto me the importance of what he was about to say.

"The very first fire in Poplar Springs took place in nineteen ninety-seven..." he sucked in a nervous breath and rushed out, "...and two people died."

5

I only had a few seconds for his words to sink in before Rowan walked up to the table with his three daughters in tow.

"There you are!" exclaimed Lucinda, who quickly sat in the seat beside me.

"Hello, Jotham," Rowan said, and then he tipped his black hat to me and added, "Serenity."

"Good morning," I chirped out, suddenly feeling slightly flustered.

Jotham stood and said to Rowan, "I have to get back to work...but I'd like to talk to Serenity in more detail later in the week."

Rowan nodded, "Of course."

Rowan motioned for Jotham to step away from the table and they began whispering. They were too far away for me to hear what they were saying, but I strained hard to listen none-theless. The bombshell that Jotham had just dropped about a possible arson with deaths that happened almost two de-cades earlier was the same as throwing a cup of cold water in my face. The man wouldn't even have mentioned it unless he personally thought that the crimes were connected in some way. I shook my head. Damn Amish. Nothing was ever simple with them.

Mareena took the other chair and Cacey climbed onto her lap. I waved down Mariah and asked her to get the children whatever they wanted. The girls cheerfully recited their orders to Mariah, who rewarded the girls with a bright smile and she even paused from her work for a moment to gossip with Mareena about a new family that had just moved to the community. Before she left the table, Mariah tilted her head to me and asked in an even tone, "Anything else for you?"

"No, I'm fine, thank you."

Mariah hesitated, and for an instant I saw a flash of uncertainty in her eyes, but then it passed and her face was emotionless once again. I was still holding my breath when she walked away and I couldn't help wondering what secrets the girl was hiding.

Rowan returned and took the seat beside Mareena and across from me.

"Jotham is an interesting fellow," I said casually.

Rowan smiled. "He's a good man. We've been friends for thirty years."

I couldn't keep the obvious question inside a moment longer and even though I already suspected the answer, I asked, "What happened to his face?"

It was Mareena who answered me. "Jotham was in the house with my mother when it exploded. She died, but he survived."

The information was swirling around in my head so rapidly that I almost felt dizzy when Rowan added, "He was holding Cacey in his arms at the moment that the house went up and he shielded her against his body to protect her."

I struggled to collect my thoughts. "Was it a gas leak?"

Rowan nodded and sagged back into the chair with a sigh. "At the time, I was working especially long hours, and even though I had smelled more gas in the air than usual, I ignored the nagging feeling in my gut and took my other children to the autumn horse sale in Michum County, thinking that I had time to check into it when I returned home."

Mareena reached over and patted her father's hand and said in a quiet voice, "It wasn't your fault, Da."

I felt a mixture of sadness for both Rowan and Jotham and also the biting suspicion that there was probably a lot more to the story than I was getting at the moment. Poplar Springs was definitely not the quaint Amish community that was being advertised to the tourists.

With the nagging question as to why Jotham was in the house with Rowan's wife while Rowan was away at a horse sale banging loudly inside of my head, I said, "Jotham must be quite the hero around here then."

Rowan's eyes narrowed as he stared back at me. I wasn't expecting that particular reaction, but figured that if I was going to find out what was going on around here, I'd have to push a few buttons along the way.

"Girls, get the sandwiches wrapped to go. You need to head back to the farm to begin your afternoon chores," Rowan said.

"But we wanted to wait a while longer to see if Elayne and Rachel come by. We haven't visited with them in some time," Mareena said in a pleading voice.

"Be on your way. There will be other times for idle chatter," Rowan ordered firmly.

I watched the emotions of anger and resentment pass

quickly over Mareena's face before she swallowed in defeat. "Up, up, Lucinda," she commanded.

Lucinda turned to say goodbye to me and then she hurried away with Mareena who was tugging on Cacey's hand.

I looked back at Rowan and snapped, "Don't Amish kids ever get a break?"

Instead of my question upsetting him like I thought it would, he answered wearily, "I've explained this too many times to count to outsiders like you, but I guess one more time isn't going to hurt me."

"Go on," I coaxed, knowing that nothing he could say would win me over.

"Our children grow up very differently than yours. They learn to work hard and take on responsibility at a young age, and it prepares them for our way of life as adults. My girls have it even tougher since they have no mother to guide them and they've taken over her responsibilities as well. But they do have some freedom." As if he suddenly really wanted to convince me, he said with more conviction, "Just last week they spent an entire day sledding at one of the neighbors."

I couldn't help thinking about Naomi Beiler and how desperately she had wanted to escape the Amish. And she had ended up dying before she had even begun to live. Naomi's story was very tragic, but I had to begrudgingly admit that a lot of the Amish kids seemed to accept their situations rather well, and maybe they even liked their existence. I guess I would just have to chalk it up to one of those things that I would probably never fully understand.

"They're really sweet girls. You should be very proud of them," I offered diplomatically. "I am." He paused for a moment. His steady and weighing gaze made me sit up straighter before he spoke again, "Are you ready to begin the investigation?"

"Absolutely," I assured him.

We rose from the table together, but when I gazed out the window one last time, I paused. Standing with the group of young men beside the barn was a couple of non-Amish men that I hadn't noticed before. One wore black boots and a black leather jacket. His face was covered with a short, clipped beard and his hawkish features made him stand out distinctly among the Germanic looking youngsters gathered around him. The other put me in mind of a chameleon as he was dressed more casually, wearing blue jeans and a brown coat. He had thick, wavy brown hair that most guys would kill for and large, black aviator shades that hid most of his face. And, whereas the alert, Taliban looking guy stuck out like a duck in a hen house, Mr. Chameleon, who was leaning back against the barn wall as if he didn't have a care in the world, blended into the group of youngsters in a very strange way.

My senses sharpened and my heart rate sped up. Something about those two men immediately put me on guard—but why?

"Serenity?" Rowan's eyebrows were raised questioningly.

I picked up my small leather purse from the table and joined him. "Yep, I'm ready."

The buggy ride with Rowan was quite a bit different than the ride I had earlier with his daughters. First of all, the previous buggy had been open and the rush of cold air had been exhilarating. This time, I was overwhelmed with the claustrophobic feeling of being closed into the tiny space of the traditional buggy. The rubbery scent of the vinyl seats was strong and I wrinkled my nose at it as I tried not to brush arms against Rowan who was unavoidably sitting very close beside me. I only thought Mareena had been flying with her little pony. The sheer power of the large black horse stretching out in front of us had me gripping the door tightly with my right hand and the thundering clip clops on the pavement made it impossible to be heard without shouting.

"Where are we going first?"

"Abner Fisher's place. He's our bishop and the last fire took his barn."

"…and that's where the body was found?" I verified.

"Yes," was all Rowan said. He pretended to be completely focused on directing the horse, but I knew better. His occasional glances and extremely rigid appearance told me that he was as bothered by our close proximity as I was.

I liked having the man off balance and tried to use it to my advantage by plunging ahead.

"I read in the newspaper that the body belonged to a woman, estimated to be between twenty-five and forty years old. But as of two days ago, the coroner still hadn't identified the body." I paused to watch four Amish teenagers riding astride and trotting their spotted horses by in the opposite direction, and then continued, "Do you have any idea who it is?"

Rowan shook his head. "I haven't got the slightest idea."

He met my gaze steadily, making me feel that he was telling the truth. "So you aren't missing any women from the community…"

Rowan interrupted, "Of course not. Why do you expect her to be Amish? I would assume that she's English."

"My experience has been that occasionally your people

run off, and when that happens, everyone ignores that they're even gone."

"Honestly, if that were the case, and one of our women were missing, I'd say so."

Rowan slowed the horse to a walk and just as quickly as we had surged forward, we were moving at a snail's pace once again.

I loosened my hold on the door frame and relaxed a little. "And what about the two people that died in the barn fire in nineteen ninety-seven?"

Rowan sucked in a quick breath and snapped his head in my direction.

"Where did you hear about that?"

The level of agitation in his voice was obvious. I picked my words carefully, too perplexed to form an opinion about either Rowan or Jotham at the moment.

"Jotham told me…and he encouraged me to begin my investigation there."

The smell of charred wood reached my nostrils just before Rowan turned the horse into a gravel driveway and I saw the wreckage of the building.

Even though fresh snow covered much of the top of the burnt pile of what used to be a barn, it was still obvious that the fire hadn't been that long ago. The remains of the bright yellow scene tape could be seen poking out here and there among the clumps of snow. The deep, muddy grooves where a fire truck had been parked alongside the road were now filling with puddles from the melting snow.

Rowan seemed to have recovered from his surprise at what his friend had told me and said, "I don't think there's any connection at all between the fire that happened eighteen years ago and the recent rash of burnings."

I gazed at Rowan, trying to get a read on his thoughts from his facial expressions, but coming up empty. Was he lying, trying to cover up some information that he didn't want me to know about? It would be hard to tell with this man. He was the type that usually controlled his emotions easily, but I had already learned that even though the Amish might be pretty good at keeping up outer appearances, they sweated the same as everyone else.

I didn't trust Jotham either, but he had thrown me a bone, so I would definitely follow up on it.

Pulling out my little notepad from my back pocket, I dismissed Rowan's intense gaze and climbed out of the buggy. The afternoon sun was shining brightly, and I reached back into the buggy to retrieve the sunglasses from my purse.

I walked a few feet and stopped. The first thing that occurred to me was that the barn was situated very close to the roadway and Abner Fisher's house sat several hundred feet up the driveway, partly obscured by patches of trees and another shed-like building. It would have been easy to pull up alongside the barn and slip in through a doorway if it had faced the road. Just as easily, someone could throw a cherry bomb into an open window while driving by.

The barn would have had "burn me" written all over it to an arsonist. But the body was another story altogether.

Rowan appeared by my side and I asked him, "Was there a doorway to this barn facing the road?"

"Yes, there was."

"And windows?"

He nodded. "If I remember correctly, there were three on each side of the door."

I quickly drew a stick image of what I imagined the barn to look like and showed it to Rowan.

"That's pretty close, except the roof line wasn't as steep."

"Do you know what part of the barn the body was found in?" I asked, stepping closer to the rubble.

Rowan didn't immediately answer and I stopped writing to look back at him. He shrugged and replied, "I don't right know. I must admit, it never even occurred to me to wonder about exactly where the woman had been found."

Not surprising at all. My prior experiences with witnesses as a cop in Indianapolis were usually the same. Most people didn't fret about the details too much.

"I want to visit the fire chief and the sheriff's department tomorrow. Are you up to that?"

"Of course I will accompany you if want me to."

Rowan's horse let out a high pitched whinny and I followed its alert gaze to see a buggy coming down the driveway toward us. Even at this distance, I was able to clearly make out Joanna Fisher sitting beside a slender, gray bearded man, who I guessed must be her husband, Abner.

The huffing sound from Rowan got my attention and I looked up at him.

"Not in the mood for company?" I asked.

"You'll understand for yourself soon enough. No need to waste my breath trying to explain."

With a heightened sense of curiosity, I impatiently waited for the horse and buggy to reach us.

When the buggy stopped, I stepped up to the open door silently, waiting for Rowan to speak first. I was surprised when it was Joanna who made the introductions.

"Abner, this is the police lady from Blood Rock," she said the words with a tight smile that was not nearly as friendly as the one she had graced me with earlier in the morning.

I thrust my hand forward. "Serenity Adams," I said and motioned with the notebook back at the debris pile. "I'm sorry about your barn."

I guessed the bishop to be in his fifties, maybe twenty years older than his wife. It wasn't a totally creepy age difference, but almost. Abner Fisher's high brows and prominent, straight nose made him look as equally aristocratic as his wife. But where she gave the instant impression of a peering hawk that was sitting on a power line, searching for a juicy mouse, Abner came off as a shy man with wandering eyes.

He waved irritably as if he was swatting an invisible fly and assured me, "It's really a minor thing to lose the building. It can be rebuilt easily enough."

Memories of Aaron Esch, Blood Rock's resident bishop, and his lack of concern about a crime, came flooding back, and I almost rolled my eyes at the thought of history repeating itself.

"True, you can have a new barn up by springtime I'd wager, but...I can't say the same thing about the woman who died in there." I tried not to sound sarcastic, but I'm pretty sure I failed.

Nodding, Abner smoothly replied, "Yes, well, that was the point I was making. The fact that a person had burned in the fire is much worse than the barn going up itself."

"Do you have any ideas who the woman was and why she just happened to be in your barn at the time of the fire?" I asked the bishop, but since he wouldn't make eye contact with me, I tried to read Joanna who didn't have such qualms about looking me squarely in the eyes.

"Haven't got a clue," he admitted.

Joanna didn't need me to ask to know that she was next

to be questioned and volunteered, "I couldn't even make a guess, and it's awfully strange that the police haven't been able to tell us yet, either." She paused and became even more focused, as if it was possible, and asked a question of her own, "Don't you think six weeks is long enough for the coroner to discover who the person is?"

Her frustration with the delay was tangible, and I completely understood her angst. I'd been there too many times to count.

"Usually, when someone's body is decayed or damaged so significantly that a visual determination can't be made, dental records are used. But sometimes it can be difficult to match records up when you have a body without a missing person. I would guess that your local sheriff is sending out information about the woman to other agencies far and wide to match her with a missing woman from somewhere else…since your community doesn't seem to have lost anyone."

I still worried a little that they were all covering up another runaway, but I was definitely getting a very different vibe in this case.

"We have to be patient, Joanna, and have faith that Sheriff Gentry is doing his best to close the case as soon as possible," Abner told his wife.

A very unladylike snort erupted from Joanna's nose and she said, "I have faith in our Lord that He'll shed light on the woman's identity in due time, but it will still be snowing in July if Brody Gentry finds it in his heart to help us."

I glanced at Rowan who had the look of a man silently telling me, "This is what I was talking about."

"Hush now, we must not talk of such things." The bishop's tone was much more forceful than it had been earlier when he had spoken to his wife. He was not a happy camper with her outburst.

Clearing my throat, I said, "Why wouldn't Sheriff Gentry be willing to help?"

"It's a long story, Miss Adams, and not one I want to get into at this time. We are late for our meeting with the Millers as it is." He tipped his hat to me, and nodded to Rowan, saying, "We'll talk later." He snapped the reins across the horse's back and they were off.

A moment later, Rowan and I stood silently together, watching the backside of the bishop's buggy getting smaller and smaller and the sounds of the horse's hooves striking the pavement becoming less distinct.

"So...Sheriff, what did you make of that?" Rowan finally breached the winter quiet of the air.

I turned to look at him and caught his appraising gaze. He was wondering himself if I was worth all the trouble of bringing me here. Honestly, at that moment, I was feeling a little overwhelmed at all the dynamics that were at play in this case. Once again, I found myself in a situation dealing with a group of people who most assuredly would lie and hide the truth from me—ironic, considering the fact that they were members of a Christian sect.

"Obviously, there is a grudge between your local sheriff and the community, maybe even Abner Fisher personally. Care to elaborate?"

"I will on our way back to the house. The day is flying by and I have a few things I have to do at the farm before dark."

I took one last look at the crime scene and closed my notebook. The place was a burnt up pile of sticks with six weeks of winter weather on it. The chances of finding any new evidence in the rubble were slim at best. I really wished I had been able to poke around the morning after the fire, and that line of thinking triggered a thought.

Climbing into the buggy, I said, "The fire happened at night, right?"

"Sure did. As a matter of fact, Reuben Lapp's sons, Jacob and Jory, are the ones who saw the flames and ran to the corner phone box to call the fire department."

I held up my hand stopping him from picking up the reins. "Where is this phone box?"

Rowan pointed down the road in the opposite direction that we had approached from, and said, "There is a phone box about a quarter mile that way on the corner of Simon Graber's land, just beside the road." My face still must have registered confusion, and he went on to elaborate, "It's a shed of sorts that several of the families use on this road."

"Aren't the families here allowed to have telephones on their property?"

"No, it's against our Ordnung," Rowan replied matter-of-factly.

Even though Jotham had explained earlier that each community followed its own set of rules, I still had a difficult time accepting the fact that this particular community allowed their boys to smoke, but telephones on their properties were against the rules.

"I see," I said with a jolt of misgiving, "Have you considered that these Amish boys might have been the ones to set the blaze?"

Rowan's eyes widened. "Why ever would you think such a thing?"

"It's not unusual for the person who set the fire to be the one who calls it in. And people who get off on burning buildings typically stick around to see their handy work."

"I would be highly surprised if that was the case. They are both good boys—hard working and mature for their ages," Rowan said firmly and then he tried to change the subject, "Now, getting back to Sheriff Gentry…"

Rowan's voice suddenly trailed off and I turned in the direction of his stare.

A newer model, solid black Dodge Challenger pulled into the driveway and parked beside us. The spattering of dusty white film over the car didn't fool me. It was a very nice sports car and not the type of ride you would see out in the country. It was much more similar to a vehicle that drug dealers in Indy drove.

But it wasn't the car that caught the breath in my throat. It was the inhabitants. They were the same two men that I had seen with the group of Amish boys in the lot behind the store. Once again, something needled me to attention and I waited for an explanation from Rowan.

"Hey, bro, haven't seen you in a while," the chameleon said.

I shot a look at Rowan, wondering at the newcomer's use of the word "bro," when he quickly said, "Serenity, this is my brother, Asher."

Things were getting stickier by the minute.

6

Asher dipped his head in greeting, but he didn't bother to remove his shades. I never liked talking to people with sunglasses on. It put me at a disadvantage when I couldn't read their eyes. That's why I rarely had mine off when I was outdoors in the daytime. But all the same, I still got the definite feeling that Asher was paying close attention to my reaction to news of his relationship with Rowan. Now that I was up close to him, I could see the family resemblance, physically. Both men had the same striking high cheek bones, but where Rowan was more reserved, Asher appeared to be extremely outgoing.

Asher continued to stare at me while he asked Rowan, "Have you been holding out on me? Are you dating this pretty English woman?"

Interestingly, the fact that Asher didn't know about me the way everyone else in the community did, signaled that there might be a rift of some kind between the brothers.

Rowan didn't beat around the bush when he said, "This is Serenity Adams. She's the sheriff in Blood Rock."

"What would the sheriff from Blood Rock be doing in our neck of the woods?" Asher asked. His tone was amicable,

KAREN ANN HOPKINS

almost teasing, but I wasn't fooled. When Asher and the man seated beside him heard the word *sheriff* they had both straightened in their seats. It was if I had just turned into a grizzly bear before their very eyes. They were suddenly extremely alert, poised for action. I'd seen this kind of reaction from plenty of people before, and it always meant they were guilty of something.

Not giving Rowan a chance to answer, I said, "I'm doing a private investigation of the recent barn burnings and the death of the woman in this particular barn." I lifted my chin toward the wreckage, but I didn't take my eyes off the men as I gaged their reactions to what I'd said.

Asher's companion's eyes widened considerably before he quickly looked away. Asher remained staring back at me, seemingly weighing my words before carefully saying, "Do you have any ideas who might be our pyromaniac?"

It was a reasonable question, but something in Asher's tone and the tilt of his head put me on edge. I also made a mental note that he had referred to the problem as *our*, which struck me as odd since he obviously had left the Amish community to become English.

With a quick glance, I saw that Rowan was waiting for my answer as well. "I just got here today, but hopefully some leads will pop up soon," I said.

Asher seemed to breathe a little easier with my answer and I decided to see how much about himself he was willing to share. "When did you leave the Amish, Asher?"

Asher leaned back and smiled broadly with the look of a man who got asked that particular question a lot. "I was about eighteen when I cut out. The Amish lifestyle didn't suit me very well," he turned to Rowan and quickly added,

58

"If you need anything, bro, give me a call. Don't be such a stranger."

Rowan nodded his head stiffly and then Asher said to me, "Have a nice day, Sheriff."

Asher's words were like rotten potatoes dripping with honey. I squinted at the sports car in annoyance as it backed out onto the roadway and drove away.

Rowan wasted no time clucking to his horse and snapping the reins. As we began building speed, he glanced over and said, "What did you think about my brother?"

"You want my honest opinion?"

"Of course," he said firmly.

"He's a jerk, but a charismatic one." As an afterthought, I added, "I can see why he didn't fit in with your people."

The farms were once again whizzing by and the breeze was getting colder by the minute. The late afternoon sun had dipped low in the sky and all the snow that had melted earlier in the day was beginning to refreeze, causing the landscape to glisten delightfully. I zipped my jacket up against the chill, and had the fleeting thought of how strange it was that I was riding around in a buggy in northern Indiana with an Amish man whom I barely knew. God definitely had a wicked sense of humor when it came to me, I thought.

"You are a very astute person. Asher was always rebellious, but he hid it well from our parents when we were teenagers. He broke the rules…but he never did get caught."

"So what finally forced him out?"

Rowan took a deep breath and his mouth quivered slightly. I suddenly became hyper aware, recognizing the imminent signs of a person about to betray a secret. I had discovered through my relationship with Daniel that both the Amish, and ex-Amish people, didn't like discussing their pasts. Then it suddenly occurred to me as if a blinding flash of lightning had struck the ground beside me that the fire of nineteen ninety-seven would have happened about the same time that Rowan and Asher were teenagers themselves.

Was it just a coincidence that Asher showed up at the crime scene today, or was there a more sinister reason for his visit to the community? I really didn't believe in coincidences and I already knew that it was very common for perpetrators to return to the scenes of their crimes. Maybe I was getting way too far ahead of myself, but I had the instant impression that Asher and his friend were not law abiding citizens. And I trusted my instincts. They had served me well thus far.

The surrendering look on Rowan's face was fleeting. It was replaced by the expression of stubbornness that I had unfortunately discovered was all too common among the Amish people. "Our ways didn't suit him, just like he said."

I leaned back and chuckled inwardly for thinking this case would be that easy. "You guys aren't that friendly anymore, I take it?"

"No. He chose to walk on a very different path than me and I couldn't have him influencing my children."

I got it. I had a sensible sister who was similar to me in everything from politics to basic values, but not everyone was that lucky. Shunning aside, it would be impossible for Rowan to keep up a relationship with a badass brother like Asher.

The horse slowed to a walk just before we turned up Rowan's driveway. I experienced a bubble of happiness for a moment at the prospect of a hot shower before I remembered that the simple luxury probably wasn't an option.

"Uh, does your family ever take showers?"

Rowan looked surprised for a second at the drastic change of direction that the conversation had taken and then he laughed. "I'm sorry, but you will have to make due with filling a bath basin with hot water."

His eyes sparkled with good humor and I wondered if he was teasing me. I really hoped he was when I protested, "You're kidding, right?"

Rowan sobered and shook his head. "It won't be as bad as you think. The girls will help you get the tub ready. It just takes a little bit longer than the instant shower that you're so used to."

I was mulling his words over when the sound of shouting mixed with the pounding of splashing hooves suddenly met my ears. We both looked quickly up the driveway.

Rowan stopped the buggy and waited for the rider to reach us. When the youth slid to a stop beside us, I guessed his age to be around thirteen. His chiseled facial features and dark brown hair told me that he must be Rowan's other son.

"Da, come quickly! It's the new black cow..." I suddenly lost understanding when the boy's words changed languages in midsentence, but I got the gist that there was a life threatening crisis going on with a cow.

Orders fired from Rowan's mouth in German as if it was an automatic weapon and then the boy was racing back up the driveway. The buggy lurched forward and I had to grab the door frame for stability.

Rowan exclaimed, "We have a cow down with a breech birth." He took a breath and glanced at me anxiously and went on, "We have to get the calf out, and it's not going to be easy. We might need your help."

Still bouncing and clinging to the side of the buggy, I muttered, "Sure thing," but I was silently thinking you have got to be kidding me.

7

When we finally reached the cow, she was obviously in great distress. Her black fur was soaked with sweat and the moisture that was rising from her wet body into the cold winter air was similar to steam that escaped from a sauna when you opened the door. She was vibrating with giant tremors of shivering and every twenty seconds or so, she'd whip her head around to her stomach and bellow out a shrill cry that made me clench my teeth. I certainly wasn't a farmer, but even I could see that the poor cow was in a very bad way.

The boy who had ridden to meet us in the driveway was now fast approaching at a dead run with a heavy, woolen-type blanket, while the older boy, who didn't look at all like Rowan, with his mousy brown hair and light blue eyes, sat at the cow's head. The boy on the ground was probably about fifteen or so, but with his wet cheeks and worried gaze, he seemed to be handling the scene worse than the other children.

Mareena stood beside me stoically holding a coil of rope tightly in her arms. Lucinda and Cacey were nowhere to be seen and I imagined that they were in the house tending to other less life threatening chores.

The sun had disappeared a few minutes earlier beyond the low hill line to the west and with its departure came a bone chilling wind that cut painfully through my jacket. I repositioned myself, turning my back to winter's onslaught, and tugged my toboggan down tighter over my ears.

I admired the way Mareena, in her black corduroy coat, could stand so straightly into the biting wind. The girl did have a thick, burgundy-colored scarf wrapped around her neck though, that completely covered her mouth. Her gaze was unflinching as she unemotionally watched the cow writhing in pain beside us.

Rowan was in the process of backing up the horse, minus the buggy, to the hindquarters of the cow. It still had the harness secured over its back and across its chest, and my imagination ran freely about what was going to happen next.

"Seth, cover the cow with the blanket and then go to her head. Gabe, come over here to help me," Rowan instructed the boys. Even though the man had probably dealt with situations like this in the past, I was still impressed with the calmness of his voice. Hysteria in an emergency certainly wasn't helpful, but unfortunately in my business, I encountered it all too often. I had to admit that when things got dicey, the Amish seemed to handle themselves better than most people did.

"Is there anything you want me to do?" I asked.

Rowan had the horse in position, and without specific direction, Mareena left my side to hand him the rope. He looked up at me as he tied a small loop at the end and said, "I need you at the cow's head. You can help Seth keep her on the ground. We don't want her to get up when we begin pulling."

Unfortunately, my assumptions had been right, I thought as I knelt beside Seth, taking the lead rope from his hands. My heart was pounding, but I focused on the cow's large eyes as another contraction racked her. Terror was easily identified in their brown depths and the sudden pang of sympathy I felt for her made me swallow hard.

When she tried to lift up, I held the rope tightly and leaned against her neck. Seth pushed in closer and placed his knee directly on her head to help me. She was incredibly strong and I began to fear that the two of us wouldn't be able to keep her still enough while Rowan and Gabe worked to free the calf.

"Take the reins, Son, and pull Dakota gently forward, just enough until the rope is taut." When Gabe hesitated, Rowan said with more force, "Go on now, we haven't got much time. You'll do fine. Go slowly now."

Another gust of wind battered my back, but this time I didn't feel the cold. I was too focused on the poor, exhausted animal beneath my hands. When the contraction passed, she laid down flat again and let out a great sigh. I had been with my sister when she delivered my nephew, Will, and the way this cow was behaving was not that much different than Laura's re-action to each passing contraction. The main difference from when my sister had given birth was that I had been in a warm, comfortable hospital room, surrounded by several gray-haired nurses and a no-nonsense type of doctor. I was just a spectator for that event and it had ended with a beautiful baby boy and an elated woman. I was afraid that this delivery wasn't going to turn out nearly as picture perfect.

"Another contraction is beginning, Gabe. Go ahead and take Dakota forward. Don't stop until I tell you," Rowan ordered.

The cow began to struggle to rise again and Seth and I used everything we had to keep her down. I even shifted positions and straddled her neck with my leg when she began to fight us in earnest. I knew that the pulling was really hurting her, but I didn't waiver, concentrating on the task I had been given.

"Good job, Serenity and Seth, we've almost got him out. Keep her down. This baby is huge and being breach, he's wedged in there pretty well," Rowan spoke with the edginess of an adrenaline saturated voice. The extra chemical rush was helping Rowan work quicker and more fluidly, and I began to feel a little hope that maybe all would end well with the cow after all.

When the horse began to strain for an instant, I held my breath and I could feel Seth beside me, poised just as nervously as I was. We all held our breaths as Dakota took a jerking stride forward, and then the rope loosened. A sudden burst of steam rose up from behind the cow as the calf finally broke free into the cold, snowy world.

"Mareena, hand me the blanket from the cow," Rowan said as he began vigorously rubbing the calf with his bare hands. An excruciatingly long moment later, the solid black calf mooed and began kicking its legs.

Rowan lifted the calf into a standing position and covered it with the blanket. "Seth and Mareena, please take the calf to barn and begin warming a bottle. Gabe, you can unharness Dakota and stall him for the night."

The kids immediately went about their jobs and Rowan came to kneel beside me. We silently watched Seth and Mareena struggle the large calf out of the field while Gabe lead the horse away. Gabe did pause for few seconds at the gate to gaze back at the mother cow before he dropped his head and headed for the barn.

"What about the cow?" I asked quietly, suspecting what he was going to say. Seeing the edges of the dark red puddle spreading out starkly into the white snow had already dashed my hopes.

"Her uterus came out with the calf, along with way too much bleeding. She'll never make it. The kindest thing to do is to put her out of her misery."

I nodded, understanding the situation full well.

Rowan gazed at me with clear eyes and said, "I'm going to the house to get the rifle. I know that it's cold, but do you mind staying with her until I get back?"

I unzipped my jacket and reached into the holster that was secured at my side, pulling out my 9 millimeter Glock.

"I think this will work." I took a second for the surprised look to pass over his face before I asked, "Where do I shoot for the quickest death?"

Rowan took a breath and then eyed me with speculation that quickly turned to a look of admiration. "Are you sure you want to do this?"

Without hesitation, I said, "It's not about wanting to do it, but more about doing what needs to be done. It might take fifteen more minutes for you to return with your gun and there's no reason to make the cow suffer that long when I can do the same thing right now." Seeing him glance at the gun in my hand, I quickly added, and there's no way that you're firing this. Go ahead and show me where to shoot so we can get it over with."

Rowan pointed and said, "The skull is the thinnest right here."

I aimed at the cow that was now lying flat. Her labored breathing and the coppery smell of the pool of blood made me a little unsteady and I took my own deep breath, blocking out the sound and smell, and staring at the soft tuft of fur curling in front of her ear.

A sudden memory of me being posed the same way, only instead of a cow, the gun was aimed at a person in a dim side street of Indianapolis, flashed before my eyes. The identical feeling of both clarity and surrealism rolled over me as my finger rested on the trigger. I had killed only once before, and it had turned out to be a teenage girl beneath an oversized Colt's jacket. That time had messed me up for months, but this was different. This was only a cow, and I was putting her out of her misery.

But when the blast of the shot echoed across the lonely field, I could admit only to myself that the act of killing the cow felt pretty much the same as shooting a criminal. It really sucked both times.

8

Rowan and I walked in silence toward the small white house that was my temporary home. Darkness had settled in, but the sparkling cover of snow was softly illuminating the barnyard and I had no trouble seeing where I was going. The calf had heartily finished the bottle of milk that Rowan had on hand for just such emergencies and it was snugly resting in a stall piled high with straw at the moment. Mareena had informed me that the little bull calf would be introduced to a cow that had lost her own calf during the bitter cold snap the week before with the hopes that the still grieving cow would adopt the orphan.

I was weary with fatigue and chilled to the bone when we finally reached the steps leading up to the doorway. Anxious to be by myself, and get cleaned up with whatever warm water I could come up with, I barely slowed when I said, "We really need to sit down and talk about the case soon. I have so many questions for you, but I'm just too tired for that conversation tonight. Honestly, I don't know how you do it. It's bad enough to feed and water all those animals, but adding the freezing weather into the mix and the drama of having to put a cow down really makes farming a terrible profession to be in."

Rowan found humor in my dead serious statement and chuckled. "Farming isn't for everyone, but I must say that you surprised me out there today. There's a lot more to you than the average English woman, that's for sure."

Gazing back at him to see if he was teasing, I discovered an earnest face. "It really is a tough life for your kind. Why do you stick with it?"

I might have been overstepping my place with the question, but I was really curious why so many people chose to remain Amish and others, like Daniel, Asher or Naomi, couldn't wait to be free from it.

"Farming is in my blood. I'd be lost without it." He paused and looked out at the wintry night and quiet barnyard, adding, "It's about the community too. We are never alone. No matter how bad things get, there's always a helping hand."

I nodded with some understanding.

"The girls should have filled up the basin with hot water for you to wash up, but I'm afraid it might be only lukewarm by now," he said.

"Don't worry, I'll manage," I said as I fidgeted in the snow, wanting desperately to get out of the cold.

"We'll have supper on in about an hour," Rowan said.

My stomach suddenly growled loudly at his statement and I hoped that he didn't hear the rumbling noise. I really was starving, but I was also exhausted from the cow incident and just wanted to be alone. That's when I heard the clip clops coming up the driveway. We both turned to watch the buggy that was being pulled by a gray horse approach.

The buggy stopped in front of us and the door popped open. A young woman stuck her head out of the doorway and said, "When I drove by earlier I saw you all out in the field with the cow. How did it go?"

Rowan took a few steps toward the buggy and replied, "The cow had to be put down, but the bull calf is robust and should survive."

I noted the soft, friendly tone that Rowan had used and was inclined to take a closer look at the woman. It was hard to tell from the long, black coat she wore, but she appeared to have a slender figure. Taking in her high cheekbones, oval face and large eyes, I realized that she was a pretty woman. A few wisps of blond locks that had escaped her cap were curling around her face and when she noticed me looking at her, she quickly moved her hand to hide them in her cap once again. When she raised her chin to gaze back at me, her cheeks were bright red.

"Oh, I'm sorry," Rowan said. "Serenity, this is Anna King. She's our new school teacher."

"Nice to meet you," I said.

"Serenity is the sheriff from Blood Rock. She's looking into the barn fires," Rowan added.

"Of course, I've heard all about you, Serenity. Thank you for traveling all the way here to help us figure out what's going on," Anna said with a reluctant smile.

"I'm going to do my best," I said.

"That's about all anyone can do," Anna told me and then she turned back to Rowan, "I worried that with the trouble with the cow, you and the young'uns wouldn't have time to prepare a proper dinner. I hope you don't mind that I brought a pot of chicken and dumplings and some fresh baked bread over."

A wide grin broke out on Rowan's face. "You're an angel, Anna. Mareena was busy helping us with the calf and wasn't able to get dinner started."

Anna beamed when Rowan added, "We'll accept your hospitality on one condition—that you join us."

"I would be pleased to," Anna glanced at me, "if it's all right with the sheriff, that is."

About the last thing I wanted to do was to make conversation with an Amish woman, but eating her chicken and dumplings was another story all together. And it was obvious that Anna had a major crush on Rowan. This might be just the chance the woman had been waiting for to make her move. Her almost pleading eyes were hard to ignore and even my jaded self couldn't help but inwardly smile at the woman's clumsy attempt to get to know Rowan better.

"Sounds like a great idea to me, but if you'll both excuse me, I really need to get cleaned up."

"We'll see you in a little while then," Rowan said to me before he offered to take Anna's horse to the barn.

I could barely hear Anna's bubbly response as I closed the door behind me. They are so hooking up someday, I thought, as I pulled out my cell phone.

I walked the room several times searching for phone service, before finally sitting down on the floor in the far corner of the room. I was grateful that the wood burning stove was still emitting heat and guessed that Lucinda must have added logs to the fire when she had arrived home earlier.

Sighing, I unzipped my jacket and enjoyed the warmth in the tiny room while I waited impatiently for Todd to answer the phone.

"Hey, boss, how goes it in the land of zero convenience?"

It was funny how the sound of Todd's voice usually irritated the hell out of me, but this time, the familiarity of it gave me some kind of weird comfort.

"Besides having to shoot a cow in the head today, everything's peachy."

"What the hell…are you joking?"

"No, wish I was. I'll tell you about it later. Right now, I need you to run a name for me."

"Sure thing, boss."

"My cell phone and internet reception here are sporadic at best, call me back with anything you find out."

"What's the name?"

"Asher Schwartz."

9

Rowan's kitchen still had the unfinished look of a just built house and I glanced around, eyeing the cabinets without doors and the particle board floor. The place certainly needed a woman's touch and turning to observe Anna hovering over the stove, I guessed that she was definitely up to the challenge.

The scent of the warming broth from the chicken and dumplings was heavy in the air and I breathed it in deeply, very happy that Anna had been keeping a close eye on the goings on at Rowan's farm.

"Will you drink water or milk, Miss Serenity?" Lucinda asked. '

"Milk would be nice," I replied.

I felt a little guilty about sitting in the rocking chair beside the fireplace while Anna, Mareena and Lucinda swept around the room, setting the table and pouring the drinks. But they had all politely refused my offer to help, so I tried to push the awkward feeling aside.

Rowan was seated on the other side of the rock faced fireplace, reading from the Bible. I caught him as he looked up nervously in Anna's direction several times. When he occasionally made eye contact with me, he'd drop his gaze to the book in his hands quickly.

Gabe and Seth were by the doorway, both engrossed in their job of oiling a western saddle that was sitting on a wooden stand. The room was relatively quiet except for Cacey's humming as she played with her doll on the floor and the constant crackling and hissing from the fireplace.

My attention was drawn back to Rowan's oldest boy and I studied his features intently. He didn't look anything like his father or brother and that made me wonder a bit. He didn't resemble his sisters either and I tried to convince myself that perhaps he favored his mother and none of the other children did, but I highly doubted it. Unfortunately, since the Amish didn't allow portraits of themselves, I had no way of even knowing what Hedy Schwartz looked like, but the thing that bugged me even more was the strong resemblance I saw in Gabe to Jotham Hochstetler. From the instant I had heard that Jotham had been in the house alone with Hedy and Cacey, I was suspicious, but it was very difficult to wrap my mind around the possibility that an Amish woman might have an affair. After seeing Rowan's oldest child first hand, I was beginning to be a believer. And the fact that Jotham had been with Hedy in the house when it blew up couldn't be ignored either.

Anna's voice broke into my thoughts, "Supper's ready."

The boys rose quickly, wasting no time at all to cross the room and pick up their plates from the table. They lined up at the stove anxiously waiting for their food when Anna cleared her throat loudly. "Boys, the English have different dinner customs than we do. I think we should let Serenity get her fill first, and then you can dish yours out."

I caught the startled looks from the boys, and the three girls, before Gabe and Seth stepped back.

Gabe graced me with a one sided smile and motioned with his hand for me to go first. Seth just slumped in defeat that he would have to wait a little longer for his dinner.

I glanced at Rowan who shrugged and said, "Usually the menfolk get their meals first, but Anna is right to change things up tonight since we have an English guest in our home."

The idea that the men fed themselves first didn't surprise me in the least and gave me one more reason to feel even more pity for the Amish women. But as I stepped up to the stovetop with my plate in hand, the look on Anna's face was anything but resentful. She accepted the way things were done and was all right with it. Who was I to complain if no one else cared? But then I thought of Naomi. I bet she'd cared.

When we were all finally seated together, Rowan and the boys were lined up on one side of the table while all the females were situated on the other. At first, I thought that maybe it was just the way it had worked out, but then I reconsidered.

Rowan said, "Let us take a moment for silent prayer."

Everyone bowed their heads and I followed suit. I had never been one to pray before meals, but sometimes at night when I was alone in the dark, I would pray to God about important things.

The weirdness of sitting at the dinner table with an Amish family that I barely knew had put me a little off balance anyway, making it impossible to focus on a proper prayer, so instead, I took a peek and was astonished to see that all the children, even little Cacey, had their eyes sealed tight.

The end of prayer time was signified with a sudden rustling of sound around the table as some of the kids reached for slices of bread and others began to dig into the meal.

I was famished myself, but I held myself in check and waited for Anna and Rowan to begin eating before I dove in. As usual, the food was amazing. The dumplings melted in my mouth and the creamy broth had a unique zing from an herb seasoning that I couldn't quite place.

I had caught a couple of shy looks from Anna in Rowan's direction, but I no longer believed her to be the sappy pushover that I had assumed earlier. Anna had taken the chance to initiate the change of dinner protocol on my account. I appreciated her thoughtfulness.

Half turning to Anna, I asked, "Did you grow up in this community?"

Shaking her head, she replied, "No, I moved here from northern Ohio about six months ago to take the teaching job."

"It must have been difficult for you to relocate like that," I said making small talk.

"Not really. I live with my aunt's family and I've made friends here quickly," she glanced towards Rowan, but quickly back at me again.

My phone vibrated in my pocket and for a second I was flushed with sudden excitement that I had reception. Unfortunately, I couldn't act on it, especially with seven pairs of eyes staring at me because of the very out-of-place noise.

"This is the best chicken and dumplings that I've ever had," I complimented Anna to distract everyone's attention.

Anna's cheeks reddened and she smiled broadly. "I am so very glad that you like it."

"Ma'am, do you know who has been setting the fires?" It was Gabe who had asked the question and I looked over at him with raised brows.

"That's not your concern," Rowan said tightly.

Gabe looked sulkily down at his plate for a moment and then he said, "I'm done eating. May I be excused?"

The boy's words were contrite, but his tone wasn't. I quickly glanced at Rowan to see his reaction and also brace for an embarrassing parental crack-down. Surprising me all the more, Rowan's expression was only tired and I guessed that he must be having some kind of ongoing battle with the boy.

"You may be excused," Rowan said neutrally.

My phone vibrated again, but this time it was an incoming text message. I couldn't put off my curiosity any longer.

"I'm sorry, I need to read this," I told Rowan.

"Go right ahead."

Holding the phone in my lap, I saw the message was from Todd and touched the screen. The content made my heart rate accelerate rapidly and I had to scan the message twice to make sure I was reading it correctly.

<This is important.>

<Asher Schwartz has long rap sheet in Indianapolis. Several drug sale arrests, including pharmies and heroin. Reckless endangerment of a minor, 2 counts felony larceny and assault on a girlfriend also on the list. Served six years on convictions. He was also convicted of selling hash oil to minors in Poplar Springs two years ago, but before he served a day, his record there was completely expunged by Judge Warren>

<This guy is badass. Tread carefully. I'll come up there if you need help.>

It was nice to know that my instincts were still right on, but the implications from the text were also quite frightening.

If Rowan's ex-Amish brother was involved with the fires, then there was a strong possibility that other crimes were also being committed in the touristy Amish town. And the question of why a judge would expunge a professional criminal's record was even scarier to contemplate.

"You're as white as the snow outside. Is everything all right?" Anna asked in a concerned voice.

I didn't have the chance to respond when loud knocks on the door sounded. Rowan rose quickly, muttering, "I wonder who that is…"

A rush of cold air slapped my face when Rowan opened the door.

When I saw who the visitor was, I felt both relief and an irritating flutter of my heart.

Holding out his hand to Rowan, Daniel said, "I'm sorry for the late arrival, but I had to finish up some business on the home front before I left Blood Rock."

While he was grasping Rowan's hand, Daniel gazed over at me and smiled.

Annoyingly, I felt at ease for the first time since arriving in Poplar Springs.

10

I stood beside Anna at the kitchen sink and glanced over my shoulder at Daniel, who was sitting at the table with Rowan. There was tension in the air between the men that I couldn't quite figure out. Maybe it was just two type A personalities clashing or possibly it had to do with the fact that Daniel was an Amish deserter. Either way, I couldn't help glancing over my shoulder every so often in rapt interest at their cautious conversation.

"Abner Fisher is our bishop here in Poplar Springs. He's the one who put me in contact with Aaron. I understand they're cousins," Rowan said.

"Aaron is a good man. He's a touch too strict with the authority in the community, but he means well," Daniel said before he took a sip from his cup of coffee.

"Personally, I think strictness is a good thing," Rowan said glumly and continued, "Poplar Springs could use a firmer hand, especially when dealing with its young people."

"Some kids are more rebellious than others. How bad can it be?" Daniel asked.

Rowan responded with a snort. "I'm not talking about the usual sneaking off after chores to play with some English kid's electronic games or getting caught kissing behind the woodshed."

I paused with the dish towel in hand and listened closer. My conversation earlier in the day with Jotham about the problems with the kids in the Poplar Springs community was still fresh on my mind, but unfortunately Anna chose right then to interrupt Rowan.

"Rowan, you don't want to give a negative impression to Daniel and Serenity of Poplar Spring's children." Anna spoke with a sweet voice, but I wanted to slap her just the same. Rowan was about to spill the beans and Anna had stopped him. Why?

I caught Daniel's gaze and saw disappointment in his eyes as well.

Rowan stood and said, "Anna is right. I probably expect too much from the young ones." He shrugged and added, "Perhaps a more traditional community might suit me better than this one."

"You don't mean that...do you?" Anna exclaimed, her cheeks suddenly flushing bright red.

Rowan's own children had left the kitchen shortly after Daniel's arrival and the question hung in the air uncomfortably. Daniel and I exchanged glances and I could tell he was clearly confused.

Finally, Rowan responded with a smile and firm shake of his head. "No worries. I have no plans to relocate. But things do need to change around here." He turned to Daniel. "It's getting on pretty late now and I have an early morning with the cows. I'm afraid you'll have to sleep on the couch tonight. Tomorrow, I'll make arrangements for you to have a room at one of the other families in the community."

"There's the trundle bed in the cabin. Daniel can use it." My words spilled from my mouth unexpectedly and after simultaneously seeing Rowan's shocked look and Daniel's huge grin, I instantly wanted to swallow them back down.

"That would not be appropriate, Serenity," Rowan admonished.

I glanced at Anna who was staring at me with a look of understanding, and maybe a bit of envy, thrown in. I narrowed my eyes at all three of them. I was a grown woman and a sheriff to boot. I didn't need to explain myself to these people.

"Look, it might be inappropriate for your Amish sensibilities, but it isn't for us. This will give Daniel and me the opportunity to discuss the case without interfering with your household," I placed the plate that I had been holding onto the stack of other dishes with a *clank*.

I walked to the door and plucked my jacket from the peg. Meeting Rowan's gaze steadily, I added, "This isn't going to be a problem, is it?"

Rowan's already dark eyes became black pools. There was an incredibly long pause before he said, "Of course not. I forgot my place. You aren't one of us and you can do as you wish." Rowan picked up his hat and told Anna, "I'll get your horse hitched up."

After saying a quick goodbye to Anna, Daniel and I followed Rowan out the door. The rush of cold air was refreshing after leaving the overly warm confines of Rowan's small kitchen. Daniel stopped at his Jeep just long enough to grab a duffle bag and then he met me at the cabin's door. I glanced over at Rowan's rigid form moving quickly towards the barn and shouted out, "Good night."

Rowan raised his hand and replied, "I'll see you both in the morning."

Once we were inside the dark cabin, I stumbled over to the bed and flopped down on it.

"The matches are in the basket on the counter," I told Daniel.

I hadn't bothered to put the sleeper sofa back together that morning and with a sudden racing of my heart, I became aware of the possibilities of what might happen with Daniel and me spending a night alone together. As I waited for Daniel to light the three oil lamps in the room, I silently scolded myself for offering the trundle bed in the corner for Daniel's use in the first place. I should have swallowed my pride and just listened to Rowan. It would have been a whole lot less complicated if Daniel was sleeping on the couch in the main house, instead of a few feet away from me.

When the lamps were glowing, Daniel went to work on the wood stove, cleaning the ashes out and adding several logs. I watched him intently as he quietly went about his business, falling right into rhythm of his old Amish ways. I admired the calm and detached way that he prepared the cabin and was also blazingly irritated that he was so easily ignoring my existence in the room. It was as if he knew we had all night together and he wasn't in any kind of a hurry.

Finally, after a very long ten minutes or so, Daniel passed by me on the bed and sat down on the trundle. When he met my gaze, he smiled smugly and said, "Cozy little place isn't it?"

His suggestive tone set me off. "Don't even think that the two of us sharing this cabin is going to lead to anything remotely romantic. We are here on business...and that's it."

Daniel didn't lose the smirk when he shrugged and said, "Trust me. I'm not delusional about our relationship in the least." He leaned back leisurely and his brown eyes were sharp when he went on to say, "But we are two consenting adults who are highly attracted to each other. I'm happy to help you in any way you need on this trip."

Part of me wanted to pull out my gun and shoot him, and the other wanted to have my legs wrapped tightly around him. The warring sides battled within me as a frustrating tingle began to develop in my groin. I looked back at Daniel, feeling confused and angry. Why did this man have such an effect on me? A mere glance from him set my body on fire. I wanted him—badly—and the feeling completely freaked me out. Before Daniel, the only time that my body had reacted so violently to a man was when I'd dated Denton, and look how that had turned out. Really hot guys were nothing but trouble. I had already learned that lesson and I wasn't about to go there again, at least not tonight.

"We are here to solve a case involving multiple arsons and a body. Let's not get sidetracked," I said. And to emphasize my seriousness, I slipped off my jacket, and then my holster. I took my time, making a big show of placing the gun on the nightstand beside the bed before I forced my attention back to Daniel.

He was staring at me with a stubborn tilt to his chin, and the look doused the flames sparking inside of me a little, thankfully.

"You aren't going to have to shoot me. I would never do anything to you that you weren't begging for."

The thought of how easy it would be to just walk over to him, climb onto his lap and press my mouth against his lips was fleeting, but poignant. I swallowed and took a steady breath, trying desperately to hide my reaction to his flirting.

Clearing my throat, I said, "We've got a lot more on our plate here than I originally thought."

"Don't we always?" Daniel teased.

"I'm serious. Listen up. Like you heard tonight, there seems to be a lot of trouble with the Amish kids in this neighborhood. Not only is Rowan worried about it, but his friend, Jotham, also gave me the heads up that something more sinister is going on with the local teens. On top of all that, Jotham was scarred up pretty badly when he was in a house that blew up from a gas leak." I paused to take a breath, and to make sure that I still had his full attention. "It was Rowan's house, and Jotham was alone with Rowan's wife, Hedy, and her infant daughter at the time. Hedy died, but Jotham shielded Cacey with his own body, and she managed to escape relatively unharmed."

"What does that have to do with the recent fires?" Daniel interrupted.

"The explosion happened at night—don't you think that it's strange that the two of them were alone together at the time?"

Daniel shrugged, "Maybe, but I still don't see how it relates to why we're here now."

"Jotham also wants me to look into a fire that happened in the area in nineteen ninety-seven. There were two deaths in that one and although I haven't had a chance to do any research on it yet, it appears that that fire might be connected to our recent ones. To me, it signals that the explosion of Rowan's house can't be ignored either. The cherry on top of all this is Rowan's brother, Asher. He has a rap sheet a mile long in Indianapolis, but for some strange reason, his narcotics convictions here in Poplar Springs were expunged two years ago."

"Why would a judge do that?"

Good question.

"My personal experience is that people who get their records expunged are either selling out someone else's secrets, or they're blackmailing or bribing the local authorities."

Daniel leaned forward. "Do you think that the law is corrupt in this town?"

I chuckled at Daniel's naivety. "Law enforcement, from cops all the way up to judges, have been known to work the system in a lot of small towns around the country. It wouldn't surprise me in the least if that's happening here in Poplar Springs."

Daniel shook his head and held up his hand. "Whoa, if that's the case, then we need to get the hell out of Dodge." Daniel ignored my gasp, and added, "This isn't your jurisdiction. You can't manipulate the case the way you did back in Blood Rock with Naomi's murder. We can get in over our heads really quickly up here."

Daniel had a point. There was a lot more going on in Poplar Springs than I ever imagined, but after spending a day here I couldn't just up and leave without at least trying to find out some answers. My mind drifted back to Cacey's stoic little round face and Lucinda's friendly smile. And I thought about Mareena baking her pies every Thursday morning and Gabe and Seth rising before the sun to do their chores in the frigid temperatures. They were great kids and I couldn't live with the thought that if I left, they all might be in some kind of danger. I had two weeks of paid vacation. Surely, in that amount of time I could figure things out enough to at least provide myself with some peace of mind that I wasn't abandoning this family to some horrible fate. And then there was the obviously troubled bishop's daughter, Mariah, who reminded me so much of Naomi. I had arrived too late to save Naomi, but not this time. There was time to help Mariah, if she needed it. I couldn't just walk away at this point.

"I'm going ahead with my investigation. What you do is up to you."

Daniel sighed resignedly. "I knew you would say that. So what's the game plan?"

"We're going to pay the local sheriff a visit in the morning and see what we can find out from him. We also need to stop by the library to search through the newspapers from nineteen ninety-seven and do a proper interview with Rowan and a few others in the community."

"Sounds as if it's going to be a full day," Daniel said thoughtfully.

"Are you up for it?"

Daniel chuckled, "Oh, you know I am." He sobered and looked back at me with tight lips and said, "Have you noticed that most of what you've told me has some connection to Rowan Schwartz?"

Daniel was definitely eye candy, but what I really liked about the man was that his mind worked a whole hell of a lot like mine. "Yeah, don't worry. At this point, he's at the top of my list."

11

T he tall cornstalks pressed in closer, their sharp-edged leaves slashing at my arms and face. I swatted them away and summoned the strength to run even faster. The muscles in my legs were cramping and my lungs burned, but I didn't slow down. I could see the tree line and knew that I was almost there.

The golden glow of the harvest moon began peeking over the tops of the trees, inch by inch its silhouette climbed laboriously into the sky. I managed to find one last surge of strength and moved forward, my heart beating madly against my ribcage, my ability to breathe almost gone.

Kaboom. The sound vibrated through my entire body as I came to a screeching stop.

I filled my lungs with a deep breath and carefully parted the last few corn stalks. A stiff breeze stirred the thickly hanging branches of the hedgerow and a flutter of leaves sprayed down in an excited spray. The moon was high enough in the sky now that I could see quite well in its buttery light, and as I pushed the last leaves aside, my senses heightened even more. The call of a bird settling in for the night whistled in my ears and the smell of decaying leaves and mud filled my nostrils, but I ignored all of it, too intent on the blurry object on the ground right before me.

With cautious steps, I walked forward, glancing up to search the shadowed trees that rose up like an impenetrable wall at the edge of the cornfield. I knew who was lurking in there, but even though fear pumped madly through me, I didn't turn and run.

The object suddenly became clear and I saw the girl lying on the ground. Naomi. She was bundled in a black coat and the front buttons were undone. A spot of dark, wet red glistened there. Her hair was pulled back, but blonde wisps framed her pale, oval face. She appeared to be sleeping as I knelt beside her.

Just as I reached for the girl, her eyes popped open and she whispered, "You're too late…"

When I opened my eyes, large hands were gently shaking me and the room was dark and chilly.

"Shhh, it's all right. It's just a dream."

Daniel's breath was warm on the side of my face and I resisted the urge to lean against his chest. Sniffing, I said, "Actually, it was a nightmare."

Daniel's thumbs pressed into the sides of my upper arms and he began to pull me to him. I really wanted to hug him at that moment. Hell, with his muscled body touching mine, I wanted to do a lot of things to him, but fortunately my stubborn nature saved me.

Squirming free from his grip, I scooted backward and rested my chin on my raised knees. Thankfully, the sweatpants and t-shirt I was wearing gave me the freedom to do so.

"I'm sorry I woke you. I've been battling with bad dreams my entire life…but this one was a doozy."

Daniel took my rebuke in stride and rose to his feet fluidly. I had to admit, it surprised me that he was so bright and alert at this hour of the night.

"Let me throw some more logs on the fire and then we'll talk."

I watched Daniel take the few steps to the stove and open it up. The glowing red coals gave off enough light that my eyes adjusted and I could see Daniels form clearly. He was also wearing a t-shirt and sweatpants, but where my shirt was two sizes too big, his was snug, outlining his wide shoulders and slim waist perfectly. Once again, warm honey pulsated through every part of my body. I quickly glanced away, fighting off the tremors.

The squeak of the stove's door closing made my heart skip a beat and I waited anxiously as Daniel returned to the trundle.

Thinking that he had decided to forego any conversation and go straight to sleep, disappointment swatted me and I began to stretch out myself. Then he finally spoke.

"What were you dreaming about?"

Daniel had been with me from the first week of Naomi Beiler's investigation. He knew all about it. But it still was difficult to talk about it sometimes, even with him.

Reluctantly, I began, "I've had dreams about Naomi's death ever since the case was closed. I'm always running through the cornfield, looking for her; trying to reach her before she's shot. Sometimes I never even find her. I'm just lost in the maze of never ending corn plants. Other times, I hear the gun shot in the distance, and when I come to the place where we found her body, she's gone. But tonight, for the first time, I almost made it to her in time to save her life."

Daniel was silent for a moment and then he said, "I guess something like that stays with a person for a long time, but you shouldn't blame yourself for Naomi's death."

"I don't blame myself," I argued.

"Obviously you do in some way or you wouldn't be having

dreams about trying to save her." Daniel paused and even in the darkness, I could see the silhouette of his head shaking, "Naomi made up her own mind to run away and unfortunately for her, she had the bad luck of having a really messed up kid obsessed with her."

"Do you really think that it's just *bad luck* that Naomi was murdered…that her death couldn't have been prevented?" I almost growled, anger coursing through me.

"Yeah, I do. Sometimes things are just fated to happen. I guess you could say that it's all in God's plan and if it's meant to be, we're just swimming against the flow of the river to stop it."

Again, silence filled the cabin for a moment and I pulled the covers up closer to my chin to chase away the chill that rippled along my skin.

"You know, you're a lot more like them than you care to admit."

Daniel's tone changed, becoming heavy with annoyance. "Why do you say that?"

"You have the same Calvinist approach to life as the Amish do—that everything that happens is preordained and we're all mindless insects scurrying around in the chaos."

Daniel snorted and replied, "Maybe your problem is that you can't accept that some things are out of your control." Daniel took a deep breath and continued more softly, "Look, I understand that in your line of work, you like to be in charge of things. Hell, you have to be. But take my word for it; you'll be a much happier person at the end of the day if you admit that some strings are being guided by a higher authority than you."

"If that's so, then why would God have allowed Naomi to die? She was a sweet girl, just wanting to find love and happiness. What good did her death serve anyone?" I challenged.

Daniel answered quickly, as if he was expecting the question all along. "It's not about whether it was good or bad or right or wrong. It was Naomi's day to die. You can kick yourself around mentally all you want and continue having guilt dreams about her, but it won't bring her back. You need to move on."

Daniel had spoken with firmness, but not harshness. He truly believed what he said and I knew that his Amish upbringing played a huge part in his outlook on life. It would sure be easier to just accept that whatever is going to happen is going to happen. I'd have a lot less stress to deal with if I took that approach. But I didn't have that outlook on life and I didn't foresee changing my mind anytime soon.

"I like to think that I can make a real difference in the lives of those around me—that I was put on this earth to be able to help people. I refuse to toss it all up to fate and destiny."

Daniel chuckled. "I hope you prove me wrong, Serenity. God knows that if anyone is feisty enough to change the flow of the tide, it's you. But in the end, I think you'll be miserable that you can't change the world. As hard as it is for you to trust anyone or anything, someday you're just going to have to have a little faith."

My face heated with the realization that his well-placed words held double meaning. All along he'd been referring to our relationship and not just my unconscious feeling of responsibility over Naomi's death. Was he right? Maybe my inability to have a little faith in the forces of the universe, and in Daniel himself, was going to turn me into a miserable and lonely woman.

A tear slipped from my eye and I quickly wiped it away, thankful for the darkness to hide it. I couldn't deny that something was off in my life, but what should I do about it?

"We have to get up in just a few hours. Let's continue this philosophical conversation some other time," I said warily.

I rolled over onto my side, away from him, and shut my eyes. Even though my body was exhausted, my mind was still wide awake. And then there were still those occasional pulsating sensations whenever I thought about Daniel being only a few feet away from me. I reckoned that sleep would be a long time coming.

"I wish you would trust me. I would never hurt you," Daniel whispered before the trundle creaked under the shifting of his weight as he settled down for the rest of the night.

Yeah right. He was already causing me pain and he didn't even know it.

12

I opened my eyes with great reluctance. If I was lucky, I may have gotten three hours of actual sleep the night before. Yawning, I pulled the covers up over most of my face and tilted my head to listen to the men talking in the doorway. Their hushed voices are what woke me in the first place. I strained to hear what they were saying.

"I'm coming with you," Rowan said firmly.

"That won't be necessary. We can handle this on our own." Daniel replied politely, but there was an icy coolness to his words.

"Serenity asked me to accompany her to town today and I've cleared my schedule to do so. Besides, since this is *my* community, it might be helpful to have me along."

"Now, you listen up…" Daniel's tight knot on his emotions was quickly unraveling.

Dammit. There was no way in hell that I going to get any more sleep anyway.

I tossed the blanket down and said loudly, "He's going with us, Daniel."

When Daniel whirled around, his gaze was unflinching, "But…"

"I've made up my mind," I told Daniel in a low, steady voice. To Rowan, I said, "Can you be at my car in half an hour?"

"Yes, Ma'am," Rowan tipped his hat to me and disappeared into the bright sunlight of the early winter morning.

Daniel closed the door and strode over to the bed. He unceremoniously dropped down on the end of it and leaned forward, placing his face in his hands.

I thought he was being overly dramatic, but I didn't say anything. I was suddenly more concerned with the state of my hair and my puffy, sleep-deprived face. And I really hated myself for even caring how I looked.

Daniel, on the other hand, was already dressed in a pair of butt-molding blue jeans and his signature red and black flannel shirt. The stubble on his stubborn chin was darker from the night's growth, but instead of the course hair giving him a ragged appearance, it only made him look even more appetizing. And somehow, his black hair was clean and perfectly in place.

"Are you one of those people who can get by without any sleep or something?" I said tartly.

Daniel raised his head. "I make do." He sighed deeply and then rattled off, "What are you thinking allowing Rowan to go with us today? He's our prime suspect, isn't he?"

I shrugged. "Haven't you ever heard the saying about keeping your friends close and your enemies even closer?"

"That makes no sense in a criminal investigation."

"Did it ever occur to you that perhaps Rowan is on a major guilt trip about something...and he wants us to discover the truth—whatever it is?"

"Is that your angle then?" Daniel said intently.

I snorted and threw my legs over the side of the bed.

"I don't have an angle. It just seems like a good idea to keep Rowan nearby at this point."

After a moment of heavy silence, Daniel said softly, "All right then. The basin is already full of hot water for you in the bathroom. I'll get the coffee brewing while you're washing up."

I couldn't keep the small grin from my mouth. I glanced over at Daniel. "Thanks."

Daniel nodded and rose from the bed. He hesitated for a second and then turned back. "You might not have any faith in me, but I do in you. However you want to handle this case is fine with me. I'm sorry I got a little wound up there."

"Not a problem."

As I was rummaging through my suitcase for clothes and shampoo, Daniel said from the stovetop, "Scrambled or sunny-side up for your eggs?"

"Scrambled is fine."

Now I knew for certain that the man was too good to be true.

The drive into town was filled with mostly uncomfortable idle chatter, but I did learn a couple of interesting things pertinent to the investigation. Rowan told us that the Church elders had recently taken action to end any contact that the teenagers were having with outsider youth. The new rule stipulated that if any of the kids were caught with an outsider, besides public events and work situations, they would be severely punished. He hadn't elaborated on exactly what punishment would be dished out, but I imagined that it would be frightening enough to keep the teens in line.

The other tidbit of information that I found interesting was that Rowan's wife Hedy was Bishop Fisher's youngest sister. I had sat and mulled that one over for a good portion of the drive while the guys reservedly talked about weather and the spring crops.

It wasn't exactly shocking that the two families were related by marriage. I had already discovered that most of the Amish in a community were connected by blood or marriage. But it did shed some light on Rowan's sour relationship with the bishop, and it made me wonder even more about Hedy's untimely death.

"Take a left at the next light. It's the first building on the right," Rowan directed.

A few stray butterflies began to dance in my stomach as I parked the car. I wasn't looking forward to meeting Poplar Springs' sheriff, and I was fairly certain that he wouldn't be too happy to have me nosing around his domain, either. I sure wouldn't if the roles were reversed and he showed up in Blood Rock.

Swallowing down the twinge of nervousness, I walked through the parking lot, measuring up the town. I had been annoyed that most of the main roads still had snow and slush on them and many of the local businesses hadn't even attempted to clear the week old snow from their parking lots. The mixture of buildings and churches that tightly lined main-street was historical, but they had the rundown appearance of abandonment and low income renters. I saw several hitching rails along the sidewalks and a black horse and buggy was tied to one of them. I got a hint of the town's by-gone glory days when I spotted a fountain in the town square that sported an icy glacier running over its sides. The fountain was surrounded by several mature, leaf-bare trees, whose tired looking branches stretched nearly to the ground in places.

I guessed that Poplar Springs had at least twice the population of Blood Rock, but unlike my own jurisdiction, this one had hit hard times. Walking past Daniel, who held the door open, and into the brick faced sheriff's department, I came to the conclusion that a sheriff in such a worn-down looking town might not have a lot of resources to investigate an arson spree and possible murder.

As if our arrival was on video surveillance, the sheriff and two deputies met us at the counter before we even had the opportunity to introduce ourselves.

The tallest man graced me with a plastic smile and held out his hand. Butter would have melted on his tongue when he said, "Why, Tony was right. You're almost a child, Ms. Adams."

The sarcastic comment about my age was nothing new and I could easily ignore it. But the mention of Tony Manning promptly curdled my stomach and gave me an 'ah, shit' moment. But I somehow managed to keep my composure. Taking a deep breath, I smiled sweetly and shook the man's hand firmly.

"Well, now, it's a small world isn't it, to run into one of Tony's buddies this far north," I said conversationally.

"Tony and I go way back. He's a good man," Sheriff Gentry said in a dare-you-to-argue-with-me sort of way.

I swallowed my pride for the benefit of the investigation and agreed with him, even though it made my stomach roll to do so. "One of the best, that's for sure." I thumbed towards Daniel, "This is Daniel Bachman. He's working the case with me." I glanced at Rowan, "I assume the two of you have already met?"

"Oh, yes. Rowan and I know each other rather well…" the sheriff turned to stare at Rowan and added, "don't we?"

"Yes, Sir," Rowan replied cordially.

Suddenly, the tension was so thick that I could have cut it with a knife. The two deputies were carbon-copies of each other; both athletically built with buzz cuts and arrogant twists on their mouths. I fleetingly thought about how well Todd would fit in with this crew when my gaze was pulled to the framed front page of a newspaper on the wall beside where we stood. The scene of a barn ablaze, surrounded by fire trucks and spraying water hoses raised the hair on the back of my neck. Without caring what anyone thought, I walked up to it and quickly skimmed the headline and then the date. With each word of the article that I read, my heart pounded heavier in my chest. Finally, I turned to face the sheriff.

"Can we talk in private?"

Sheriff Gentry's mouth tightened before he sighed loudly. "That's probably a good idea." He flicked his hand for me to follow him. I took only a second to glance over at Daniel and Rowan before I left them standing in the lobby with the deputies.

The sheriff's office was spacious and decorated in a western style that would have looked perfect in a Texas sheriff's office, but felt pretty out of place in northern Indiana. I tried to relax in the brown leather seat and set my thoughts in order while Sheriff Gentry poured me a cup of coffee. I was a little worried that after Daniel's strong brew only an hour ago, any more caffeine would peel my skin back, but I had accepted the offer anyway. It gave me a chance to study the sheriff keenly for a moment before we got down to business.

Brody Gentry was probably in his mid-sixties. His arrogant

confidence put me in mind of Tony, but where the former Blood Rock sheriff was tall and wiry, like Clint Eastwood, this man was built similar to a polar bear. His gray haired head actually looked too small for his large body.

I also noted that he wore a wide banded wedding ring and that there were several group family pictures around the room. From the sheer number of grandkids, and people in general in each photo, it was safe to assume that the sheriff was quite the family man.

Sheriff Gentry handed me a cup and then took a seat behind the desk. He sipped his cup of Joe and waited for me to speak. His silence didn't really bother me. I used the same tactic myself sometimes to intimidate people.

"You have a beautiful family, Sheriff Gentry," I said.

"Brody, just call me Brody from now on." The lines on his face seemed to become deeper when he went on to say, "So what exactly do you want to talk about?"

I ran my fingers through my hair and replied carefully, "Well, my original intent was to discuss the recent rash of barn burnings. As you already seem to be aware, the Poplar Springs' Amish community searched me out and asked if I would check into the case for them on the QT."

"And now…?" Brody appeared as relaxed as a cat sunning itself on the windowsill, but underneath the calm facade, I knew he was coiled as if he was a snake ready to strike. The occasional twitch at the corner of his mouth and the constant tapping of his foot was a dead giveaway.

"My condolences on the death of your grandson and his girlfriend in the nineteen ninety-seven barn fire; it's a horrible crime for two young people to die like that," I said steadily.

Our gazes locked for a second before Brody looked away

and sniffed. The moisture I had seen in his eyes was real and for the first time since walking into the building, I felt a little kinship to the man.

"The kids were fooling around in my son's storage building late one night. They must have nodded off. The fire spread quickly. The coroner told us that they died from smoke inhalation."

"Was there an arrest?" I said bluntly.

"No. And that's the most frustrating part."

"I can relate. My own house burned down last year from arson, and it's still unsolved."

"Really?" Brody's brows were raised, "Surely you have some inkling to who did it—right?"

"Yeah, actually, I know exactly who was responsible." I paused and narrowed my eyes. "And I'd guess that you have a pretty good idea who set your son's barn on fire too," I prodded softly.

Brody nodded his head wearily and said, "It's nice to know that we're on the same page, Serenity. I was a bit worried that you were going to come trotting into town like a pent up race horse, so fixated on these new burnings that you wouldn't even think to look into the town's past." He leaned over his desk. "The Amish are keeping secrets about that night eighteen years ago, protecting their own, I reckon. And until they open up to help me solve that case, I won't lift a finger for them."

I shuddered. The sheriff hadn't minced any words. That the proclamation was coming from an elected official who was sworn to serve and protect his constituents was scary enough, but that was only a shard of what was on my mind. Poplar Springs was turning out to be a much more intriguing town than I had thought, and quite possibly a dangerous one.

I knew to tread very carefully. "Do you mind if I take a look at the file?"

He quickly opened up the top drawer of his desk and pulled out a manila folder. He unceremoniously dropped it in front of me. "It's all yours." He swallowed. "I really hope that you get the answers out of them people that I wasn't able to. Austin was a good boy. Everybody loved him and his poor momma was never the same after he died. My daughter-in-law got all depressed, couldn't take the thought of her oldest son burning up like that. She overdosed on prescription meds two years after the fire, leaving my only son, Michael, to care for Austin's little brother on his own."

I could feel my eyes widen and I didn't even try to hide my shock.

Brody paused in thought and then he added, "My family needs closure, Sheriff. Any which way we can get it."

"I understand. And I promise you, I'll do my best." I picked up the folder and glanced back up, asking, "Is it possible for me to take a look at whatever you have on the recent fires?"

Brody spread his lips tightly, clearly agitated. Scoffing, he said, "I don't think it will help with the cold case, but you're welcome to what I have."

Feeling as if I was treading on thin ice, I pressed forward and asked, "There's one more thing. Do you know anything about the gas explosion that killed Rowan's wife?"

Brody's expression changed so dramatically that I quickly leaned back and poised my hand close to my jacket opening. I had the hesitant feeling that the topic was probably a sore subject for the sheriff, but I wasn't prepared for such a violent reaction.

"That was just an accident. And you would be well enough to leave that one be and focus on the true crimes that we're dealing with," Brody warned me.

I shrugged. "Fair enough, I have enough to keep me busy."

I left Brody Gentry with an unspoken truce and a loose alliance that could swing either way, depending on what I kind of dirt I dug up. But as I walked down the corridor alone toward the lobby, I knew one thing was for certain. There was no way in hell that I was ignoring the fire that killed Rowan's wife.

If anything, I was now more convinced than ever that there was foul play involved, and that there was a connection to the barn fire that had killed Brody's grandson and the recent rash of fires.

And who the dead woman was in the bishop's barn wasn't far from my thoughts either.

13

I pushed the file folders aside and took a sip from the water bottle that Daniel had just returned with. I glanced at Rowan, who was still pressing his face up to the news article displayed on the computer screen in front of him. I had to smile. It had taken about ten minutes to explain the basics to the Amish man, but once he'd gotten the hang of it, he cruised through the news articles quicker than I had.

The Poplar Spring's library turned out to be a much better source of information than either the sheriff's department or the fire department. Besides the extensive file that Brody had on the fire that had killed his grandson in ninety-seven, the other folders on the arsons only contained a single page report each. I did manage to glean some useful names and addresses, but other than that, they weren't very helpful.

The newspaper articles were a different story, though. After sifting through them for over an hour, I came up with a clearer picture of a troubled town with high unemployment and a seedy, trailer-trash element on its eastern side. My reading branched out from the arsons, to twenty years of burglaries, vandalism, domestic violence, and assault. Looking at a plot map, I was shocked to see how close the Amish community was to the criminal hot spots.

The town had been bustling back in the eighties, but when several factories closed down in the early nineties, the place became a mid-western ghost town. Businesses closed, people had to go on government assistance to survive, and subsequently lost hope. I had seen firsthand in Indy how the downfall of the economy affected the very core of society. People became depressed, they drank more, played around with drugs, and soon enough violence and crime sprang up in previously calm areas.

Except that Poplar Springs' hardships hadn't affected the Amish in the same way they had everyone else. The Plain people's businesses were flourishing from both a steady growth of families and the ever increasing tourist trade. It now occurred to me that there could be a lot of disgruntled, jealous and vindictive people out there who would want to hurt the Amish and their prosperity.

Taking a deep sigh, I frowned at Daniel.

"Not finding anything helpful?" Daniel asked, taking the seat across from me.

"On the contrary, I found out more than I bargained for."

I quickly jotted down a couple of sentences on the paper before me and shook my head at Daniel's raised brow. I wagged my thumb towards Rowan, who was still fully immersed in reading the screen.

Daniel got my drift and with a curt nod, he reached over and picked up the notebook that I had shoved his way.

After reading the note, Daniel's eyes met mine. His mouth was set in a grim line when he said loudly, "I saw a little diner on the corner. Is it any good, Rowan?"

Rowan reluctantly looked away from the computer and replied, "I've eaten there a time or two. It's decent food."

"Sounds perfect to me, I'm famished." I stood and quickly gathered the folders together in a neat stack.

"All right then. How do I turn this thing off?" Rowan asked, putting his hat back on. He watched over my shoulder with rapt interest as I logged him off.

"Now that you know the basics, you can come here any-time to do research," I told Rowan.

"Yes, thank you for taking the time to get me started. No one has ever actually taught me how computers work." Rowan walked beside me and we followed Daniel out into the bright sunlight of the library parking lot. The air was still cold, but the rays made all the difference in the world. I slipped my sunglasses on and tilted my face to the little bit of warmth shining down.

"I didn't think that you had many opportunities to use a computer," I said absently.

Rowan shrugged and kept perfect pace with me as we headed towards the diner. "From time to time I've needed to check in-formation about farm equipment or livestock sales. Usually one of the drivers will look everything up for me, but it's nice to actu-ally know how to do it myself. I won't be as dependent on others that way." He glanced down and said softly, "Thank you."

I noticed Daniel look over his shoulder, but I ignored him. "You're welcome."

The cheeseburger and fries were extra salty, just the way I liked them and as I took a bite of the burger, I waited for Rowan to answer Daniel's question.

Rowan shifted in his seat across from me and Daniel uncomfortably for a lingering moment and finally said, "Yeah, I knew Austin Gentry."

Motioning for more with his hand, Daniel prompted, "Were you friends?"

Rowan glanced out the window beside our table. "Not exactly friends. But we knew each other. He was spoiled and a bit arrogant, but he was all right." He looked back at us and met my gaze evenly. "He shouldn't have died that night."

I swallowed down my food and quickly admonished, "Of course not. It's a horrible way to die and he was still just a kid."

"No, that's not what I meant," Rowan shook his head. "Austin shouldn't have been sneaking off to a barn in the middle of the night with his girlfriend. I'm sure that he would still be alive today if he had a little more sense."

The callousness of his words chilled me and I glanced sideways at Daniel to see his reaction. Daniel was shocked, too.

Daniel beat me to the punch. "Wow, man. That's pretty damn cold."

Rowan's dark eyes looked away. "It is what it is."

I pressed forward, "Do you have any ideas who might be the culprit?"

Rowan rounded on me, and with steel in his voice, he demanded, "Why are you so focused on something that happened nearly two decades ago, while we have burnings from the past few months that we need to solve?"

I didn't waver. Calmly I said, "I think they may be connected."

"Really?" Rowan stretched the word out, making it clear that he didn't agree.

"And then there's the explosion that killed your wife," I plowed on, staring unflinchingly into Rowan's eyes.

Rowan let out a breath and shifted forward to rest his elbows on the table. He pressed his fingers into his head as if he was trying to remove a deep pain before he met my gaze once more.

Rowan's discomfort was pulsating in the air, but I was able to push aside any sympathy that I might have and patiently wait for him to answer me. Rowan was definitely hiding something. I was sure of it now.

The plastic covered blue booth seats were small and Daniel was sitting close enough that our legs pressed against each other. Even for the dramatic conversation and my desire for answers from Rowan, I was hyper aware of Daniel's close proximity and how weirdly right it felt. We were literally on the same side this time and it shamed me to admit that it was a wonderful feeling.

Rowan's gaze finally rose from the table top. In a quiet voice, he said, "There was a gas leak, I already told you that."

Just as softly, I said, "Did it ever occur to you that foul play may have been involved?"

"No."

I squinted and bit my lower lip. It was a pivotal moment. If I said the wrong thing, it would screw up any chances of Rowan opening up. But then again, if I said the right thing, a big piece of the puzzle might fall into place.

"I'm sorry to bring up bad memories. It was just a thought, that's all," I assured Rowan.

Rowan's gaze became fierce and he said, "We need to find out who is setting these recent fires before someone else gets hurt."

I didn't like being spoken to in such an angry tone and I couldn't help but narrow my eyes and lean in toward Rowan, who held his ground, returning my heated glare with his own.

"I've been here for a total of two days and I'm doing the very best I can to sift through all the information. If you don't like the way that I'm handling the case, then go ahead and send me home. But if you do that, I can almost guarantee you that with this town's climate of bad blood, secrecy and poverty, you'll never find out the truth."

My words hung in the air the same as the foul stench of decaying flesh. I didn't like the way Rowan stared at me, his mouth slightly gaping. And I certainly didn't like having to go all Clint Eastwood on the Amish man, but my patience was wearing thin. I couldn't shake the needling sensation at the back of my mind that something very dangerous was on the horizon. Poplar Springs definitely had bigger issues than just the barn burnings.

"I understand, Sheriff Adams. I wish you to stay, and I will interfere with your investigation no longer." He placed his hat on his head and abruptly stood up. "I have chores to do at the farm. Can we be going now?"

I inwardly smiled at the win, but I managed to keep my face blank. I nudged Daniel as I quickly wrapped my burger and fries in a napkin to take for the ride back to the Amish community.

Sometimes things worked out perfectly, I thought. Next stop was going to be Joanna Fisher's place, and I definitely didn't want Rowan hanging around in the shadows for that conversation.

14

"You sure didn't hold anything back with Rowan," Daniel chuckled when we were finally alone in the car.

I pulled out on the roadway, remembering the way Rowan and I had gone the day before to get to the bishop's farm, but going in the opposite direction instead as I listened to my phone's robotic voice guide me.

"Of course not, he has his own agenda, the same as everyone else in this town and it needed to be reined in."

"I thought you've already been to the bishop's place?" Daniel asked as he glanced out the window in confusion.

"Yeah, I remember how to get there. But we're making a couple of other stops first."

"Mind if I ask, where?"

"I think we need to check out the other three barns that burned down. There's so much going on around here that it's difficult to make sense of it all, but there's one thing I'm fairly certain of. The recent fires *are* connected to the one in ninety-seven that took Sheriff Gentry's grandson and his girlfriend."

"What makes you so sure about that?"

"Mostly just a gut feeling at this point—nothing concrete

—but the bad blood between the sheriff and the bishop, and even Rowan, is unmistakable."

"They definitely don't trust each other. That's for sure," Daniel commented.

"No, they don't. And those types of feelings arise from deeds done to each other or believed to have been done."

"And how do you think Rowan's own house fire plays into the intrigue?"

I sighed deeply and glanced at Daniel. He had been staring at me for an unreasonable amount of time, and it was beginning to get on my nerves.

"Honestly, that's the only wild card in the theory I'm beginning to develop. There's something I'm missing."

"It's damn strange, is what it is. Don't get me wrong. I've personally heard of several Amish houses going up in gas explosions over the years."

"So what makes this one strange to you then?"

"Well, for starters, that it happened at night, and Rowan wasn't there—too convenient if you ask me. Then there's the fact that Jotham Hochstetler *was* there." He paused and eyed me with a very serious look, before continuing. "It's not normal for a married Amish woman to have another man in her house in the middle of the night. I hate to say it, but it looks as if Hedy Schwartz was having an affair."

I thought for a moment. If the woman hadn't been Amish, I would have agreed with Daniel wholeheartedly, but she *was* Amish and I was still having a difficult time wrapping my mind around the idea that an Amish woman who was married to a good looking and intelligent man, like Rowan, would cheat. Unless, maybe Rowan wasn't as he appeared.

"It seems to be the thing these days," was all I said on the matter as I turned into the gravel driveway of the farm. "This is where the first fire took place. Shem Yoder's hay barn went up on October fifteenth of last year."

Daniel slowly nodded and then turned to look out the window at the newly constructed barn on the right. I followed his gaze as I shut the engine off. Most of the roof was under cover, but at the far side of the framed in building, there were several exposed joists and a deep snow drift rose below them.

There were a few men hammering boards up and a young girl was in the shadow of the structure pulling two smaller children through the snow on a sled. The sun was hidden by thickening clouds that were spreading out across the sky, making it feel as if the possibility of snow flurries was very real.

A black Labrador greeted me as I shut the car door. Absently, I reached down to scratch his head before I joined Daniel and headed towards the barn. A short man with a long, brown beard that was heavily speckled with gray stopped working and came forward to greet us.

"Ah, you must be the lady sheriff from Blood Rock," he said in a friendly manner. "I've been expecting your visit. I'm Shem Yoder."

After we had all shaken hands and I introduced Daniel, I asked, "Is the new barn on the same site as the one that burned down?"

"Yes, Ma'am, it sure is. I was in the middle of harvesting the corn when it happened, and I didn't get around to excavating the area until well into November." Shem pulled a handkerchief from his pocket and wiped his brow before finishing, "With the weather the way it's been, I really regret that I didn't get the new barn built sooner."

"I thought that the entire community would get together to have a barn raising sort of thing," I ventured.

Shem laughed. "Well now, you do know something about our ways. I've had a lot of help here with mine and about a month ago, we all got together to put up Elijah Mast's buggy shed and Samuel Miller's stable, but the snow has put my construction off schedule."

I pulled out my small notebook and checked the names I had written down at the library. "The Miller's buggy shed was the second fire, right...back on October twenty-ninth?"

Shem scrunched his round face up in thought for a minute and then answered, "Why yes, I believe that was the date. My sister-in-law had her baby that day, and the wife and I were heading up the road to see the newest family member when we saw Elijah's barn on fire in the distance."

"It happened during the day?" The wind was gusting again and I took a step closer to Daniel to use his large frame as a wind block. I caught his grin from the corner of my vision, but I let my annoyance slip away as I paid closer attention to Shem.

Shem nodded his head. "I reckon it was about dinnertime when we passed by Elijah's driveway and first smelled the smoke. We continued on, rushing to the phone box and called the fire department, but by the time they arrived, the barn was gone."

"Was that barn as far off the road as yours is?"

"Yes, maybe a little further. Samuel's stable is about a quarter mile back and it was set alight too."

Daniel and I exchanged glances. "Samuel Miller's stable went up on November eleventh. Was that during the day also?"

"I wasn't personally there when it burned, but I arrived in

the early evening to help clean up. So I reckon it was in the middle of the afternoon."

I took notes and tried to control my building anxiousness. With control, I asked, "Were there any horses in the stable at the time?"

Shem shook his head, "The Lord blessed Samuel that day. He had turned all the horses out in the field to muck the stalls that morning. Usually, they would have been in."

I thought for a moment and said, "So, out of all three fires, no animals were killed."

"No. Of course, that wasn't the case with Abner's barn." Shem's face was already red from the stiff, cold breeze, but I could have sworn that it turned a shade even darker when he shrugged and said, "But I'm sure you already know about that."

I nodded. "Yeah, I know all about it." Closing the notebook, I went out on a limb and asked, "Do you have any idea who would want to burn Amish barns, Shem—any ideas at all?"

Shem fidgeted and wiped his face once again. The poor guy was a nervous wreck, but what—or who was he afraid of?

Finally, he shook his head firmly. "That's why you're here, Ma'am, to figure out what's happening."

Irritation shot though me, warming my face. "Usually in cases like these, the victim has an idea of who might be the perpetrator. That kind of information helps law enforcement solve the case." I took a deep breath and asked once again, "Are you sure you don't have any information that will help me to help you?"

"Sorry, Ma'am," Shem said. He tipped his hat and returned to the other three men who had paused from their work to listen in on the discussion.

I caught a glimpse of Daniel's amused smile as I got into the car, but was thankful that he didn't say anything obnoxious.

"I guess there's no point stopping by the other crime scenes if they've already been cleared and have new barns erected," I sighed.

"Afraid not," Daniel had lost the smile when he turned to me. "You're not surprised that Shem Yoder didn't have your answers, are you?"

I shrugged as I pulled out onto the roadway. "He wouldn't be an Amish man if he wasn't being difficult. But I did get some of my questions answered…and I'm fairly certain now that Shem's and the other two barn fires were not set by the same person who burned down the bishop's barn."

"How did you come to that conclusion?"

I purposely eased my foot off the gas pedal to make the short trip to the Fisher's last even longer.

"They just don't match up. The first three fires were all set during the day, to barns or buildings that were set well off the road. There were no animals or people in any of the buildings. Whoever committed those arsons did it in rebellion or animosity, not with serious malicious intent." I paused and thought for a moment and then continued. "The bishop's fire happened in the middle of the night and to a barn that was a stone's throw from the road. And of course there was a body."

"Do you really think that we're dealing with two arsonists? That's crazy," Daniel scoffed.

"Maybe so, but that's sure what it looks like to me. Think about it for a minute. Whoever set the fire at the bishop's was very careful to pick a barn that he could get in and out of easily and did it in the middle of the night so that he would have the best chance of not getting caught. The person who set the other fires was much more emotional about it. He wanted to create a spectacle or maybe even make a point."

"*He?*" Daniel questioned.

"I read up on it. Most arsonists are male."

"It's starting to make sense, but why would a random person set fire to the bishop's barn?"

I smiled for an instant at Daniel's naivety and then quickly sobered, saying, "To hide the body, of course."

15

We passed Mariah on the bishop's driveway and a shiver of anticipation ran up my spine. The sour look that darkened the girl's face when she saw me confirmed that there was definitely something going on with her.

I parked on the other side of the club cab pick-up and glanced over at Mariah, watching her ignore our arrival, as she leaned into the truck and chatted with a young English man. Her brazen behavior confused me. An Amish girl who was also the daughter of the bishop wasn't supposed to be so openly conversing with a guy, especially not an outsider.

I raised a questioning brow to Daniel who only shrugged. He looked about as surprised as I was.

"You heard Rowan last night. This community is a little more laid back than Blood Rock," Daniel offered.

I snorted. "My guess is that this girl gets away with a lot more than any of the other kids do."

"Why, because she's the bishop's daughter?" Daniel asked.

"That, along with the fact that she's an only child, and a beautiful girl to boot."

"I bet you always got what you wanted growing up, too," Daniel said with a mild smirk.

"This isn't about me...but no, I didn't," I said forcefully.

It was a good time to get out of the car, before I really got mad at Daniel. When I walked over to greet Mariah, I didn't miss the stiffening of her posture or her exhale of breath.

Mariah offered me a plastic smile and said, "My mother is in the house waiting for you."

I couldn't help bristling at the girl's rude tone. "Well, hello to you too."

Mariah rolled her eyes ever so slightly and she completely lost the fake smile. She began to open her mouth to speak, but her companion interrupted her. "You must be the Blood Rock sheriff everyone's talking about." He reached out of the cab and I shook his hand. "I'm Damon Gentry."

I had already taken in the guy's fair hair, bright blue eyes and all-American good looks. He was in his mid-twenties making me automatically assume that he was a little too old for Mariah, but not by everybody's standards.

"Are you any relation to Sheriff Brody Gentry?" I asked.

Damon smiled with embarrassment and shrugged a little. "He's my grandpa."

I exchanged glances with Daniel and saw the spark of curiosity in his brown eyes. I thought quickly and nodded towards Daniel and said, "This is Daniel Bachman. He grew up Amish, but left when he was nineteen. He's helping with the case."

As I spoke, I watched Mariah's face intently and was relieved when my suspicions were confirmed by her sudden change of posture. She relaxed and gazed up at Daniel with great interest. The girl definitely wanted out.

In a hushed voice, she asked Daniel excitedly, "You used to be Amish?"

"Yes, I did."

"Do you miss it?" Mariah rushed out.

Daniel paused with a long breath and then said, "Sure, sometimes I do. But to be honest, I've moved on and am happy."

The way Mariah was gazing at Daniel with a look of total admiration and envy was almost jolting.

"You're so lucky," Mariah whispered.

Daniel leaned a little away from Mariah and said in a low voice, "Whoa, you don't mean that."

Mariah's lips thinned into a grim line and her blue eyes darkened. She thought for a moment and then suddenly giggled. "Of course not, I was just joking."

Like hell she was joking. But the girl's face was a mask of emotions once again.

I turned to Damon and said, "Was Ashton Gentry your brother?"

My question caused a heavier chill to ascend than the winter wind already carried. Mariah's single eyebrow raised, and Damon's white face made me regret asking the obvious question. But I had just wanted to be sure before I drew any conclusions. The pair's relationship was still unknown to me and even though I was pretty good at picking up on other people's attraction to one another, these two were coming up blank in that department for me.

"Yes…why do you ask?" Damon said slowly.

I didn't answer him, instead, asking a question of my own. "You must have been about five or six when the fire happened that took his life."

"I was seven, and I still distinctly remember the barn in flames and the line of fire trucks parked bumper to bumper in the driveway." Damon's face flushed with color as he spoke. The young man obviously carried the same bitterness that his grandfather did.

I decided to take a chance. "Do you have any idea who set the fire, Damon?"

Damon laughed. The sound was so abrupt and unexpected that I glanced up at Daniel to for his reaction. But he only stared at Damon with quiet intensity.

"Believe me, if I knew who did it, they'd be dead by now," Damon said with steely sureness.

"He doesn't mean it. He's just angry, is all, *Sheriff*," Mariah stressed my title for Damon's benefit.

"Sure, I do," Damon growled with benevolence.

"Damon, you had best be heading over to the Lapp's place. Margaret wanted you to take her and the boys to the store this afternoon." Joanna's voice startled me, but I noticed her reproving tone.

"Yes, Ma'am," Damon said sweetly before turning to me and saying, "Later, Sheriff."

I nodded and stepped back. Damn. I was on to something here.

"Mariah, that cow still needs milking," Joanna told her daughter firmly.

"Sorry, Damon was telling me all about how he saw Hope and Sarah out by the road talking to those English boys again."

Joanna eyed her daughter silently for a moment, before she said in the cool and collected voice of a very pissed off mother. "You know that I don't like you gossiping with that young man."

"But...I thought that you'd want..." Mariah stuttered.

Joanna placed her hand out to silence her daughter. "I will not have it. Do you understand me?"

Mariah took a breath and looked away. "Yes, Momma."

"Get on with your chores," Joanna ordered.

Mariah hurried away without a backward glance.

In a blink of an eye, Joanna was honey sweet once again. "Come on in. It's mighty cold out here."

Daniel and I mirrored each other's quizzical expressions as we followed Joanna into the warmth of her kitchen just as the first, puffy snowflakes began falling.

"Do either of you want a cup of tea or coffee?" Joanna asked.

"Coffee would be wonderful," Daniel replied.

"I'm good," I added, sweeping my gaze around the kitchen.

I joined Daniel at the table and sat beside him. There was an open Bible in front of me and I couldn't help craning my neck to take a closer look. The page said, Psalm 7, Prayer and Praise for Deliverance from Enemies.

My curiosity was suddenly heightened. Just as my finger touched the leather bound book to inch it closer, Joanna said, "Are you a believer, Serenity?"

The Amish woman set a cup of coffee in front of Daniel and took the seat across from us. The laser sharp focus that I had seen on her face the day before abruptly returned.

"Ah, well, kind of," I stumbled, "I mean I believe in God, just not necessarily all the stories that come along with the Bible."

"Stories?" Joanna smiled kindly, making me feel as if I was a small, naughty child who needed a stern lecture. I glimpsed Daniel wiping a smile away with his hand. Now he seemed to be waiting anxiously for the conversation to continue.

"Why, the Bible is truth, not stories. It's the Word of our Lord Jesus and His Heavenly Father." Joanna lightly shook her head as she continued, "I am always pained to meet an unbeliever—because I know in my heart what you're missing."

Her consolatory tone made my skin crawl and my blood pressure rise. I was respectful and held in the snort that threatened to escape my lips, and said, "I've always found the Bible fascinating, though." Losing all inhibitions, I picked up the book and began reading, "like this for example. *If I have repaid evil to him who was at peace with me, Or have plundered my enemy without cause, Let the enemy pursue me and overtake me; Yes, let him trample my life to the earth, And lay my honor in the dust.* What exactly does it mean?"

Joanna's face darkened for an instant. It was as if a storm cloud had suddenly closed in around her. But she quickly regained her composure and said, "God forgives those who sin. Sometimes it takes a while for judgment to be rendered, but no one escapes evil deeds without retribution of some kind."

I couldn't help glaring at the woman. It was the same religious zeal that I had dealt with in Blood Rock, all over again. Bishop Esch and his followers justified having Tony Manning, the town's former sheriff, punch me and hold a gun to my head when they thought it served some ordained purpose.

Daniel cleared his throat and saved me from getting into a philosophical battle with Joanna by quickly changing the subject.

"Is Damon Gentry a driver for the Amish around here?"

Joanna turned her attention on Daniel. "He's been driving in the community for a few years. He's a nice young man. I really wouldn't take his vengeful words from earlier seriously."

"Threatening to kill someone in front of a sheriff is serious business," I countered.

"Of course it is," Joanna agreed wholeheartedly, "but since he isn't targeting a specific person, they are just frivolous words."

Something about Joanna Fisher reminded me soundly of Aaron Esch, and I took a deep breath at the realization. She wouldn't be the easy nut to crack that I had originally guessed she'd be.

"Maybe he suspects someone?" I offered.

Joanna shifted in her seat uncomfortably. "He was only a boy at the time. I don't believe he knows anything." She paused and forced a smile. "But aren't you here to discuss the recent fires and not one that happened nearly twenty years ago?"

Joanna was smooth, very smooth. But I did have other questions for her, so I went with the flow and asked, "Do you know anyone who would want to do your family personal harm, Mrs. Fisher?"

"Joanna, please call me Joanna." She thought quickly and replied, "No one that I can think of. We get along quite well with all of our English neighbors and Abner teaches at the schoolhouse, so he doesn't do business with outsiders."

It was curious how she had automatically assumed any threat would come from the outside.

Daniel must have picked up on my exact thoughts. He asked, "What about anyone in the community, maybe one of the more rebellious kids?"

Joanna's eyes widened to saucer size. "Are you insinuating that one of our own is doing these burnings?"

Daniel shrugged, "Just a thought."

"I have no worries whatsoever that our young ones are

involved with the fires," she said angrily and then faced me. "That is exactly what Sheriff Gentry suggested and he refused to look any further than our own homes. Are you going to do the same thing, Serenity?"

The heat in her voice was genuine. Joanna Fisher might be a little over-the-top religious by my standards, but it was obvious that she was a good woman, and extremely worried about what was going on in her community.

"I have no intention of eliminating *any* potential perpetrators. I swear to you that," I promised Joanna.

Joanna nodded in relief, "I'm glad to hear that. I really am. This bad business is beginning to keep the tourists away," her eyes were desperate, "and that's a good portion of many of our family's livelihoods. And then who knows who will be next—maybe the schoolhouse or one of the barns with livestock in it. This has to stop."

"I'm doing my best, Joanna." I stood up. "But it certainly wouldn't hurt for you to keep on praying we catch a break in the case. Because, trust me, we're going to need one."

Joanna came quickly around the table and hugged me. Her sudden movement caught me off guard and I could only stand rigidly while she squeezed me tightly. Daniel looked amused.

"Thank you for coming to our aid. The Lord is with you— I can sense it." She pulled back to meet my gaze and said, "You and Daniel are welcome to our Sunday service tomorrow morning. We normally don't allow Englishers to attend our Church, but we'll make an exception in this case. It will also give you both the opportunity to meet the other elders in our community."

Inwardly, I was very pleased with the invitation and the access that I was being given to the entire Poplar Springs Amish community, but I kept my face steady when I said, "We'll be there."

My boots crunched on the thin layer of fresh snow already coating the ground as Daniel and I walked to my car. The snowflakes were coming down heavier now, and the entire countryside was becoming obscured in a dull, gray haze.

I lifted my face, enjoying the shiver that the wet flakes striking my face caused, and said, "That was weird."

Daniel grinned. "It always is."

We reached the car and I was about to reply when Mariah appeared out of the gloom and touched my arm. I turned around and immediately recognized the expression of a person wanting desperately to share some kind of news.

"I'm sorry about the way I acted earlier." She shrugged. "I didn't know what to expect...and I didn't trust you."

"And you suddenly do now?" I couldn't keep the sarcasm from my voice.

Mariah stepped closer and I watched the snowflakes gathering on her black coat as she spoke. "Please don't say anything to Momma, but I was listening to you talk in the kitchen." She must have seen my confusion, because she quickly added, "You see, the window is always cracked a little to cool down the room when the wood stove is cranked up."

"That's convenient for you," I smiled. Mariah's changeable personalities were annoying, but I had to give the girl credit for bravery.

"I wanted to make sure that you weren't like Sheriff Brody before I talked to you."

"I understand. Go on," I urged.

"There are things going on with the Amish here...things that the sheriff, the elders...even my parents, don't want to believe or concern themselves with. But it's serious, Miss Serenity, you have got to listen to me."

The urgency in her voice added to my own well-hidden feeling of panic.

"Why don't we get in the car? It will be easier for us to talk inside," I suggested.

"No," she whispered harshly. "We don't have time. Momma will catch us."

I held up my hands, "All right then. Go on."

"You need to arrest Asher Schwartz. He's an evil man," she said in a low, feverish voice.

"Arrest him for what?" I spoke while holding my breath.

Mariah almost got the words out before Joanna called her daughter loudly from the porch. I glanced over to see Joanna standing with hands on her hips, just as the wind gusted, picking up the snow in the driveway and spraying it around in a momentary white-out.

Mariah looked at me with determination and hissed, "Please, just do it if you can."

Mariah twirled and ran to the porch. I remained standing there in the frozen wind, watching as Joanna hugged her daughter briefly before the two of them went into the house arm in arm.

"You drive," I tossed the keys to Daniel.

He didn't complain and started up the engine while I climbed into the passenger seat.

"Where to?" Daniel asked as he backed up.

"Back to Rowan's, thanks for driving. I have an important call to make."

I listened intently to Bill Sherman on the phone as the icy landscape became whiter. The pavement of the roads was completely hidden by the white stuff now and visibility was less than a mile.

"Thanks, Bill. You've been a big help."

I tucked my cell back into my coat pocket and said, "Bill is a former colleague of mine at the precinct in downtown Indy. I had a hunch that he would know Asher Schwartz personally, and I was right."

"Small world," Daniel said.

"Bill is an undercover narcotics agent, that's why I called him. And you know what?" Daniel was waiting for me to respond, but he was also paying a lot of attention to the worsening weather conditions. "Asher is big-time dealer…and Brody Gentry knows all about it." My voice began rising with the heat of my anger. "As a matter of fact, Indy contacted Sheriff Gentry personally to discuss their suspicions that Asher was extending his business into the countryside. But Bill said that Brody didn't want to hear any of it, even after Asher was arrested two years ago for selling BHO—you know, hash oil—to some minor in the next county over."

"Why would the sheriff ignore Asher's record?"

"Oh, he didn't just ignore it. He pressured Judge Warren to completely expunge his record in this county. He was protecting Asher for some reason."

"He had a record here?"

I nodded. "Along with the rap sheet in Indy, he had a slew of misdemeanor possession convictions and an assault on a jacked up girlfriend that nearly killed the woman."

"It sounds as if Mariah is on to something. I think we need to have a little talk with Asher Schwartz."

We came around the bend slowly and I looked up the hill at Rowan's farm. The snow was coming down in buckets, but there was something else in the wind that I could also see—*smoke.*

"Oh…my God," I stammered.

The flames shooting from Rowan's main barn suddenly pierced clearly through the storm.

"Dammit," Daniel exclaimed as he pressed down on the gas pedal and we lurched forward up the driveway.

16

By the time we slid to a stop alongside the barn that was on fire, I had already called 911. The backside of the barn was engulfed in flames and the plume of smoke that a minute before had been wispy tentacles on the wind was now a giant black cloud rising from the structure.

"Where's Rowan?" Daniel shouted at Gabe as he grabbed the boy by the arm and held him in place.

"He went in after Dakota and the calf. They're in there!" Gabe struggled against Daniel's firm hold.

"You stay here with your sisters and Seth. I'll go help him," Daniel released the boy and plunged through the open doorway.

My heart pounded in my chest. I took a breath and calculated the speed of the growing fire and weakening of the structure. Lucinda suddenly had her arms wrapped tightly around my waist.

The little girl's red face was soaked with tears. She looked up and cried, "Da's going to die trying to save Dakota and Midnight."

Mareena was standing a few steps back, holding onto Cacey, and watching the spectacle with the blank face of complete shock. Seth was crouched beside her. His arms encircled the dog tightly as it barked relentlessly at the doomed barn.

Midnight—the calf had a name now? Shoot. Anger nearly glazed my vision. Why were those stupid men risking their lives for a horse and a cow? Deep down I totally understood, but still, seeing Rowan's children lined up and knowing that they might be orphans in the next few minutes made it unconscionable. And now Daniel was in there, too.

To hell with the Amish's ideas about God's will and preordained fate. I certainly couldn't stand by and let it happen on my watch.

"Stay here and wait for the fire trucks!" I shouted at the kids.

I relished in the wet splatters of snow that hit my face just before I ran through the doorway of the barn. The aisle was dark with smoke, but I could still make out the frames of the stalls as I held my breath, stumbling along. I counted the stall doorways, trying to remember which one Dakota had been in.

Muffled voices reached my ears and a surge of hope sprang to life inside of me, but it was short lived when the barn's interior was suddenly illuminated by a spout of blazing flames wicking up the wall. I could clearly see the fire dancing in between the skeletal remains of beams and joists that were left in the far part of the barn. I was betting that in less than a minute that section was coming down.

Daniel was struggling with Dakota's lead rope as the terrified horse jumped away from Rowan's hands. I quickly assessed that he was attempting to cover Dakota's eyes with a cloth of some kind.

"Get him against the wall, Daniel. I almost got it that time!" Rowan called out.

Daniel pushed Dakota forcefully into the wall. The lines on his face popped with strain when he looked over at me.

"Get the hell out of here, Serenity!" Daniel shouted.

Instead of running for safety, I joined him alongside Dakota's quivering, sweat soaked body. With all my strength, I pushed against Dakota's side, helping to hold him in place while Rowan reached up and secured the cloth onto the horse's halter.

It probably only took a few seconds to get the job done, but as I shoved Dakota with everything I had in me, time seemed to slow down. I noticed that we were in a small pocket of smokeless space that was surrounded by a billowing black and gray monster. Besides seeing the explosions of flames from the rapidly expanding fire, sweat trickled down my chest into the cleft between my breasts at the ever increasing rise in temperature. The deadly scent of hot, scorched wood was held somewhat at bay as the smell of the sweat soaked horse hair bombarded my nose.

"I got it!" Rowan took the lead from Daniel and signaled for us to follow him as he tugged on Dakota. Amazingly, the horse that had been too paralyzed with fear a moment ago to save himself was now prancing beside Rowan, almost knocking him over with his sudden desire to run.

The bright light from the snowy afternoon beyond the barn door shone through the opening, as if it was a lighthouse beacon in a raging storm. I could see Rowan's kids silhouetted against the white background and the dog's barking reached my ears once again. Everything inside of me was focused on that place of cold, wet snow and safety.

At some point after Rowan had taken Dakota's lead rope from Daniel's hands, Daniel had grabbed me, tucking me under his arm as we fled the stall just when the boards ignited with a sizzling hiss.

Daniel and I clutched each other as we ducked and surged forward. We were only a few steps behind Rowan and Dakota's shadowed forms when I heard the calf bellow.

The sound was sharp and loud in my ears, hitting me like an invisible bullet. I dug my heels in and pulled Daniel to a stop.

"What the hell?" Daniel exclaimed hoarsely.

"The calf is in this one!" I twisted away from him and grabbed the latch to the stall door, turning it.

At the exact instant that the door flung open, the fire reached the hay bales stacked in the loft. With a horrifying *SWOOSH* the loft went up. The ceiling was breaking up above my head as I touched the warm fur of the calf's neck. It bucked, recoiling from my touch, but luckily Daniel hadn't left my side. He grabbed the calf around its chest and buttocks, restraining it with his strong arms until I positioned myself on its other side.

"This is a big calf—too big for me to carry," Daniel coughed, "We'll have to scoot him out."

There wasn't any time to discuss the logistics of it. I absorbed what Daniel said and placed my arms around the calf the same way he had. As the back half of the barn came crashing down, we worked side by side, pushing and pulling the calf with all our might.

Death was just behind us and I didn't dare to glance over my shoulder. The barn's structure shuddered at our backs for an agonizingly long second before it splintered. The roof smashed into the loft's floor, the fire devouring the ceiling above us in a mighty gulp of smoke and debris.

Rowan met us at the doorway. He flung his arm around me and helped shove us all clear of the threshold, just as it gave way. It barely missed us as it crashed to the ground at our backs.

The calf bucked up at the shattering sound, breaking away and running freely towards the house. The momentum carried me and Daniel forward and we stumbled into the wonderful, welcomed coldness of a drift of snow.

"Your back is on fire!" Mareena screeched, pointing at me.

Daniel rushed onto his knees in amazing speed and rolled me sideways, pressing my back into snow. He grabbed the sleeve of my coat with one hand and gripped my shoulder with the other. In a quick tug, I was free of my coat and in Daniel's tight embrace.

Gabe came to our side and shed his own coat, placing it over my shoulders in a sweeping motion.

Daniel continued to squeeze me against his chest for what I thought was a completely unnecessary amount of time, but I didn't protest. My gaze quickly passed over Seth who was standing well away from the wreckage with Dakota in hand, and the three girls who were kneeling in the snow beside their father.

Rowan was staring at the enormous pile of burning wood and metal that had once been his stable with a strange look of calm acceptance that sent a chill racing through me. The rush of heat coming from the shooting flames was so hot that it was melting the snow where we sat, so I knew that the chill that I suddenly felt was not from the cold. It was my gut telling me that Rowan had expected this all along.

When the two volunteer fire department trucks and the three police cruisers arrived, Daniel, Rowan and I were standing in the driveway. Rowan had ordered the girls into the house and the boys to catch the calf.

It had been less than ten minutes from the time that we had pulled in the driveway for the entire barn to be lost. There was no way that any emergency response by authorities could have saved the barn. The Amish community was just too remote for the fire department to reach it in time, especially during the snow squall that had suddenly whipped up. And the fact that the barn had been mostly made of wood and filled with highly flammable dry hay had added to the speed of its demise.

I buttoned up Gabe's borrowed coat and waited for Sheriff Brody to reach our little group. Smoke was heavy in the air and the wind shifted, bringing a rush of the fumes over us. I coughed. Daniel tentatively reached over and stroked my shoulder. I took one step back and glanced up at him. He scowled for an instant and then looked away, shaking his head.

Rowan didn't miss the interchange. His brows rose quizzically, but I ignored him, bringing my full attention to Sheriff Gentry when he finally stepped up to us.

"How many more barns are going to burn before one of you finally talks?" the sheriff asked in a raised voice.

Brody was speaking to Rowan and I closely observed his face go from curiosity about my relationship with Daniel to guarded disinterest with the sheriff.

"I've told you everything I know already. What more do you want from me?"

"Dammit, the truth," Brody growled. He looked at me in annoyance and said, "I believe Rowan here, along with several others in this community, know who set the fire that killed my grandson."

"Excuse me," I thrust my finger forward, pointing at the giant bonfire that used to be a barn and seethed, "Don't you think that we should all be focused on who lit *this* fire at the moment?"

"Maybe they're all connected somehow, Miss Adams. I don't know. What I am sure of is that the Amish have never been upfront with me during any of my investigations, past or present. How am I supposed to help them, when they won't help themselves?"

The sudden appearance of a long line of buggies speeding up the driveway added to the surreal feeling of the scene. We paused from our conversation as two of the buggies pulled up almost beside us, the steam rising from the horses' backs indicating the fast pace that they'd set to get to Rowan's farm.

Jotham jumped from the first buggy and ran over to Rowan. He placed his hand on his friend's shoulder and gushed, "I came as soon as I heard. Did you lose any of the horses?"

Rowan shook his head and glanced over at me and Daniel, "I was blessed to have these two. They helped me with Dakota and then they got the calf out, all on their own."

I probably reddened a little at the flash of admiration I saw on Brody's face and the genuine thankfulness reflected on Jotham's.

Bishop Fisher joined us with another man who was unknown to me. The newcomer looked to be in his forties and sported a shorter beard than the others. I only spared him a glance, though. Anna King was on his heels and her flushed, anxious face got my attention.

"Rowan, is everyone all right?" she rushed the words out, as if saying them faster would get her an answer sooner. Anna stood beside the bishop and the newcomer, making no attempt to move any closer to Rowan.

"We're all fine," Rowan looked at me and said, "This is Mason Gingerich, one of our ministers and Anna's uncle."

I nodded at Mason, who favored me with a quick smile before telling Rowan, "I see you lost the buggy. I'll send Jacob and Jory over this evening with our extra one. You may borrow it for as long as you need."

Rowan looked genuinely touched when he replied, "I appreciate that very much."

A minute later, Shem Yoder appeared, along with the same group of men that had been working on his barn with him earlier in the day.

I patiently listened to the Amish as they talked to each other in German for a moment, not understanding a word of it. Brody didn't look very patient, though. In between barking out a few orders to passing fireman and pulling the fire chief, Bill Doherty, aside to whisper back and forth, he stood silently, tapping his foot.

With a flurry of movement, most of the Amish men disbanded, leaving behind only the bishop and Jotham. I had already watched Anna slip away, heading towards the house soon after the other men began arriving. Fleetingly, I admired how the Amish handled an emergency. Several men, along with Daniel, were clearing out the shed on the side of the house to create a temporary stable for Dakota and the calf. I imagined that Anna was helping the girls with dinner, and the two teenagers that I assumed were Jacob and Jory, had already arrived with their extra buggy, before their father had even instructed them to do so. The Amish's no-nonsense approach to a crisis was definitely impressive.

Rowan finally returned his attention to Sheriff Gentry and asked, "Did Chief Bill say anything about the cause of the fire?"

Brody rolled his eyes and snorted. "He assumes that it was purposely set, but he won't be able to test for accelerant until it cools down. He found what looked to be a trail of prints on the backside of the barn that led out through the field, but the falling snow is quickly obscuring them."

I processed what he said quickly and asked Brody, "Was there snow on the ground with the other fires?"

"Nope, this is the first one. Mighty lucky if you ask me for the guy to have an unexpected blizzard pop up to cover his tracks."

"And you think it was just one person?"

Brody paused in thought, glancing at the burning scene and then back at me again. He shrugged, "Honestly, it just seems to me that it would be a hell of a lot easier for a single person to sneak across that snow white and barren field without being caught. But who knows. There certainly could have been an accomplice."

Jotham looked between Brody and me and said, "So we aren't any closer to finding out who's been setting these fires?"

Brody answered, speaking to the bishop alone. "I'm willing to bet that the day you tell me what you know about the fire that killed my grandson is the day that we'll have some clarity about this fire," he nodded towards the debris pile, "and the others."

"That sounds a lot like blackmail to me, Sheriff," I spoke up.

Brody fixed a steely gaze on me. "It's simply the truth."

As I watched Sheriff Gentry walk away, I was more conflicted than ever about the case. As much as I wanted to distrust Brody, I couldn't find it in my gut to do so. There was something genuine about the man that made me reluctant to brand him as a bad cop. He was definitely a good old boy, but I really didn't think that he was behind the fires, or that he knew who was doing them for that matter.

"If you need anything at all, let me know, Rowan. We'll talk more after the service tomorrow," the bishop said before he tipped his hat to me and walked back to his buggy.

Jotham turned to me and with a high-pitched whine, said, "Do you see what we're dealing with here?" he motioned at the sheriff's retreating form and added, "He won't help us."

Swallowing first, I glanced between Rowan and Jotham before saying, "Why don't you just tell him the truth about that fire that happened eighteen years ago?"

Jotham sighed loudly and ran his hand through his hair. Rowan continued to stand as if he was a statue, staring at the firefighters while they hosed down the burning debris.

When Jotham began to speak, Rowan abruptly came out of his daze and raised his hand to stop him. Rowan looked over at me and said, "Whatever happened back in nineteen ninety-seven has nothing to do with what's going on today. I only hope you can figure out who is doing this before something really bad happens. Now if you'll excuse me, I'm going to help the others with the shed."

Rowan left us with the straight-backed posture of a man who wasn't anywhere near bending.

"Don't blame him for his rudeness. He's overly emotional right now. It wasn't so long ago that Rowan returned to this very property to find his house in ashes and his wife gone."

I took the opening that Jotham's words gave me and asked, "Why were you in the house with Hedy Schwartz in the middle of the night?"

Jotham didn't hesitate. He almost sounded relieved when he said, "I needed to talk to her about something very important. But we never did get the chance."

"Do you think it was an accident?" I pressed.

Jotham swallowed and then frowned. "I always thought that it was, but lately here, I've been wondering…"

"Jotham will you help us?" Gabe called out. Seth had a halter on the calf and was tugging on the rope as Gabe pushed the animal's rear end up the driveway.

A slight smile teased at Jotham's face when he looked at Gabe. I could now see the eerie resemblance between Jotham and Gabe, from the tawny hair and sky-blue eyes to the straight nose and square chin.

"Of course I will, one minute!" Jotham called out.

Jotham turned back to me with a little wetness in his one good eye. The wintry wind had battered the scar tissue on the side of his face to an even deeper, beet red color and I tried not to stare at it. Suddenly, I recognized his pleading look.

"Does Rowan know that Gabe is your son?" I whispered.

Jotham wasn't surprised, only resigned when he smiled sadly. "I think he does…but after he lost Hedy, he didn't want to lose Gabe too."

I nodded with some understanding. Jotham left me standing in the driveway to jog over to help the boys with the calf.

As a heavier, wetter snow began falling, I muttered under my breath, "The truth always comes out, in the end."

Then I spotted Daniel talking to a couple of firemen near one of the trucks. As if he felt my gaze on him, he looked up and smiled. My very core trembled as warmth spread through my veins.

How am I ever going to stay focused enough to figure this craziness out with Daniel turning me into hot molten lava with a mere glance, I thought to myself. Shaking away the uncomfortable sensation the best I could, I began walking to the house. I needed to call Todd and attempt to help Anna and the girls with supper. I raised my face to the snow in an effort to cool my desire and wipe away the touch of death that had grazed my skin when the barn had collapsed nearly on top of me.

17

When I opened the door, the warmth of Rowan's kitchen, along with a dozen pairs of eyes greeted me. I quickly recovered, taking note of Mariah's presence in the room as the teenager gently rocked Cacey on her lap in the corner of the room. But I singled out Joanna Fisher, when I said, "Well, I guess my help isn't really needed in here."

Joanna left the counter to grasp my hand and say, "I heard all about how you charged into that burning barn to help the men get the animals out." She smiled. "Seems to me that you've helped out enough already today."

The room suddenly seemed smaller and warmer too. I shrugged, feeling my face tingle with heat. "It wasn't a big deal. I'm just glad that we got the horse and calf out safely."

Anna handed me a warm, wet wash cloth. She pointed to her own face and said, "Your face is smudged."

I touched my check questioningly. Lucinda giggled and held up a shiny pot for me to get a distorted view of my face. Sure enough, Anna was right. My forehead, nose and left cheek were sooty. Damn men. Not even one of them had the decency to point out that I looked like a chimney sweep.

I vigorously wiped my face while Joanna guided me to a seat. She gently pushed me into it as Mareena handed me a tall glass of water. Catching a glimpse of Mareena's and Lucinda's worried expressions, I was once again reminded of the amazing resilience of children. Their barn had just been burned to the ground by some nutcase, and here they were, all concerned about my well-being.

Joanna briefly motioned to each of the other women in the room, naming them off, before she turned her attentions back to me. When Joanna leaned in and began whispering, I'd already forgotten the women's names, being much more focused on the intensity of the look in the bishop's wife's eyes than anything else.

"You see, I warned you that it would happen again."

I tilted my head, "I need some help on this, Joanna. I've only been here a couple of days, and no one in your community is willing to point the finger at anyone. Surely, you have an idea who is doing this?"

Anna joined us at the table, sitting close beside me on the bench. She glanced between Joanna and me and urged softly, "We can trust her, Joanna. Go on…tell her."

The other women in the room, along with Mareena and Lucinda, were now busily making sandwiches at the counter, seemingly ignoring our conversation, but I wasn't fooled. They were all listening. Mariah didn't even try to pretend. She just stared directly at me while she continued to rock Cacey in her arms.

Joanna's face twisted with intense thought and I almost felt sorry for her confliction. But I didn't say anything, hoping desperately that she'd spill the beans.

With a heavy sigh, Joanna said resignedly, "Our men make most of the decisions in our lives, but they certainly aren't always right. I'm afraid this is one of those situations." Her face sobered even more when she added, "You, or Rowan or Daniel could have easily been killed today. This must end."

Carefully, I nodded my head.

"Our men don't want to point blame at anyone. They are afraid that it goes against our spiritual convictions to get involved in the goings-on in the outside world, and its system. They are also afraid of what might happen to some of our own people if the box of truth is flung open." In a firmer voice, Joanna continued, "But enough is enough. We must act."

Joanna met my gaze unblinkingly and said, "Eighteen years ago, Sheriff Gentry's son's barn burnt down. His grandson and a girl were killed in that fire."

"Yes, I already know that."

Joanna ignored my comment and went on, "The Sheriff believed that Amish teenagers had something to do with it. Our elders at the time didn't like the accusation. They chose to hide whatever knowledge they may have had to protect the young ones in the community who were being singled out."

She must have seen the question in my eyes, because she hurriedly said, "Abner and I don't know anything about it. I wasn't much beyond my teen years myself at the time and Abner wasn't even a minister back then. But what I do know, is that a lot of animosity from the English towards our community began building after Austin Gentry died…and I think the fires that we're having now are in retribution for his death."

The room was silent, except for the slight clinks of the dishes being moved half-heartedly around on the counter by the eavesdropping women. The theory wasn't far off from my own, but there was one thing that I was now certain of. The bishop's wife herself believed that Amish kids had set the barn on fire that killed Brody's grandson and another girl. But why would they have done such a thing in the first place?

"Will that help you to find the person who's setting the fires now?" Anna asked in a hopeful voice.

"I already had this pegged as retaliation crimes. What I need to know is if you have any idea who might be involved—in both the Gentry fire and recent ones?"

Mariah spoke up from across the room. "I already told you who I thought it was."

"Hush now, Mariah. This is not your concern," Joanna chastised her daughter.

I met Mariah's hot gaze. The girl was angry at the world. But maybe it was just because no one was listening to her.

"Trust me, Mariah. I'm looking into what you told me."

"There are some people you ought to talk to," Joanna said hesitantly.

I pulled out the notepad and pen from my back pocket and waited.

Joanna lowered her voice and leaned even closer. "There is a group of English teens…"

"Momma!" Mariah shouted, waking Cacey when she bolted right out of the chair.

"Don't interfere, Mariah. If they're innocent, then Serenity will find that out. But if they're not…"

"I don't believe you're doing this," Mariah hissed. She abruptly deposited a confused looking Cacey onto the rocker and grabbed her coat from the peg by the door. "You're all going to regret this."

There was a brief blast of cold air as the door swung open and then slammed shut.

Anna looked away in embarrassment, but Joanna held my gaze firmly. "Don't mind her. She's a rebellious girl and she's gifted her loyalties falsely." She took a breath and said, "Cody Buffet, Lyell Simmons, Nathan Tucker and Brandy Warner. Those are the people you need to speak to."

As I wrote the names down, I immediately pictured the group of teens that I had encountered at the gas station convenience center on my first night in Poplar Springs. Sure, the one boy had attempted to shoplift a pack of gum, but I definitely didn't get the vibe that any of them would be running around setting Amish barns ablaze. But I'd been fooled before.

I closed the notepad and rose.

Anna bolted up beside me, "You aren't going out on a night like this and after everything you've been through?"

I chuckled. "I only have twelve days left of vacation before I have to return to Blood Rock. I can't afford to waste any time."

Mareena handed me a brown paper bag. "At least take sandwiches for you and Mr. Bachman."

The simple gesture affected me more than I cared to admit. For all the backward thinking, secrets and vigilante tendencies, the Amish were good people.

"Thank you," I told the girl.

I opened the trunk of my car and grabbed my spare coat and quickly slipped it on. It wasn't as warm as the other one, but it was better than nothing.

"Where are you going?"

Daniel's voice made me jump. "Dammit, I wish you'd stop sneaking up on me."

"Maybe it's a guilty conscience making you jumpy," Daniel accused.

I faced him with angry determination that quickly turned to a giggle when I saw the black smudges on his face as well. Pulling an old, but clean napkin, from my pocket, I handed it to him. "Your face could use a little cleaning."

Daniel took the napkin without argument and began rubbing it all over his face.

"Seriously, are you leaving?"

"The bishop's wife just gave me the names of some possible culprits."

"Really, that's surprising." He paused and lifted his brows. "And you were going to sneak off without me?"

I exhaled warily. It was true, I was definitely trying to get away without him noticing, but I wasn't exactly sure why. Most of the time, I really liked having him beside me during my interviews, but there was still that part of me that felt all too vulnerable when he was around. For all of my tough cop bravado on the outside, I was a bowl of mush on the inside when it came to this gorgeous man.

Not wanting to hurt his feelings because of my own issues, I said, "I thought you'd be a while longer with the make-shift building project."

"We've got the buggy horse and the calf under cover for the night. Tomorrow we'll have some more work to do, but for now it'll do." He grinned. "So, I'm all yours."

I handed him the sandwich bag and said, "Then get in. It's almost dark and the roads aren't getting any better."

18

I hung up the phone. "The girl lives at thirteen Mulberry Road. Can you put that into my GPS, please?"

"Sure thing," Daniel replied. "Todd can certainly be handy sometimes."

I eased up on the gas pedal as another squall of snow whipped up in front of us from a drift on the side of the road. I narrowed my eyes and leaned forward over of the wheel to see a little bit better.

"Damn, I can barely see thirty feet in front of the car," I grumbled.

"Do you want me to drive?"

Daniel was just trying to be helpful, but I snapped back at him anyway, "Why? Do you have better eyesight than I do?"

The rumbling snort that he answered me with made me feel bad. Trying to smooth things over, I said, "Yeah, it's convenient to have a partner who doesn't mind bending the rules to get inside information. Todd's loyal to a fault sometimes."

"I still think that he has the hots for you," Daniel growled.

I chuckled, "He's getting married this spring."

"He was supposed to marry her on New Year's Day, wasn't he?"

I shrugged. "He had to work. Besides, he isn't due for his vacation until March. Who wants to tie the knot and then go into work the next day?"

"He might have other reasons to delay," Daniel suggested.

I took the risk of glancing away from the swirling snow to look at Daniel, wondering if he was actually serious.

"You can't be jealous of Todd."

Daniel was silent a moment, and then he said casually, "It's not jealously, it's more concern that you're so distracted all the time solving cases that you don't really notice what's happening with the people around you."

Irritation swelled up inside of me. "I'm more aware than you give me credit for. But honestly, Todd and I have known each other since middle school. It's just an excess amount of familiarity that you're picking up on."

The GPS warned me to turn in five hundred feet and I pumped the brake softly to test the traction. Thankfully, my tires gripped the fresh covering of snow easily and I made the turn without any issues.

"Do you really think these kids are the arsonists?" Daniel asked as I pulled into Brandy's driveway.

The neat looking brick rancher was covered in multi-colored Christmas lights and there were several cars already parked in front of the garage. The place was pretty much as I imagined it would be.

"No, not really, but I can't completely cross them off the list either." I shut the engine off and leaned back, suddenly anxious to discuss the case with Daniel before I bothered the girl and her parents. "In a lot of cases like this, it is rowdy neighborhood kids setting the fires."

"Then why are you so reluctant?"

"I actually ran into this same group of kids at two o'clock in the morning at the gas station the same night I arrived," I admitted.

"Seriously? That's kind of coincidental. And the fact that they were out in the middle of the night doesn't bode well for their innocence either," Daniel observed.

"I don't agree. I overheard them talking and they did mention the Amish community, but they seemed to be good kids for the most part. As far as being coincidental, that seems to be the story of my life lately."

"Somebody snuck across a snowy field and set fire to Rowan's barn today. That doesn't sound to me like something an adult would do."

"You wouldn't believe half the crap I've seen adults do while I've been a cop. And I get what you're saying, except that I'm just not convinced yet that it's the English kids doing it."

Daniels eyes grew wide with expectancy. I savored the moment and said, "Let's go have a talk with Brandy Warner, shall we?"

The snow on the pathway to the front door was trampled flat from a lot of traffic and adding to the sparkling festive lights hanging around the porch, the inside of the house was also lit up brightly. I knocked a few times on the door and then took a step back, eyeing Daniel with a here-we-go look.

The woman who opened the door had red hair that was streaked with gray at the temples. I immediately guessed her to be Brandy's mother, or possibly another relative. She smiled tentatively and said, "May I help you?"

"I'm Serenity Adams, the sheriff from Blood Rock, and this is Daniel Bachman. I've been asked by the Amish community to investigate the arsons."

She nodded in quick succession. "Oh, I see. It's terrible, I know, but why are you here?"

"Another barn went up a few hours ago—Rowan Schwartz's. I understand that Brandy is friends with some of the Amish teenagers. I'd like to ask her a few questions if it's possible."

The woman's face lost some of its color and she glanced over her shoulder nervously.

"I don't know. I mean, my niece certainly doesn't know anything about the fires."

"Aunt Iva, it's okay. I'll talk to them," Brandy squeezed her aunt's shoulder affectionately and then glanced at me with the bland expression of inevitability.

"All right then. I'll be in the kitchen," Brandy's aunt said as she opened the door wider and motioned us inside.

"Are you Brandy's guardian?" I asked the woman. When she nodded, I added, "I would really rather that you're present while I talk to Brandy."

The woman looked relieved and quickly sat down on the recliner beside the sofa. I wasn't at all surprised to see Nathan Tucker and Cody Buffet already sitting on the sofa. The TV was on and there was a bowl of popcorn and several opened cans of pop on the coffee table. How incredibly convenient, I thought, as I took the only other free chair available. Brandy hurried out of the room and returned a moment later with a kitchen chair that she set down beside me for Daniel's use.

When Brandy was finally seated on the sofa beside the boys, she said, "I heard you tell Aunt Iva that the Schwartz's barn burned down. Is everyone okay?"

There was genuine curiosity in her voice. Nathan's mouth dropped at her words and Cody's face lit up with disbelief.

I was convinced that this was the first time that the boys had heard the news.

"Everyone's perfectly fine, even the animals," I assured her and then as casually as possible, I said, "What have you guys been up to today?"

"They've been sitting in this very room, watching movies all afternoon," Aunt Iva told me enthusiastically.

"We did go into town to rent the movies and get snacks this morning, but other than that, Aunt Iva's right, we've been here," Brandy added.

They were telling the truth. I'd bet money on it. But still, Joanna's insistence about the English kids was fresh in my mind. "What about Lyell. Where's he?"

Nathan answered me. "His sister had a baby late last night. He went with his folks to the hospital today to see it." Nathan came to the edge of his seat, leaning forward even more towards me and added, "Look, I know you probably don't think much of me cause of the other night at the gas station, but none of us had anything to do with those fires and I'm telling the God's honest truth."

"I'm not making accusations here. I was hopeful that you may have an idea about who's behind the fires."

"You should be interviewing the Amish kids," Nathan blurted out.

"Nathan, shut up," Brandy scolded the boy beside her. She met my gaze evenly and said, "I don't think they're doing it any more than we are."

I looked at the three teens sitting on the couch and carefully said, "What about Asher Schwartz. Do you know him?"

Brandy and Cody visibly tensed and glanced quickly away, but Nathan puckered his lips as if thinking hard. Their reactions to the name were interesting to say the least.

Nathan brushed the blond hair back from his forehead and exhaled deeply. When his gaze met mine again, he looked resolute. "Asher's a bad dude. He could be in on it."

"Nathan!" Brandy threatened.

"I'm not afraid of him," Nathan retorted.

"You should be," Cody muttered.

For the first time, Cody had my full attention. The tall boy was tapping his foot nervously and avoiding eye contact with me.

"What did you say, Cody?"

When Cody didn't answer me, Brandy's aunt ordered, "Cody, answer the lady!"

He shrugged. "He killed a man in the parking lot at Hochstetler's Country Store last year."

"What?!" Daniel had suddenly found his voice.

"The cops said that it was self-defense. He was never even charged," Cody said weakly.

I twisted and looked at Aunt Iva. "Is that true?"

She sighed, "Yes, it was in the newspapers and everything. This Schwartz fellow smashed a man's head into a hitching rail and killed him. Supposedly it was in self-defense. The police never pressed charges."

I exchanged wary glances with Daniel and then turned back to the teenagers who were still tensely sitting on the sofa.

"Do any of you ever come into contact with Asher Schwartz?" I asked, looking around the room.

Brandy answered, "I see him around sometimes with that friend of his...Julian West."

Their silence told me that they were finished talking. Reaching into my pocket, I pulled out a few business cards with my cell phone number on them and passed them around.

"If you think of anything else, please call me," I said rising.

Brandy and Cody nodded, but Nathan seemed lost in thought. When we stepped out into the moonlight, the snow had stopped falling and the night was crisp and clear.

Daniel waited until we were back on the road to finally speak. "So what did you make of all that?"

"For the most part, those kids were telling the truth. I don't think that they had anything to do directly with the fires, but I am concerned with Brandy's and Cody's aversion to talk about Asher."

"Again, it keeps coming back to the Schwartz family," Daniel offered.

"Yes, it does," I agreed. After a pause, I asked, "Why would the Amish kids want to burn barns down?"

"Maybe for a thrill, I'm not sure really. I think it's odd that the bishop's wife was pointing the finger at the English kids and in return, they were singling out the Amish kids." He turned to me and said more directly, "Is it possible that Asher Schwartz really killed a guy and didn't even get arrested."

"Absolutely, I've heard of many instances where small town authorities deem a killing to be self-defense and no charges are filed. But in the same breath, when a person is involved in violent situations, it's usually a tell-tale sign that they're walking on the wrong side of the law themselves. Asher's rap sheet in Indy includes battery assault on a girlfriend, and a slew of drug offences. He's not a good guy."

"Then why would Sheriff Gentry let him off the hook so easily?"

"That's a question that I don't have the answer to. I can imagine a few reasons why, and none of them paint the sheriff in a very good light."

"Are we going to pay Asher Schwartz a visit tomorrow after the church service?" When I glanced at Daniel, he wore a small grin and his eyes were bright.

"Why the corny face?" I asked suspiciously.

Too quickly, he said, "No reason."

Yeah, right, I thought as I pulled into Rowan's driveway. It was after nine o'clock and there were still a half dozen buggies in the driveway and the house was lit up brightly. I needed to talk to Todd again and attempt to pull some information up on my phone. If I was lucky, Daniel would hang out with the Amish until I was already in bed. I was exhausted from the insane day and the last thing I wanted to deal with was his smoldering glances and sexual innuendos. I was in no mood for it tonight. But bothering me something fierce was the awareness that my mind could be changed quickly.

Even heavier on my mind was Asher Schwartz, though. Could he be responsible for the arsons after all? I hadn't been completely honest with Daniel. I actually had a pretty good idea why he had literally gotten away with murder, and couldn't help but shiver at the thought of what was going to happen if my suspicions turned out to be correct.

19

My butt was sore and my legs were cramped from sitting on the hard wooden bench for nearly three hours. I glared across the room at Daniel, who was wedged in between an old man with a long, snowy white beard and a middle aged, chunky fellow wearing glasses. Now I knew why he had been so damn amused the night before in the car.

The weirdness of being separated into two groups, the men all on the left and the women on the right, had finally worn off, but the drone of the bishop's sermon in German and awkwardness of being pressed up against an old Amish woman still made the ordeal torturous.

The one good thing to come from being trapped in Elijah Mast's cold buggy shed during the overly long and boring service was that it gave me the opportunity to really think about the case. The night before when I'd finally gotten off the phone with Todd and re-read Brody's files, I was too exhausted to put all the information into perspective. And then there had been Daniel.

Sharing a room with the man was driving me insane on top of everything else. His close proximity through the night had kept me awake for hours, even though he had annoyingly fallen asleep fairly soon after he'd laid down on the trundle.

My thoughts disappeared when Abner Fisher abruptly stopped talking and the congregation began singing. Without the accompaniment of instruments, the music was rather dull, but it was more the somber tone that the Amish sang than the song itself that bothered me. If I closed my eyes, I would have thought that I was at a funeral in Germany, instead of an Amish church service in Indiana.

The cold breeze slipping through the gap in the shed's door made me shiver, even though I was sitting close to the generator-run heater in the corner. In all, there were probably about one hundred and fifty people crammed into the new construction. Before the service began, Rowan had introduced me to Elijah and I asked him a few questions, but the skinny man with the medium length black beard didn't enlighten me with anything new. The only thing that I took away from the conversation was that Elijah had a more difficult time keeping his emotions hidden than the other Amish I'd encountered. He'd spoken angrily about losing his own barn and the local sheriff's inability to solve the case.

It was nice to know that some of the Amish were emotional about the crimes. At least it made Elijah seem more human.

The song finally came to an end while I was still deep in thought. I began stretching my sore limbs the same as everyone else. I blinked and searched for Daniel in the crowd. He was waiting by the door and I wasted no time meeting up with him there.

"Thanks for the warning," I said tersely.

Daniel shrugged and grinned broadly. "It's really impossible to prepare someone for such an experience."

No kidding. Briefly I wondered how he managed to keep the dark bristles on his chin at the perfect cropped length, before I asked, "Did you find anything else out from the other men?"

I watched the steady stream of women passing by us in an orderly line, and I thought I recognized a couple of them from the gathering in Rowan's kitchen from the night before. Mareena and Lucinda had already passed, both smiling warmly. Anna slowed long enough to point towards the Mast's house where she had already explained the lunch would be served in the basement. She was holding Cacey's hand and for the first time the little girl actually acknowledged me with a slight wave of the hand.

"I did get some more information about Asher," Daniel whispered, leaning in closer. "It seems that Rowan and Asher's father was diabetic. Since the two were the oldest, it fell on their shoulders to keep the family business going when he was sick. At about the same time that their father lost his leg to the disease, Michael Gentry, Brody's son, outbid the boys on a big construction project. I guess losing the contract put the Schwartz family in a difficult way for a while and there were bad feelings between the two families." He took a breath and glanced around before continuing, "Asher might have been a rebellious kid, but he still worked hard alongside Rowan to support the family."

I looked up at Daniel with a narrowed gaze. "You sound like you respect the jerk."

Daniel glanced away and then back again. "I wasn't that different when I left the Amish. I'd grown up quickly, doing a man's job while I was still a child. I helped to put food on the table and then when I left, I was shunned, just like Asher. I bet he has a lot of pent up resentment about it, the same as I did."

My voice raised a little and I had to consciously tone it down. "That's no excuse for becoming a professional criminal. There are a lot of people out there who were dealt hard-knocks when they were kids and they didn't grow up to sell drugs, beat up their girlfriends, or kill a man. Look at yourself, for example."

"Things aren't always black and white."

"In my world, gray isn't a color."

The bishop paused beside us with questioning brows. "I hope you'll be staying with us for dinner. It's just a simple fare, homemade peanut butter sandwiches, but there is more than enough to fill your bellies."

"Of course we will. I was just answering some of Serenity's questions about the service.

Abner looked more closely at me and asked, "Is this your first time?"

I nodded, "Yes. It was…very long."

Abner laughed out loud. "That's what all the English say. I would have thought that Aaron would have invited you to attend one of Blood Rock's services by now."

"Actually, he did. But there was a traffic accident that I was called into that morning."

Abner smiled again and motioned for us to follow him.

The area between the transitional buggy shed/church building and the other metal sided barn was crowded with people. It surprised me that each group was still strictly segregated between men and women, even after the service had ended. After a moment of observation, it didn't seem that the separation of the sexes was being enforced, more just expected.

"Why aren't the men and women mixing?" I whispered to Daniel as we fell a few more steps behind the bishop.

Daniel smiled fondly, and not for the first time, I got the impression that there were some aspects of the Amish lifestyle that Daniel missed.

"The men enjoy talking to the men and the women like female companionship."

"That's all? There must be more to it than that. I certainly don't enjoy female companionship that much," I argued.

"Most women do. Besides, it only causes problems when men and women are socializing together. Just look at your friends Denton, Jory and Ruby. Maybe if they didn't spend so much time together, Denton wouldn't have hooked up with his best friend's wife."

I rolled my eyes and scoffed, "Good people can control themselves. Trust me. Denton has never been a *good* guy. I know from personal experience."

"You'll have to tell me that story sometime," Daniel chuckled.

"Not on your life."

It was about noon and the sun had finally burned away the thick cloud cover that had made the morning especially dreary. I reluctantly stepped over the mound of snow to enter the other building, really hating to leave behind the bright rays of sunshine that were finally warming my face.

My eyes quickly adjusted to the dim interior of the room as I looked around. There were women and teenage girls bustling around, pouring glasses of water and setting out platters of very plain looking sandwiches. The bishop guided us to the corner and motioned for us to sit down. Once again, he was trying to be subtle about seating us off to the side, but I certainly caught on to what he was doing.

Mareena appeared at my shoulder and leaned down, "I see you survived the service," she smirked.

I had to give the girl credit for a sick sense of humor. "I've lived through worse."

Mareena gave us glasses of water and moved on. I watched the girl balancing the tray on one hand while she continued to deposit the full glasses of water along the table.

"Rowan's kids are tough," I said out loud, but mostly to myself.

"Amish kids usually are," Daniel replied.

"It's truly amazing that more of the kids don't runaway in the night."

"It's really not so bad, Serenity. There are a lot of good things that come along with being Amish."

I sighed with irritation, "Yeah, you've already told me all about the wonderful large families and how close-knit the communities are. How you're never alone…but what about those loner-type kids who have independent spirits?"

"It's not easy being a kid anywhere nowadays. At least most of these kids have support from their families and friends."

"Naomi sure didn't," I said bitterly.

"Hey, I didn't say that the Amish have it perfect. I know that better than most. I'm just trying to get you to understand that freedom and technology aren't the only things that make people happy."

I met his gaze squarely, taking a breath to calm myself before I responded. "Don't paint me as a shallow person. I'm not." I leaned in and whispered fervently, "I'm more interested in these kids' lack of higher education and life choices. I don't give a shit about the absence of cell phones, internet and big screened televisions in their lives."

My voice rose a little higher than I intended and several pairs of eyes looked our way. I shrugged off the uneasy sensation rising in my gut as I took a sip of water.

Daniel spoke with calm understanding, which annoyed me even more. "You aren't going to be able to help these people if you don't try to understand them better. Naomi's situation was atypical. These families love and nurture their children. They would do anything for them. They provide them with the skills and knowledge that they need to be successful in *their* world. For most of the young people here, it's all they need to be happy."

"I don't think Mariah is happy."

Daniel looked away for a long moment and then met my gaze again. "So you feel the need to save her...because you couldn't save Naomi?"

I wasn't sure what to say and that didn't happen very often. As much as I hated to admit it, maybe Daniel was correct about my Amish-bashing mind. But he wasn't the one who had been held captive one night in a darkened barn, surrounded by a group of Amish vigilantes. I had every right to feel the way I did. But it was unsettling to think that I might be unconsciously imposing Naomi's craziness into Mariah's life.

While I was lost in thought, I caught a glimpse of Mariah following someone out the door.

I grabbed Daniel's wrist and whispered urgently, "Come on!"

Daniel didn't question me and I really appreciated it at that moment. He simply rose as suddenly as I had and joined me when I left the building.

Mariah was now walking alone down the steep driveway, but I wasn't fooled. Asher's friend, Julian, was about forty feet in front of her. To anyone else, the English man was just heading to his car, the same as any of the other Amish drivers.

I slowed a bit, using the line of parked buggies and the occasional white van as cover. As long as I kept the girl in my sights, I breathed easier.

When I glanced up and saw Daniel by my side without question, I suddenly realized how extremely patient he was being with me.

"We're following Mariah," I volunteered.

"I see her. Do you mind me asking why?"

When we reached the last buggy, I stopped Daniel with my hand on his arm. He followed my gaze to the black charger that was parked beside the road. Mariah was too smart to stop at the vehicle, though. She continued walking to the little white board telephone shed at the corner of the yard. Mariah took the time to look all around before she stepped into the building and closed the door behind her. Julian was sitting in the passenger side of the sports car and no one was in the driver's seat.

My heart rate quickened.

Daniel's hot breath was close to my ear. "What's going on?" he whispered.

"That's Asher Schwartz's car," I nodded at the vehicle and then back at the shed, "and Mariah is in there with him."

Daniel's eyes widened in surprise. "Not much gets by you does it?"

"Nope," I sighed.

"Let's go talk to him," Daniel said, taking a step forward.

I stopped him, "Wait."

Mariah emerged from the shed alone. She walked purposely back the same way she had taken on the way to the shed. I motioned to Daniel to continue waiting, and then lifted my chin towards the shed again.

A minute later, Asher finally came out, and we met him just as he reached his car.

"Hello, Asher. Do you remember me?" I said sweetly.

Asher hesitated for a step and then fully stopped. He was dressed the same as I had seen him before in khaki pants, brown coat, close cropped brown beard—Mister Chameleon.

A wide and very phony smile erupted on his face. "Of course, I do. How are you, Sheriff?"

"I'm great," I pointed at Daniel, "This is Daniel Bachman."

"Hello," Asher said, reaching out to shake Daniel's hand.

At that moment I wished very badly that we were standing in my own jurisdiction so that I could *officially* bring Asher Schwartz in for questioning. Unfortunately, I had no power to do anything in Poplar Springs. The sudden realization of how out of control the situation really was hit me as if I was just smacked in the face.

"Do you have a minute to talk?" I asked.

Asher began backing away from us. "You know, really, I don't have the time today."

"Maybe you'll be a little more willing to talk to me if Sheriff Gentry is by my side," I threatened.

Asher's abrupt laugh surprised me. He smirked and met my gaze. "I'm not worried in the least about that. But you can go ahead and try." He turned and moved quickly around the side of the car. Before he climbed in, he said, "Enjoy your dinner with the Amish. You might want to plan to hit the steak house by the interstate afterwards. I remember the Sunday noon meals to be quite unsatisfying."

Daniel and I watched the Charger pull away in silence. Once the black car had disappeared around the bend in the road, Daniel said, "I was wrong about him. He really is a bastard."

I would have laughed if I wasn't so angry. I began walking up the driveway toward the car. I glanced at Daniel who was even with me. "We need to pay Sheriff Gentry a visit."

Daniel smiled. "I knew you'd say that."

I tossed Daniel the car keys. "I'm calling Todd."

"You came up with twenty-six missing women in a four state region that are possible matches to fit our burn victim?" I asked Todd in astonishment.

I immediately figured half of them had purposely vanished on their own accord, and the rest were probably involved in their own criminal behavior that added to their disappearances. But still, it was a large number of women to work through.

"Let me work on it for a couple of more hours. I think I can whittle it down to about nine possibilities. Three are from the Indianapolis metro area," Todd said.

"Start with them first." I could hear the muffled background noise of people talking and knew that Todd was sitting beside Rosie at the front desk of the Blood Rock Sheriff's Department. Rosie was our elderly receptionist and unofficial personal therapist. The woman was incredibly wise and she wasn't shy about telling everyone else that they were idiots. A small stab of homesickness washed over me and I asked, "How's Bobby doing?"

Todd snorted, "As annoying as ever. He's still in a tizzy trying to get last year's files sorted."

I smiled into the phone picturing Bobby exhausted and rubbing his eyes with a pile of folders on the desk in front of him. Bobby put everything off until the last minute and then he completely freaked out when the mayor came storming in wanting to see this or that. It was really quite comical to watch the two old men bantering back and forth. It was something that I didn't realize I enjoyed so much until this very moment.

"I'm glad things are quiet there for you guys. Tell Rosie, I said, hi." I heard Todd immediately relay the greeting to Rosie and then Rosie said loudly enough to clearly penetrate the phone line, "You tell Serenity to hurry up and get her skinny butt back here. I'm tired of being surrounded by a bunch of idiot men." Todd quickly said, "Ah, Rosie says, hi, too."

I chuckled as I looked out the window at the sun glistening off of the snowy field that we were passing by. The bottoms of the corn stalks poked up through the snow, making me think of rows of skeletons littering a battlefield. Once again, Naomi popped into my thoughts. I shivered and had to blink away the image of her body lying among the dried up, autumn cornstalks.

"I really appreciate this, Todd," I said.

"No problem. It's been incredibly boring around here anyway. I'll call as soon as I have something for you."

When I hung up, I glanced over at Daniel.

"What's wrong?" Daniel asked, taking his eyes off the road for a moment to meet my gaze.

"I came up here to investigate some barn burnings, but it's grown into something much more sinister. And I don't like it one bit."

"I really don't know how you're keeping everything straight in your head. There's a lot going on in this town," Daniel snorted.

"Brody's department could be doing the same kind of research that I'm having Todd do right now. The fact that they aren't, is ringing an alarm bell in my mind."

"What do you think the story is with the woman's body?"

I took a deep breath, "The woman was dead when she was placed in the barn. The fire was set to get rid of her and any evidence on her body."

"How can you be so sure?"

I shrugged. "It just makes the most sense."

"But what about the other fires, and Rowan's house explosion?"

"I have some ideas, but I need more time...and answers from the sheriff."

A few minutes later, we parked in the little parking lot beside the sheriff's department. As timing would have it, Brody was walking out of the building by himself as we approached. We intercepted him on the sidewalk.

"Sheriff, do you have a minute?"

Brody stopped, but said, "It's a busy Sunday. What do you need?"

With the sun out and the milder temperatures, it wasn't uncomfortable having a conversation outside, but it still irritated me that Brody wasn't showing any inclination to invite me into his office for a meeting. I caught a glimpse of Daniel peeking at me with one eyebrow raised. I ignored him. This had to be handled extremely delicately.

"All I have is one question. It won't take long." I tilted my head and watched his expressions closely. "What's the deal with Asher Schwartz? He has a rap sheet a mile long in Indy and he's been involved in criminal activities in Poplar Springs that include murder. Why aren't you gunning for him? If he was in my jurisdiction, I know I would be."

A curious flash of fear passed over Brody's features and then, just as quickly, he relaxed. "It was self-defense. No witnesses and Asher's word against a dead man's, who had an equally long rap sheet of his own. Some cases just aren't worth the tax payer's money."

Brody sniffed and shifted on his feet. He was a really big guy, and standing in his shadow would have been intimidating if he had been a different sort of man. But I was convinced that he was the type who would rather run from a fight than make a stand. I knew a lot of guys like him. The easy way was always the best way in their book.

I raised a questioning brow. "On a first name basis with him?"

Brody cracked a little smile and said, "I know everyone in this town…and I'm a friendly man. You might learn a thing or two from my actions, Serenity."

I gave him my deadliest stare and asked, "I need to know, Sheriff, before I bother going any further with this investigation, whether you'll prosecute Asher Schwartz if I discover that he's involved with the arsons in the Amish community… and possibly other criminal acts?"

I had to give Brody credit for not blurting out what I wanted to hear, just to pacify me. He hesitated for a long moment before he steadily met my gaze. "There are a lot of factors in play here that I'm not going to discuss with you. But I will say this. Asher has a big mouth and he won't be taken quietly." Brody took a step closer, leaning down to the side of my face. He whispered so quietly that I wasn't even sure if Daniel could hear him. "Asher is a cancerous wart on my community. He needs to be brought down, but as long as he's able to talk, I won't touch the man."

Brody stood up tall again, and tipped his gray hat to Daniel. He left us alone on the sidewalk just as an uncomfortable burst of apprehension struck me. It was the same type of feeling you get when you're swimming in the ocean and you suddenly have a horrible feeling that something is beneath you in the dark, greenish water, and it's about to bite your foot off.

I finally breathed again and looked up at Daniel. "This town is a lot more messed up than I originally thought."

Without hesitation, Daniel said, "I'm right here with you, however you want to proceed."

Daniel was watching me with a still, unreadable face. His eyes were warm and alive, though, and for a moment, I was completely at a loss. I certainly wasn't used to the sickening feeling of trepidation spreading quickly inside my gut, but having Daniel standing there at attention, waiting for me to make my move, was encouraging. Suddenly a thick knot lodged in my throat and I struggled to swallow it down. Oh, how I wished that Daniel and I really were more than just partners. I was tiring of the cat and mouse game. Even now, sparks were tingling inside of me as I gazed up at his handsome face.

But I couldn't mention to him what Brody had just insinuated. It was just too dangerous. I still wasn't sure what I was going to do, but the less Daniel knew about it, the better for him. I was about to go down a very slippery slope, one that I wasn't even sure myself if I would be able to climb out of.

I cleared my throat. "Todd gave me Asher's address. That's our next stop."

Daniel's smile and his immediate willingness to follow me deeper into the mud gave me a burst of hopefulness for an instant, but as I turned away and walked to the car, I wondered if I should just keep on driving, right out of this town for good.

20

It was a typical trailer park, only with the snow and the bare, skeletal trees, it was even gloomier than usual. Absently, I had already counted a dozen different dogs chained to dog houses in the front yards and there were enough older model cars in the driveways to fill a junk yard. Children's large, plastic toys littered most of the simple porches and even on this cold day, several people were outside on those porches smoking cigarettes.

This was the perfect place for Asher Schwartz to blend into. People that lived in places like this didn't snitch on each other. They had unwritten rules that everyone automatically knew and followed. And with the depressed, chipped paint look of most of the homes, the main portion of the inhabitants of the East Side Trailer Park were probably unemployed and living on government assistance. They were trapped in a vicious cycle of poverty. Asher would be king in such a place.

"This neighborhood has a rough look about it," Daniel commented.

"No kidding," I muttered. In the academy I had been trained to trust my instincts, which I usually did. But I knew cops that were by nature jumpy, and ended up making the wrong call in a sticky situation. I certainly didn't want to wind up on the evening news for shooting an innocent person. The thought made my hand inadvertently slip into my jacket. I touched the cold steel of my gun, and immediately, my heart rate calmed.

I turned two more times before I saw the black Charger parked on the one lane road. The trailers were lined up tightly along the lane, and I had to slow the car down considerably to maneuver through the parked vehicles making the lane even narrower. The trailer that the Charger was parked in front of was a little better kept than most of the others. The bushes were trimmed neatly and the stone walkway from the carport to the house was shoveled free of snow. It occurred to me that even though Asher had strayed as far away from his roots as a man could, he had maintained the same compulsiveness to have a very clean and manicured property that all Amish people seemed to have.

"Here we are," I said with exaggerated flourish as I parked behind the sports car.

Before I had a chance to touch the door handle, Daniel touched me. He swallowed and said, "Are you sure you want to confront this guy without the local authorities here?"

I searched Daniel's eyes, looking for fear, but found none. He was just worried about the legal consequences that I might have to deal with. He had no idea what kind of hornet's nest we were walking into. I hesitated. Again, the thrum of wrongness shook me.

But I ignored the sensation, remembering the pasty shade of Mariah's face when she had exited the telephone shed after meeting secretly with Asher. If I didn't intervene, something bad would eventually happen to Mariah and maybe other kids in the Amish community, too. And then there was Cody's obvious terror of the ex-Amish man. Asher Schwartz had gotten away with his corruption long enough. I still wasn't sure what he had over Sheriff Gentry's head, but whatever it was, I didn't really care at the moment. The Sheriff had not-so-subtly given me his blessing to take matters into my own hands, and I had the distinct feeling that it wouldn't take much to put Asher into a situation where he forced my hand. Daniel might have felt some kind of comradery with Asher since they both shared the experience of leaving the Amish, but that didn't play into this at all as far as I was concerned. Brody was right—Asher was a disease that wouldn't stop until he had infected everyone he could in Poplar Springs.

"It will be all right. I'm just going to put Asher a little off balance, see if he'll break."

Daniel nodded and once again, without question, he walked beside me up to the trailer. When I knocked on the door, a fluffy gray and white cat strolled up the steps and stopped at my feet. It pushed up against my legs and I could clearly hear its loud purring.

Daniel reached down to stroke the cat, but I stayed alert. I stood sideways at the door, darting my eyes from the carport back to the road. I was listening hard for any sound of a possible ambush or escape. But the only thing I heard was the muffled noise of a children's program on a television inside the house and dogs barking from behind the house. With my bad luck as of late, the dogs were probably all Pit Bulls or German Shepherds. The blinds were pulled tight. I couldn't see into the rectangular shaped window to the right of the doorway at all.

I knocked again, a little louder this time. My heart began

pounding in my chest and I glanced at Daniel wondering how he could be so relaxed.

"Maybe he's not home?" Daniel suggested.

"He's here," I said with sureness.

The door finally opened a few inches and a gauntly thin woman stared out with pure venom in her eyes. Her hair was dyed an outrageous orange color and the mascara around her bloodshot green eyes was smudged. It was well past one o'clock in the afternoon, but the woman was still in satin pajama bottoms and a white tank top. She wasn't wearing a bra and her nipples were clearly visible through the thin fabric.

With a slight drawl to her words, she growled, "What do you want?"

The child peeking around her legs was probably around two years old. The girl's wispy blonde hair was greasy and her face was smeared with something yellow. The strong smell of a soiled diaper wafted off of the girl and I wrinkled my nose for an instant.

The woman was high. No doubt about it. I kept the sympathy that I felt for the child at bay. I had been on a lot of domestic violence calls in Indy, and there was almost always a rag-tag child like this one hanging onto her mamma's leg. Social services were overrun with these kinds of cases. They could hardly keep up with the number of kids in the system, and sometimes foster care was even worse than the circumstances that the kids were already living in.

I put on my stony, cop face and said, "I would like to talk to Asher."

"He's not here." She began to slam the door, but my hand was quicker. With a thump, I braced the door open. I saw the heroin tracks on her arm.

"I don't believe you. And if there is even an ounce of you that wants to do the best thing for your daughter, you'll leave that man. You need help and I can get it for you—if you'll just go get Asher for me," I tried to convince her.

"I don't need your help, bitch!" the woman shouted.

The scurrying sound in the snow by the carport got my attention. Daniel bolted up and I released the door, letting it slam shut. The cat hissed, and like a flash of smoke, it was gone just as the dogs rounded the corner. My mind only had a split second to register that they *were* Pits. The brindle one hit us first, snapping its jaws around Daniel's leg.

The acidy taste of bile rose in my throat as I freed my gun in one smooth, fluid motion, and fired at the black dog that was a just few strides behind the first. The disgust of having to shoot a dog flowed through me, and an almost blind rage toward Asher followed next.

The black dog rolled into the snow and was dead by the time its momentum stopped. A gush of dark red spread onto the snow beside it. Between the shot blast and Daniel striking its head with his fists, the brindle let go of Daniel's leg and backed off the porch, barking at us.

Under the circumstances, I would have been within my rights to shoot that dog as well, but as long as it was holding its position, I decided to take my chances and leave it alone.

"Get in the car, Daniel, and call 911," I ordered.

"What about you?" Daniel demanded. He clutched his bitten leg, trying to slow the bleeding, but his hands were already covered with blood. Fear was now flashing in his wide eyes.

"Right behind you," I lied.

As Daniel limped across the yard, I kept an eye on the dog that hadn't moved, but was still barking up a storm, and ran to the carport. I was sure that Asher was running out the back door, and was ready for pursuit on foot, when another gunshot blast split the air.

Twisting, I saw Daniel go down beside my car and I stopped breathing altogether.

21

I ran to Daniel with my gun raised, alternating my focus from Daniel's crumpled form on the ground, the barking dog, and side of the trailer where I suspected the shot had been fired from.

When I reached Daniel, he mumbled for me to "take cover," but I completely ignored his plea. My gaze was still darting around when I grabbed Daniel's coat and turned him over so that I could see his wound. I quickly looked him over and began breathing again when I saw the bloody hole in his coat was at the edge of his shoulder. He had been winged by what I guessed to be buck shot from a shotgun.

I touched Daniel's chin and made him look at me. "Hold on, Daniel. Your shoulder's just been grazed."

The adrenaline rush caused the words to shoot from my mouth, but I was glad for the extra blood flow. It made me see a lot better and react quicker, too. Pulling the cellphone from my pocket, I called it in while I held my scarf against the wound. Fortunately for Daniel, by the slow leaking of his blood, I judged that an artery or vein hadn't been nicked.

When I slid the phone back into my pocket, Daniel managed a weak laugh, "Well, this didn't go very well, did it?"

I took the chance to look down and search Daniel's eyes. His pupils were dilated, but they were still sharp. "It's not funny, dammit. You could be dead right now if whoever shot at you had better aim."

Daniel smiled and my icy heart thawed a little bit more. "You sound as if it would actually bother you if I died. That's a surprise."

At first the wailing sirens were very faint, but within seconds, they became louder and louder still. The sound was music to my ears.

"Of course it would bother me. Do you think that I'm completely heartless?"

"I was hoping it might be for other reasons." Daniel began to grin, but then winced in pain.

"Serves you right," I scolded. "This is definitely not the time to go there."

I bolted upright and aimed my gun at the door as it began opening. The orange headed woman took a step onto the porch. She was holding the small girl in her arms as protection. The toddler was crying and the tears were mixing in with the yellow matter on her cheeks making her look even worse than before. The sight made me want to vomit.

"Hey, don't shoot. Let me get Zeus in the house so them Po Po don't shoot him, too," the defiance in the woman's voice grated on what was left of my nerves, but she was right. The police would shoot that dog before they even got out of their cruisers.

I lowered my gun a foot, but still kept it poised. "Go ahead and get your dog, but be quick about it." Just as the woman got a hold of the dog's collar with her free hand, I shouted, "Was it Asher or Julien who shot my friend? You're fooling yourself if you think that you can protect them. And you shouldn't want to. They probably ran off into the woods out back and left you to deal with the aftermath of all this."

The woman didn't respond, and managed to struggle the dog into the house and have the door shut by the time the three cruisers pulled up, followed closely by the ambulance. I kneeled back down beside Daniel and waited for Brody to approach me with the two paramedics.

I rose and began to step away as the first of emergency personnel squatted beside Daniel, but he grabbed my leg and said, "You're coming to hospital, aren't you?"

I couldn't hide my smile. Daniel was just too large of a man to need me as an emotional crutch. "You're in good hands. I'll be there as soon as I can."

Daniel rolled his eyes, but he was quickly encircled by the medical staff, and I made my escape.

Two deputies were on the porch and three more were moving stealthily through the carport. I shouted out, "There's a woman with a toddler inside, along with an attack dog. She's not the one who shot him. The shooter probably ran into the woods, but I think that he was only trying to scare us away. Daniel's a big target and it's pretty hard to miss a killing shot at that close range."

Brody looked at me with disgust and I couldn't help glancing away to take a breath and collect myself before turning back to him.

"Did you at least get a shot off at Asher?"

I shook my head, but didn't look away this time. I was keeping up a pretty good appearance of calmness, but inside, I was a jar full of jelly. Brody had better not push my buttons too hard. I was not in the mood for it.

"Got the dog, though," Brody sighed.

"We were on the porch trying to talk to that smackhead," I pointed at the orange haired woman who was now outside being questioned by a deputy, "When the dogs came around the corner. One of them got a hold of Daniel's leg. We couldn't handle them both, so I shot that one. Thirty seconds later, Daniel was heading to the car and I was going through the carport for a chase. That's when Daniel was shot."

Brody's lips tightened, but he held his tone level when he said, "Chase? You aren't one of my deputies and you certainly aren't the sheriff here. You have no business trying to apprehend a criminal in this jurisdiction."

Our gazes locked. Once again, I wasn't exactly sure what he wanted of me, but I did breathe a little easier when he went on to say, "I think it's best if you return to the Amish community…or go see your boyfriend in the hospital. I don't really care what you do, as long as you aren't blatantly stepping on my toes."

I dared to pester the man with one more question. "Are you going to sweep this incident away under the carpet?"

"That's none of your concern. I've already told you what you can and can't do here. And I won't be able to protect you if you ruffle the wrong person's feathers. You're on your own now."

Brody walked away without a backward glance. The fact that six deputies were swarming over the front yard and all of them were careful to not look my way gave me the heads up that I wouldn't even be formally questioned. And I thought that Tony Manning was corrupt.

I hated paperwork anyway, I convinced myself, as I got into my car. I wasn't headed in the direction of the hospital, though. Daniel's life wasn't in jeopardy, but he'd need surgery to remove the pellets from his shoulder and a lot of stitches to close the dog bite wound, along with a rabies shot. I figured he wouldn't even be awake and open to visitors for a few hours, at the least.

When I pulled out into traffic on the main road, I took a trembling breath. The East Side Trailer Park was more than just depressing. It was a snake's nest of criminal activity. I would bet that there were a dozen emergency calls or more to that place each week. What a headache it would be to police it.

I drove through the industrial section of town, watching the empty buildings pass by as if they were a long line of broken dreams. Rusted brown steel and broken windows were brightened occasionally by bright red, green and blue graffiti. The symbols and dimensional words were similar to those found in Indianapolis or any other city center, and I found it interesting that the country kids had mastered the art just as well as the city dwellers. And I admitted that it was a form of art, just one that also signified depression and chaos.

The brick buildings began to thin out, until finally the open fields began appearing again. The transition from the run-down ghost town of Poplar Springs to the windswept snowy openness was almost startling. The cropland, dotted with pristine white farmhouses and red gambrel barns, brought with it a sense of hopefulness that the town completely lacked.

I lowered the window to allow the cold, wintry air to blow in for a moment. The fresh, country wind erased the decay that still clung to me from the trailer park. I thought about the dirty toddler and her smackhead mother, already guessing the child's fate in the world. The cycle of drug addiction, poverty and lack of education was vicious and continued to fester in family lines for generations. It was highly unlikely that the child would escape the same fate as her mother.

Daniel wasn't far from my thoughts, either. The sickened feeling I'd experienced when I saw him crumpled on the ground kept replaying in my mind. As much as I wanted to, I couldn't deny that the thought of losing the man before I ever even had him, terrified me.

I slowed the car when I approached Elijah Mast's farm. There were still a few buggies parked in his driveway, but the majority of the crowd that had been there in the morning were now gone. I decided to pull in anyway, just to make sure that Rowan and the kids had already left for home. Buggies weren't like cars. I couldn't pick one out from the other.

Surprising me, Rowan had allowed Mareena and Lucinda to ride in the car to the church service. During the drive over, the two girls had really loosened up for the first time since I'd met them. They giggled and talked non-stop the entire way. I wasn't sure if they finally felt comfortable with me and Daniel or if they were just so thrilled to be in a warm, cushioned vehicle, instead of a cold, hard seated buggy for a change.

I had to admit the girls were beginning to grow on me. Even Gabe and Seth were friendlier now that I had run into a burning barn to save their horse and calf. Cacey was the only one remaining aloof. But even she had shown a couple of signs of cracking.

I parked in the gravel turn around and hurried out of the car when I spotted Jotham hitching up his horse. I reached him just as he had secured the last strap.

He looked startled to see me, but he straightened up and smiled anyway.

"Are you heading home?" I asked.

"Actually, I'm on my way to Rowan's. I want to help him begin piling up the barn debris."

"I didn't think that your kind worked on Sunday," I commented.

"We do sometimes, when our friends need us," Jotham said quietly.

"We never did have the talk that you promised me," I reminded him.

He nodded. "You're right. I have a little time now," Jotham suggested.

"Perfect," I said. "Is my car all right?"

Jotham chuckled, causing the side of his face to crinkle. I briefly wondered if it hurt for him to laugh.

"I can only imagine what the others will think," he lifted his chin toward the few stragglers who were late to leave, just now walking their horses to their buggies. "But I'm willing to chance the gossip."

We sat in the front seat in silence for a moment. I watched a young woman help her husband with a bay horse while another horse was being harnessed by several children working together. It crossed my mind how tedious it would be to have to go through such a timely and difficult process every time you wanted to go somewhere. It was way too much work, even if you loved horses, I thought.

"Did you look into the barn fire that happened in nineteen ninety-seven?" Jotham asked with a guarded voice.

I glanced at the man. Even with a half scarred face, his quiet confidence made him formidable. I quickly thought about several ways to proceed, and finally settled on the path of pure honesty.

"Yes, I did. I even talked to Sheriff Gentry and Damon Gentry about the incident."

"And…?" Jotham urged.

"I think that the Gentry barn was set on fire as retaliation for stealing business away from the Schwartz family. I would like to believe that the person who set the fire didn't realize that Austin and his girlfriend were inside the loft of the barn, and was horrified to later find out that two people were killed. Because of the obvious grudge between Sheriff Gentry and the Amish community, I can only assume that the Amish elders knew who had done it, but kept the information to themselves. Taking matters into their own hands, so to speak."

Jotham was so tense that I could almost feel the fear jumping off of him. Why he was afraid, I could only guess, but I did sit up straighter, suddenly fueled by my own rapidly beating heart.

Finally Jotham said evenly, "That's a good story. Do you have any actual proof of what you just said?"

I couldn't stop my eyebrow from lifting. Jotham's passive aggressive behavior was not something I expected at all.

"Right now, it's just hypothetical, but if you have any information to add, it could easily become a solid case," I challenged.

"Are you a Christian, Serenity?" Jotham suddenly asked.

The swift change of subject made me lean back against the headrest. Wariness had settled deep into my bones by the time I responded. "Yes, I consider myself one. But I don't go to church on a regular basis, and I've seen enough horrible things during my time as a cop that I am somewhat a bitter believer. But what do my religious beliefs have to do with anything?"

"It might help you understand our people a little bit better. For instance, I know that God is real and that He affects everything that happens everywhere. And that *He* punishes those who sin against His laws, not the Amish elders or your judicial system."

I shook my head slightly and smiled tightly. I was too exasperated to respond right away. I thought for a moment and then said with a measured sigh, "I'm sure God punishes sinners in His own way, but without law and order, humanity would slip into sheer chaos. The good people would be cut down by the bad guys. That's why I became a sheriff. I wanted to help people. And I want to help you, Jotham. I can see that something is weighing heavily on your mind. Why don't you just let it go, and do the right thing?"

Jotham turned to stare at me. His one good eye shined extra blue as the sunlight shone in through the window. He smiled sadly. "There isn't always agreement about what is the right thing." He gripped the door handle and said, "I really should be going. I'm sure Rowan is wondering where I am."

Knowing that I was about to lose any chance of help from Jotham, I blurted out, "Asher was the one who set the Gentry fire, wasn't he?"

Jotham paused, his back to me. I could feel the heavy weight of his thoughts in the air as if they were raindrops in a summer storm. When he finally spoke, disappointment washed over me in a cold rush.

"I have nothing to say regarding Asher."

Jotham abruptly left me alone in the car, the thump of the door closing loudly in my ears. I continued to watch him walk to his horse, untie it and hop into his buggy. He snapped the reins and sped away at a hasty trot down the driveway.

I sighed. Dammit.

The sight of Anna King running a few steps and then stopping on the gravel in front of my car caught my attention.

I opened the door and asked loudly, "Were you trying to catch Jotham?"

Anna's face brightened when she saw me. She walked over and shifted her weight, hoisting a large box onto her hip. "Hello, Serenity. I wondered where you had gotten off to. I think Rowan and the girls were curious also."

"Something came up and I had to go check it out. Do you need a ride?" I asked hesitantly.

Anna smiled. "Oh, that would be lovely." She made an effort to take a breath as she moved the obviously heavy box to her other hip. I jumped out of the car and went to open up the trunk for her.

"This is supper for Rowan, his family and everyone else working over there." She paused from talking to ease the box into the trunk. "Libby Mast and Martha Yoder helped me prepare the food in Libby's kitchen after the service," Anna went on to explain.

Once Anna was seated in the passenger seat that Jotham had just vacated, I nodded for her to put her seatbelt on.

She blushed. "Yes, silly me. I always forget to do that when I ride in cars." As she was buckling, she asked, "Where's Daniel?"

Some of the Amish had stronger accents than others. Rowan and Jotham, for instance, spoke with a strong foreign lilt, while Anna sounded the same as any Midwesterner. The comparison briefly passed through my mind as I glanced at Anna and replied, "He's in the hospital. He was shot this afternoon."

The look on Anna's face was priceless. Her jaw dropped and her gray eyes widened. I quickly added, "He'll be all right. It was only a grazing wound."

"Why did someone shoot him?" Anna exclaimed.

"We went to Asher Schwartz's trailer to ask him a few questions. Asher never came to the door, but two very large Pit Bulls attacked us and then Daniel was shot by an as-of-now unknown assailant."

"Oh, my," Anna said as she glanced out the window. After a moment of silence, she found her voice again. "Asher Schwartz is a troubled man," she paused and met my gaze with frightened eyes, "He's been hanging around with some of the teenagers lately. And I don't like it one bit."

I suddenly realized that maybe I'd been talking to the wrong people all along. Anna was new to the community and she had a certain measure of normalcy about her that most of the other Amish whom I had come in contact with were absent of. The pretty young woman might actually help me.

"Anna, I'll be honest with you. Asher has some serious convictions against him, which include narcotic sales, battery assault and domestic violence. I already know that he's a bad guy. What I don't understand is why your community is tolerating his presence here…and why Sheriff Gentry is afraid to go after him, too."

Anna's mouth spread into a grim line. I could tell by the faraway look in her eyes that she was in deep thought. When she finally came out of her trance, I was happy to see steady determination on her face.

"I don't know anything about the sheriff, but I can tell you that Bishop Fisher and the other ministers don't want to deal with him on any level, even to protect our young ones."

"How do you know this?"

"Several meetings have been held on the subject. There are those in the community who are willing to go against

Asher Schwartz, but the leadership will have none of it. I personally had to speak to the congregation about some of the interchanges that I'd witnessed going on around the schoolhouse after hours. But Abner wasn't interested in listening to anything I had to say."

"You've seen Asher talking to the kids after school?" I said the words slowly enough to emphasize the importance of my question.

"Yes, I have. I've even seen some of the English kids with him," she took a deep breath and admitted, "I don't know this Asher fellow at all, but there is just something about the man that makes me very uncomfortable."

"You have good instincts," I told Anna.

Even before I pulled into Rowan's driveway, I quickly counted up nine buggies parked beside the house and a flurry of dark clad men with beards moving about the barnyard. Out of the corner of my eye, I caught a glimpse of Anna quickly smoothing her blonde hair neatly beneath her cap. She then flattened the front of her dress in an anxious movement. I didn't even try to hide my smile.

"You obviously have a thing for Rowan, so why don't you go ahead and tell him," I said seriously.

Anna's pale cheeks suddenly heated to a cherry red color as she exclaimed, "Is it so very noticeable?"

I nodded nicely. "Yeah, to me anyway, but who knows about Rowan. Men can be awfully dense in that department."

I parked in front of the cabin and turned off the engine. Anna reached over and touched my arm. "I don't know what to do. Sometimes I think that he may be fond of me, but other times he seems so distracted."

I absorbed what she said. There were two Amish men who

I wasn't familiar with pushing debris around with Bobcats and several other men putting the last strips of tin on the brand new framework. Rowan had mentioned that morning that the men would be constructing a temporary shed that would be large enough for him to park his borrowed buggy and harness in, but I was surprised to see it almost completed only hours later.

Rowan was up on the ladder, and Jotham and Gabe were working together to hand the tin up to him as sprays of snow gusted up around them from the wind. The sight of the man who was Gabe's biological father working so closely beside the only dad Gabe had ever known was brow rising, for sure. Perhaps everyone would be better off if Gabe never knew the truth. In the real world, father and son would never have moments like this, but here in the Amish one, there would be a lot of opportunities for interaction on a regular basis. I dismissed the thought, feeling the twinge of a headache blossoming. There were just too many issues to think about around here. It was almost maddening at times.

I turned back to Anna's expectant face and said, "Rowan has secrets that are eating him up inside. I don't believe that he'll ever be happy or at peace until he faces his demons. Maybe you can help him along with that."

Anna slowly nodded. "That's very sound advice from an Englisher," Anna commented and then added, "I'll see if he'll talk to me."

"I hope that once he's opened up to you, he'll be willing to talk to me about it. I think his demons are shared by a few other people as well."

"I understand. And I'll do what I can," Anna assured me. Almost as an afterthought, she said, "You'll stay for dinner won't you?"

"No, I'm going to head over to the hospital to check on Daniel."

Anna smiled mischievously. "I know you told me earlier that he wasn't your man, but I must speak up and say that I think he very much wants to be."

I glanced away and then back again. "I'm kind of in the same boat as you are, Anna. I'm afraid to take the plunge."

"If I can do it, so can you. We both deserve to be happy, don't you think?"

I smiled at her naivety. "I'm not really sure if true happiness exists."

"Of course it does!" Anna exclaimed. "You mustn't lose hope."

After I opened the trunk, I found myself suddenly in Anna's tight embrace. I wasn't used to being hugged by near strangers, and women even less so, but I swallowed down the discomfort and returned the woman's squeeze anyway. I wasn't sure who needed the hug more, me or her.

After we said our goodbyes, I gladly jumped back into the car. The sun had just dipped behind the low rise of hills and with the darkening sky, came an even more bitter cold. I turned around in the driveway, shaking my head at the men who were still working, but impressed at the same time.

I had to slow and pull off to the edge of the driveway as an oncoming pickup truck passed by. There was a dent on the backside of the bed that grabbed my attention and I only caught a glimpse into the cab, but it was enough to see Mariah sitting in the passenger seat beside Damon Gentry. Seeing the pair together again instantly bothered me in some inexplicable way that I couldn't quite put my finger on. And then something else teased at the corner of my mind, trying desperately to open up into understanding.

I continued to think on it until I was about a mile from Rowan's farm and then it hit me with the force of a train wreck.

I had seen that exact same blue truck earlier today—parked not too far behind Asher Schwartz's black charger in the trailer park.

22

The smile that lit up Daniel's face when I walked through the door into the hospital room warmed my insides. I crossed the room quickly and pulled up the hunter green plastic wooden-armed chair to the bed. After I was sitting down, I finally met Daniel's hopeful looking gaze.

"How are you feeling?" I ventured.

Daniel shrugged. "Not too bad. The nurse was just in here. She gave me some more pain meds. Reckon I won't feel anything for another day or two."

"Do you know when you're going to be released?"

Daniel's smile faded. "I think if you talk to the doctor, you might be able to spring me sooner, but right now, he's talking about tomorrow morning."

"That's not that long," I scoffed.

Daniel looked at me pleadingly. "I don't want to stay in here until then. You need my help."

Now it was my turn to smile. The last time that I had seen Daniel, his face had been ghostly white and there had been pain in his eyes, but at the moment, his face was flushed with healthy color and his eyes crinkled at the corners in annoyance. I took the chance and continued to meet his steady gaze. I was almost distracted by his sculptured, full lips and the thought of kissing them, but I controlled myself.

"You were shot today at close range with powerful ammo... and you were severely bitten by a large Pit. You're lucky that you aren't dead," I chastised. It was much easier to be harsh with Daniel then to risk being nice and having him start flirting all over again.

"The shooter obviously didn't want to kill me or I *would* be dead," Daniel smartly pointed out.

I was impressed. "That's a very good assumption and one that I've already made." I paused and leaned back in the incredibly uncomfortable chair. "It was Asher, Julian...*or* Damon who shot you."

Daniel's eyes widened considerably. "Damon Gentry— what does he have to do with any of this?"

"I don't know yet. But afterwards, I saw Damon in Rowan's driveway with Mariah again, and it was definitely his dark blue extended cab pickup truck that I'd seen parked in front of Asher's Charger." I sighed heavily in irritation and went on to say, "I've ran it through my mind a hundred different ways and I still can't come up with any logical reason for his connection to Asher. Well, besides buying drugs of course."

"What did the sheriff say about all this? He must have recognized his grandson's pickup parked at the scene," Daniel said as he sat up straighter. The cords to his IV got tangled around the armrest to the bed and he snorted and tugged them free.

"Oh, I'm sure old-man Brody knows that his son is involved with Asher. That might even be the reason that he seems to be protecting Asher at every turn. Asher probably has some major dirt on Damon…and maybe even some of the police and officials in this town. What I don't get is how any of this ties into the arsons."

Daniel thought for a moment and then said, "It must be Asher burning the barns down as revenge against the Amish for shunning him."

"I don't think it's that easy of an answer." I twirled a blonde lock around my finger, thinking. "There must be something that I'm missing."

"Well, we know that Asher is into all kinds of criminal activities, so it's probably safe to assume that he's our man. Can't you go over Sheriff Gentry's head on this, and bring in other law enforcement?"

I really liked the way Daniel's mind worked. He was similar to me in many ways, but he wasn't going nearly deep enough on this one.

I nodded slowly. "Sure, I can get the Indiana State Police involved…but I'm not ready to do that just yet."

"Why not—if the sheriff isn't cooperating with you and you know that his own grandson is involved with our main suspect then he's completely compromised. Meanwhile, barns are still burning down, and I was even shot. Something has to be done quickly, Serenity," Daniel implored.

"You're absolutely right. I'm just waiting on a phone call." Was it just mere coincidence, or something more that caused my phone to suddenly vibrate in my pocket at that very moment? I'd never know for sure, but when I pulled the phone out, it was just the person I wanted to talk to.

"Todd, what do you have for me," I said without wasting time with a proper hello first.

Todd took it in stride and said, "I think I have your woman."

I held my breath while Todd told me the name and information that I needed, only exhaling when I said, "Thanks, Todd. You should get a raise for this one. I think that I'll be home sooner than I originally thought."

I hung up and put the phone back into my pocket. My gaze met Daniel's anxious face.

What did Todd say?"

"You were right. Asher is our man," I replied, standing up.

"Whoa, where are you going now?" Daniel lightly grasped my arm and tugged me in closer. The worried frown on his face made me pause. It felt good that he seemed to care so much.

"I have enough information for an arrest." Seeing him about to rise, I put my hand out to stop him and my fingers touched the hard warmth of his chest. But I didn't flinch away this time. "Don't worry, Daniel. I have this under control. If Brody won't help me, the state bureau and the FBI are on my speed dial. You have to stay here and rest. My plan is for us to be on our way home by tomorrow evening."

Daniel hesitated for a moment. When his brown eyes suddenly darkened, I knew exactly what he wanted before he said a word.

"I already know that nothing I have to say is going to change your mind on this one. But it sure would be nice if you gave me a little kiss before you left," Daniel said softly.

The tentative way he spoke made me feel a mixture of guilt and stupidity. Daniel had proven himself in many ways since I'd first met him, and here I was still giving the man a hard time. I wasn't just attracted to Daniel; I was reluctantly falling in love with him. And even though I was completely jaded and messed up in the relationship department, I was beginning to lean towards at least giving him a chance.

My thoughts were still waging war as I leaned down. I caught a whiff of the musky cologne that had become so familiar, and for a moment, I forgot everything else. My lips softly touched Daniel's forehead. I savored the instant of having his warm skin beneath my mouth and then I began to pull back.

Daniel's hold on my arm tightened and he reached up with his free hand, placing it behind my head. For a second we made eye contact, and the next thing I knew our mouths were moving against each other. The pressure of his hand tangled in my hair and the movements of his tongue with mine sent mini jolts of pleasure coursing through my body.

I was losing myself to him when I heard a vague noise somewhere way off in the distance. The second time the throat clearing sound was easily recognizable and I pushed away from Daniel in a hurry. Daniel must have heard it too. He let me go without complaint for a change.

When I turned around, I felt a hot flush spreading across my cheeks.

"Have you ever heard of knocking first, Sheriff?" Daniel said in a half teasing, half serious sort of way.

Brody gave a short laugh and came fully into the room. "Glad to see that you're doing so well, Mr. Bachman." Then he turned to me and said, "We need to talk."

"You can say anything in front of Daniel. Trust me. I'm going to repeat everything you tell me to him anyway."

Brody shrugged, and placed his hands on the rail at the bottom of Daniel's bed. The big man moved in a casual way, but I'd already noticed the tight set of his jaw. My heart sped up as I waited for Brody to speak.

"Do you have any idea where Asher Schwartz and Julian West are?"

His question completely took me off guard. I exchanged glances with Daniel and replied, "Ah…I wasn't really convinced that you were even going after him. You weren't very responsive about the shooting…and the dogs being turned out on us earlier," I stammered, quickly trying to collect my thoughts and read Brody at the same time.

Brody nodded impatiently. "Don't even go there. I've been around awhile and I'm aware of the fact that if you want to, you can bring in higher authorities to clean this mess up. But you're not exactly working within the confines of the law yourself, and you certainly aren't in your own jurisdiction."

"Are you threatening me?" I interrupted.

"No, not at all, I'm just pointing out the obvious, clearing the deck so to speak." He rose back up to his full height and took a step closer. The constrained desperation in his voice was barely noticeable, but I picked up on it. Once again, I had the distinct feeling that Brody wasn't a corrupt cop, just a man who was used to working out of the box to take care of his business.

"No, I have no idea where they are."

Brody hesitated and rubbed his hands through his cropped gray hair, before he took a measured breath and said, "What about Damon? Have you seen my grandson?"

It was as if a brighter light was turned on in the already well lit hospital room. Everything suddenly became clearer, even the poor quality water color painting on the wall and the vivid blue hue of the walls. The hearty beeps of the monitoring machine that was hooked up to Daniel pounded in my head and the nurses talking at the station right across from the open door were noisy chatter.

In an indirect way, Brody was admitting that he had lost

control of the situation and he needed help. Inwardly, I sighed satisfactorily.

"I saw your grandson about an hour ago. He was driving Mariah Fisher up Rowan's driveway at the time. I don't know if he's still there, though."

Brody breathed a little easier at the news, but not enough to slow my own rapidly beating pulse.

"We may have a problem on our hands." Brody met my gaze steadily.

"Oh, we definitely do. As I'm sure you already know Damon was at Asher Schwartz's trailer today." I shook my head warily and continued, "Your grandson isn't hanging around with a good crowd."

Brody nodded. "I've been doing my best to change that, but there are a lot of factors involved that you don't understand." He abruptly tilted his head, looking at me intently. "I get the feeling that you're a common sense type of person— not some idiot paper pusher. You're willing to skirt the rules to get the job done. Am I right about you, Serenity?" Brody said the last part with the sternness of a father asking a child if he could trust them, while at the same time desperately wanting to do so.

I had an instant of misgiving, but went with my gut and said, "Yes you are, Sheriff."

"All right then. Asher Schwartz has been selling Hash oil to the local kids for a while now, but recently he's pushed his dealings into the Amish community. My grandson is involved, but I'm not sure to what extent. I've been waiting for Asher to screw up and give me an opening to bring him in, but the man's squirrely as all get out. He's made it known to me that he won't be taken down easily—or alone."

"Dabbing is serious business. People can die from a bad batch of butane."

"I understand that." Brody said in a tired voice. "I was hoping to get Damon to work with us on the case…but he refused to. Frankly, I'm at my wits end." Brody flicked his thumb at Daniel. "After today, I realize how truly dangerous Asher Schwartz is."

Daniel laughed. "He killed a man in a parking lot with his bare hands. Why on earth did you ever doubt what the man was capable of?"

Brody looked away in embarrassment. "Well, now that was a different thing. I mean, the guy that Asher did in was a rotten cracker. Schwartz was doing the community a favor at the time."

My eyes narrowed and I quickly reconsidered my assessment of Brody Gentry. He was a good old boy after all. "And you gave him carte blanche to kill a man because it was convenient for you. And that's the big dark secret that Asher has over you. I'm sure you've been worried about your grandson, but it sounds as if you're really more worried about spending the rest of your own life behind bars."

"It's his word against mine. You don't have anything on me, either," Brody said defensively.

"Maybe not, but we have more important things to worry about at the moment. That badass who got his head caved in by Asher isn't the only person he's killed." Brody's eyes widened with sudden understanding, but I said the words anyway. "The woman's body in Fisher's burned out barn was none other than Asher's ex-girlfriend."

23

I let out a relieved sigh when I parked by the cabin. At least all of Rowan's helpers had finally gone home. The night seemed extra crisp and there was a stark contrast between the frosting-like layer of snow on the ground and the inky blackness of sky. There was a soft light shining in Rowan's kitchen and I purposely headed in that direction. The dog, who I had found out earlier in the day, was called Ben, trotted up to greet me in the driveway. I reached down and stroked his thick black and white fur as I glanced up at the sky. Pausing for a moment, I gazed at the twinkling stars that seemed to shine so much brighter during the coldest part of winter, and thought about what I was going to say to Rowan. There wasn't going to be any easy way to break the news to him, but the right words and a gentle tone might just make it a little easier to hear.

I knocked a couple of times and then opened the door a little ways and peeked in. Cooking smells of whatever the family and workers had eaten for dinner still lingered in the air and blissful warmth radiated from the room. It was only nine o'clock, but I worried that everyone was already in bed. I'd already discovered that the Amish usually turned in early.

"Hello," I whispered loudly, chancing to open the door further still as I stepped into the room. The kitchen was so warm that it was almost stuffy. As the heat absorbed into my skin, I was suddenly so tired that I yawned.

"You look exhausted, Serenity," Rowan's voice slipped up from the side as he walked quietly into the room from the hallway.

"It's been a long day."

"How is Daniel doing? Anna told me that he was shot," Rowan said cautiously.

I raised my brow at his tone and studied his stoic features for a moment before I answered.

"He's doing all right—probably be out of the hospital to-morrow," I paused and weighed my words carefully, "but it could have been a very different story."

Rowan ran a hand through his thick, dark hair and then leaned heavily on the table. It was obvious that he was quite disturbed, but I still wasn't sure exactly why.

Finally, he glanced up and said, "I'm sorry for what my brother did to Daniel. It seems that I've spent my entire life apologizing for him. He's a restless spirit, always has been."

Anger flared inside of me. "Restless? He's a damn crimi-nal, Rowan. He's killed people—yes, plural. That woman who was found in the bishop's barn is your brother's ex-girlfriend."

Rowan's eyes widened at the news. He pulled the chair out that he had been leaning against and sat down. "Are you sure?" he asked.

I nodded. "My partner back in Blood Rock has been work-ing on this since I arrived. By process of elimination, he inves-tigated all the reported missing women in a four state region. At the same time that he came up with the name, Kristen

Humphrey, a buddy of mine in the Indy police department touched base with my partner. They compared notes, and it turns out that the last time your brother was arrested in the city on drug charges, the girlfriend was brought in too. She was a real smackhead, but she also liked her hash oil. It was difficult for the local coroner to establish the exact method of death, but he was sure that she was dead before the fire. The coroner also stated that there weren't any definitive signs of blunt force trauma or asphyxiation, which leads me to think that maybe it was an overdose and Asher was trying to hide the body in a burning building."

"I met the woman one time. She was not right in the head. I suspected that she was on something at the time, but wasn't sure," Rowan admitted.

"By all accounts she was pretty much a transient—born in California, but had lived in nine states in the last four years. That's why she was so difficult to track down. No one really missed her. The only person who even bothered going to the police was an elderly landlady in Indy who became suspicious when Kristen didn't show up for some kind of weekly card game," I told him.

Rowan shook his head. "It's sad isn't it?" He looked up with bright eyes and added, "What about the other barn burnings...and mine. Why would Asher have set those fires?"

"He didn't, at least I don't think he did." Seeing the confusion on his face, I took the seat beside him and said, "All along, I suspected that you had two arsonists on your hands. The first three fires and your barn were completely different than the Fisher burning. That one was the only one to happen at night and it was the only barn that was right on the road. The location of the bishop's barn first made me think about a teenage prank, but the body didn't fit into that theory. The puzzle pieces began to fall into place when I saw Mariah Fisher meet privately with Asher after the church service this morning."

Rowan's eyes widened and he blurted out, "Why would she have any dealings with my brother?" The horrified look on Rowan's face made me feel a little better for some reason.

"I hate to say it, but I think Mariah and some of the other Amish kids have been buying drugs from Asher. He's a smart dude. He probably figured that if he hid Kristen's body in the bishop's barn, Mariah and the others would be more likely to make an effort to cover for him. I'm making presumptions on a lot of this, but one thing is for certain, my own eyes don't lie. I saw Mariah meet with Asher in the telephone shed at the Mast's farm today."

Rowan swallowed and met my gaze with moist eyes. "Our community is festering, rotting from the inside out. God is punishing us for our sins."

I couldn't breathe. At the same time that curiosity was blazing inside of me, dread of what Rowan was about to say was even stronger.

"Go on," I urged in a whisper.

Rowan gazed off into space for a moment and then abruptly turned to me again. His face was open and I took a shallow breath, preparing for whatever the truth was.

"It all started back about twenty years ago, around nineteen ninety-five…"

Even though I was immediately mesmerized by Rowan's quiet voice, when my phone vibrated in my pocket, I couldn't help but look at it, immediately worried that it might be from Brody or worse yet, the hospital. I reluctantly held up my hand to stop Rowan. I didn't know the number on the screen, but it was a local Poplar Springs' area code. As I gazed at the number for an instant, my heart began banging against my chest.

I swallowed hard and brought the phone to my ear. "Hello…"

"Ms. Adams, this is Brandy—Brandy Warner."

The girl's rapid, distressed voice immediately registered and I made eye contact with Rowan. Judging from his worried eyes and slightly gaping jaw, he was as concerned as I was.

"Yes, Brandy, what can I do for you?" I said steadily, not allowing the spastic racing of my own heart to affect my voice.

"I need your help. Nathan and Cody went to stop them, but he's going to get really mad, and I'm worried about what he'll do to them if they confront him…"

Brandy's voice had reached an almost hysterical pitch when I interrupted her, "Whoa, wait a minute. You're talking too fast. Who are they trying to stop and who is going to get mad?"

The silence lasted only a few seconds while Brandy hesitated, but it was an eternity. "The Amish kids—Mariah, Jory, Jacob and the rest. They were going to meet Asher Schwartz in the woods tonight…to buy some new stuff he has."

"Do you know where they're meeting?"

"Yeah, it will be hard to find in the dark, but I can find the place."

"Are you home right now?" I asked as I stood up and motioned for Rowan to do the same.

"Yeah…"

"Listen up, Brandy. I'll be there in fifteen minutes. Get a piece of paper and draw the very best map you can to show me the way to this meeting place."

"But…"

"No, you're not coming with me. But your map will get me there and I'll take care of everything. I promise."

I hung up and met Rowan's anxious gaze. "I'm going with you," he told me.

I nodded slowly, "I'm not going to argue with you on this one. I think I'm going to need your help anyway."

Rowan quickly scribbled a note to his kids telling them that he had gone with me to talk to someone about the fires. He left it on the kitchen table, tucked up neatly beneath a plate with a slice of wrapped pie that Mareena had probably made earlier in the day.

He picked up his hat and sighed heavily, "I'm ready."

"You had better be. This isn't going to be pretty," I said honestly as I opened the front door and we rushed out into the cold night.

And then the snow began falling again.

24

T he snow was coming down in heavy, wet sheets that made the going even tougher. Brandy's directions had been right on, but now that it had been snowing steadily for nearly half an hour, the barely-there path was all but nonexistent. I could see well enough from the hazy glow of the white all around, but I was afraid that we had lost the trail a while back and were now aimlessly stumbling over roots and downed branches, going in circles.

I pulled my toboggan down lower and trudged after Rowan, acutely aware of his labored breathing as we began to go uphill again. Our huffing and the rhythmic crunching of our boots in the snow were the only sounds in the woods. The winter storm seemed to have draped the entire area in a heavy blanket that silenced the world around us in a very lonely and creepy way.

I instinctively reached into my coat and touched my gun. The action calmed my nerves somewhat. I left my hand pressed against it while I looked around, squinting to see through the quietly dropping, large flakes that relentlessly continued to fall from the sky. Dammit. As if our job wasn't difficult enough, now we had a mini-blizzard to deal with.

At least the physical exertion was keeping me warm. I was actually sweating under the black coat. My thoughts had been jumbled ever since we had left Rowan's place. He was about to tell me something very important when Brandy called, but the moment was long gone now. We were both too busy worriedly listening for any sign of a group of teenagers to chat. We certainly didn't want to accidently stumble right into them or worse yet, have Asher see us before we saw him. As I took quick intakes of cold, wet air, I wondered if Asher would actually harm his own brother. When I'd met him the very first time, the animosity between the brothers was tangible, but how far either of the men were willing to take it was anyone's guess.

I inwardly prayed that when the time came, Rowan would support me in anything I had to do. Brody's earlier suggestion that taking Asher down floated around statically in my mind. It certainly wasn't an ethical thought, but in reality, it might truly be the only way to get the community back on track. Not only had Asher murdered before, but he had no qualm about selling his wares to kids and using violence to save his own ass. A part of me acknowledged that he had signed his own death warrant, but the other more practical side, still wanted to follow the rules and bring him in alive to face a judge and jury of his peers.

Of course, the ultimate outcome might be out of my hands anyway.

Rowan suddenly stopped and I nearly bumped into his back. I was close enough to his tall form that the wool fibers of this black coat tickled my nose. I took a step back and looked carefully around.

Rowan lifted his hand, bringing his gloved finger to his lips, holding me silent. I tilted my head to listen.

Faintly at first, but gaining volume, I heard the muffled sound of voices. The same as a jolt to the heart, I stopped breathing altogether. In the back of my mind, I had thought that maybe Brandy had led us on a wild goose chase, or perhaps the weather had ultimately foiled the kids' plans, but now I had the sickly realization that a group of Amish and English kids were out here in the woods with Asher.

Not taking any chances, I brought my gun out and aimed it toward the sky in a holding position. Rowan's brows raised, but he didn't say a word. He motioned for me to follow him and together we climbed up a steep ridge. At one point the grade was too much and I had to put the gun away to grab a sideways growing thick sapling to pull myself up behind Rowan. When we finally reached the crest of the hill, I was out of breath and dropped into the welcoming snow. I crawled to the edge to take a look around.

Down below in the wooded hollow was a small, rough looking cabin. Smoke puffed out of its stone chimney and light shined from the only window on this side. There wasn't a porch, just a simple, solid wooden door at the top of several steps that were already pretty much covered with snow.

The shadows of several people moving about inside the cabin were clearly visible, but I ignored them, focusing instead on the three figures that were arguing in the small clearing in front of the cabin. I pulled the small recorder from my inside pocket and held it out in front of me. Sure, there were laws against such measures, but this conversation might definitely come in handy in the future. If Rowan noticed, he didn't acknowledge it, more interested with the goings on below us.

Asher said, "Damon, you aren't going anywhere. Just like I told you, you're my lucky charm."

"I'm only your insurance that my granddaddy won't go after you," Damon shot back.

He was almost as tall as Brody, but wiry thin, where his grandfather was thickly built.

I glanced at Rowan, but he was still gazing intensely at the scene below as if I wasn't even there.

"Call it what you want to, I don't care. The sheriff can't touch me or Julian here, as long as you're knee deep in the shit right along with us." Asher laughed. "Hell, don't go acting all innocent on me. You're the one who helped us get in with this group anyway." He thumbed toward the building.

"That was when it was only weed. This dabbing shit is dangerous. Look what happened to Kristen…"

Damon didn't get to finish his sentence. Julian's fist met his face in a quick, solid punch that knocked him backward. Damon caught the ground with his hand and righted himself without completely falling down.

Rowan began to rise and I grabbed his arm. "No, not yet— Damon's all right. It's a bloody nose, that's all," I whispered, shaking the recorder in front of him. "We need to hear what Asher has to say."

Rowan looked as if he was about to argue and I braced for a struggle, but after a few seconds, he relaxed and settled back into the snow.

Asher stepped up to Damon. The two men were of equal height and build, but Asher carried himself with a lot more confidence and authority than the younger man would probably ever possess.

Asher thrust his finger at Damon's face and snarled, "Listen here, you don't ever talk about that whore. She was so juiced up on pharmies that she was a ticking time bomb. It was just a matter of time before it happened."

Damon straightened and for an instant I was suddenly impressed with his bravado.

"Julian said that it was a bad batch of butane that did it," he countered.

Julian's fist hit Damon's stomach this time and he doubled over with a loud gulping noise.

"Now…?" Rowan's eyes implored, but I shook my head.

The sudden gun shot that *boomed* through the trees made both Rowan and I immediately drop down deeper into the snow. I quickly put the recorder safely into my pocket. I needed both hands free for my own gun.

Searching the hollow again, I discovered that all three men had scattered. Asher and Julian were behind a stack of firewood beside the cabin and Damon was using a tree for cover, pressed up tightly against its trunk.

Whoever let the bullet fly wasn't a very good shot, and I quickly had an idea who it was. I rose to my knees and searched the ridgeline, only having a few seconds tick by before my suspicion was proved correct.

Cody and Nathan were quickly making their way down the snowy bank, sliding in a few places, but managing to keep their footing until they hit level ground. Nathan had a .22 caliber rifle raised in his hands. He flicked the barrel left and right when he shouted, "Mariah, you come on out of there. I'm taking you home."

I rolled my eyes at both Nathan's words and his choice of a gun to take out a professional criminal as I jumped to my feet. "Now it's time," I whispered to Rowan, motioning for him to get behind me.

Luckily, I still had the element of surprise, but I was out of range and I feared that I wouldn't be faster than the bad guys. As I ran swiftly down the slope with Rowan close on my heels, I saw Asher and Julian both rising. Like me, they had quickly judged the teenagers to be no real threat and were preparing to take the offensive. Asher reached down his leg and pulled his own gun from a holster fastened around his calf. Julian already had his freed from his jacket.

Only a few more feet and I should be good.

"What the fuck, you little shit! Are you crazy?" Asher shouted.

I was close enough to the standoff to see everybody's breath in the air and even to smell the faint scent of men's cologne coming off of one of them when I stopped and aimed. Nathan, Asher and Julian were too focused on each other to notice me at first, but Cody saw me. Thankfully, the kid didn't give me away.

I had to get off two shots quicker than Asher and Julian could get one off each. I didn't think about the odds, instead going to that place where the dark tunnel stretched to a pinpoint place of bright light before me.

Boom...Kaboom.

Julian hit the ground, clutching his leg and screaming, "I'm shot...my leg..."

Rowan had the presence of mind to surge forward and grab Julian's gun from the snow and aim it at him. I only caught a glimpse of this happening as I walked cautiously towards Asher. His hand was so completely covered in blood that I couldn't even see any skin at all. But he had dropped his gun just below him and I could read from his pale face that he was seriously thinking about making a move for it. Whether he could shoot it with his left hand was anyone's guess, but I wasn't going to take any chances. I'd been good and purposely aimed at non-life threatening parts of their bodies, but if Asher tried to shoot me, I was going to kill him for sure.

"Stay there boys," I ordered Nathan and Cody. I probably didn't even need to tell them, but they'd already proven that they were capable of moronic acts of heroism, so I was a little concerned that they might do something stupid.

"Don't do it, Asher," Rowan pleaded with his brother at a brief moment when Julian wasn't loudly crying out in pain.

"It'll be the last thing you ever do," I told Asher with my gun aimed at his chest this time. I couldn't keep the slight smile from my lips. I wouldn't admit it out loud, but deep down I really wanted him to do it.

Asher's blue eyed gaze met mine and for a moment we were the only ones there. He sniffed in what was sure to be pain shooting up his arm and he regarded me steadily. "I do believe that you would gladly kill me, Sheriff." He shrugged loosely, and added, "That's what your kind does, shoot first and ask questions later. Just because you're the law, you think you're above it…that you can do anything you want. Hell, I've had to deal with it from Gentry for years. And you know what? He's the one who taught me how to work the system."

I didn't have time for his speech. I interrupted him, "You aren't going to get any sympathy from me, so don't even waste your breath."

He nodded slowly and then a wicked grin erupted on his lips. The look made my heart skip. I'd seen that expression before. It was of a man who suddenly thought he had the upper hand.

"Even the Amish have their own set rules to protect themselves and screw everyone else…just like Rowan here."

He looked at his brother with pure ice and said loudly, pointing his bloody hand at Rowan, "He's the one that lit the match that killed your brother Austin all those years ago. I was there...with Jotham...and I saw that fucker do it."

What happened next was too fast for me to even barely comprehend, much less adjust my strategy for. Damon rushed out from behind the tree and ran straight for Rowan, knocking into him with such force that the two men fell into the snow together in a heap.

Damon had his hands on Julian's gun and Rowan grappled with him for control of it. The second it took for me to see this, Asher was diving for his own gun.

A gunshot echoed through the winter night. I stopped breathing and turned my head towards Rowan and Damon, while keeping my gun aimed straight at Asher who was in the exact same stance as me.

Damon rolled away from Rowan and quickly jumped up. Rowan's hand came away from his stomach, covered with blood. For a sickening instant, I saw each bright red drop hit the pure white snow. No one moved. There was only the sound of heavy silence from the falling snow in my ears and time seemed to have stopped all together.

The sharp intake of breath from the doorway of the cabin pulled me from the partial trance. Jory Bontrager was standing there staring at Rowan with his mouth gaping. Knowing that there wasn't much time, I tilted my head towards Asher again. I was surprised to see a flash of shock pass over his features, before his mouth twisted again and his gaze met mine.

He began backing away with his gun raised. The fleeting thought that I was trapped in an old western movie occurred to me before I sucked in a breath and challenged Asher, "Don't move…or I will shoot you."

I quickly calculated my chances of success. I reasoned with myself that I was shooting with my good hand and Asher had only his left hand to fire with, putting me at a definite advantage. It was still a risk, but I had the law of averages on my side for a change. I was very close to making my move.

Asher didn't stop his backward momentum. Clutching his ruined hand to his side, he suddenly turned his gun on Cody and smiled back at me. "You might be crazy enough to risk your own life with a ridiculous shoot out, but I don't think that you'll risk that kid's life over mine."

Nathan swiveled, raising his gun at Asher and for a split second, I thought that maybe between the two of us we had a chance to bring the son of a bitch down, but the thought left me as soon as it arrived. Nathan's fingers were trembling, causing the rifle to vibrate in his hands. Even if he did manage to get a shot off, did I really want to be responsible for how messed up the kids would be if he met his mark or if he missed altogether and his friend was killed in the process. No. As much as I wanted Asher's head on a spike, I couldn't risk the boys and Rowan needed to be rushed to a hospital if he had any chance of survival.

"Don't, Nathan. Let him go. He's not worth any more blood being spilled here tonight," I told the boy in a firm voice.

Asher's eyes darted toward his brother lying on the ground and then back to me. A smug expression erupted on his face and he nodded once at me before he began jogging sideways into the thick stand of trees. Asher never took his gun off of Cody while he stole into the night, erasing any hopes that I might still get a shot off at him.

A moment later, when it was safe to assume that Asher was gone for good, I yelled over to Nathan, "Hey, Nathan, come over here and point your gun at Damon. Do...not...shoot, unless I direct you to."

Nathan did as he was told, with Cody shadowing him as he walked over.

Damon, said, "He deserved it. He killed my brother. I learned the truth that the Amish did it a few months ago when I was driving old lady Yoder to the store."

I quickly searched my memories of the church service and recalled meeting a very old woman who was suffering from Alzheimer's disease. I remembered the woman because at the time that I met her, I was impressed that her family was taking care of her on their own instead of shipping her off to a facility.

Ignoring Damon's zealous reasoning, I made certain that Nathan had Damon covered and then I dropped to the ground beside Rowan, pressing my scarf over his wound.

Julian's cries had turned to a constant drone of painful murmurings and I spared a glance at the swath of red snow beneath his leg. I couldn't manage both of the men's injuries and I certainly wasn't putting any of the kids at risk.

Rowan's eyes were dilated and his face was drained of any color whatsoever.

"How do you feel?" I asked softly as I brought the phone up, relieved to see that I actually had a couple of bars.

"Oddly, I don't feel much at all," Rowan whispered.

I made the call to emergency dispatch quickly, giving the location, type of injuries and a warning that a shooter was still on the loose. When I hung up, I asked Cody to take my place, which he did without question. I stood up and contemplated my ability to easily track Asher in the snow when Jory's stammering voice got my attention.

"It's Mariah…she's not doing…so good,"

Oh my God. I sprang forward and dashed into the cabin. I only half registered that Jacob was at the table with his hands on his face and two other boys who I didn't recognize were sitting on the floor in the corner. The only boy in the room who wasn't high was Jory, and he was standing protectively over Mariah. I dropped to the floor beside the girl and felt for a pulse. I found it, but it was very weak.

The smell of Mariah's vomit from the puddle beside her head mixed in with a metallic, burning chemical scent that permeated the air. I caught a glimpse of the bong on the table just before I began CPR on Mariah.

"The other times it wasn't like this. We never meant for anyone to get hurt," Jory cried out beside me.

I ignored the distraught Amish boy and focused on the job at hand. I wasn't going to let Mariah die because of a teenage moment of terrible judgment and rebellion.

I wasn't there for Naomi, but I still had a chance to save Mariah.

25

I held Mariah's hand as the ambulance made a safe effort to speed along on the snow covered country roads. I spotted the flashing lights that were well ahead of us and I sighed heavily wondering whether Rowan would even be alive when he finally reached the hospital. The wait for the paramedics to make it to the secluded cabin in the woods seemed to take forever, but in actuality, they had made amazingly good time in spite of the weather. If the snow hadn't been falling so heavily, I was certain that the county would have sent a helicopter to airlift Rowan, Mariah and Julian from the patch of woods that was about a half mile from a gravel road that intersected a main roadway. But it was too dangerous, so the paramedics had to drive in as far as they could go without getting stuck and make the rest of the way on foot. I was really impressed when the three pairs of medics and the troop of twelve uniformed officers came sliding down the embankment.

Brody had been with them too and I couldn't help but shiver when I remembered the guarded look he gave me when he saw his grandson in handcuffs. Nope, nothing had worked out the way I hoped it would. Asher was still on the loose, Mariah had OD'd, Damon, who had seemed to be a fairly nice young man, was now going to be charged with attempted murder, or maybe even murder, depending on if Rowan survived. Either way, I didn't think that Brody was going to be able to protect his grandson from jail time on this one.

And worst of all, Rowan was probably going to die, leaving his children as orphans. My throat constricted as the fleeting image of the three little girls' teary-eyed faces rose before me.

I shook the vision away and glanced at the medic beside me, who was monitoring Mariah's vitals and then down to Mariah again. Her face wasn't as pale as it had been in the cabin and it was relaxed in sleep. After she had thrown up the second time, right before everyone arrived, she had come alive in a sudden rush of tears and apologies. I had pulled her into a tight embrace and told her that it would be all right. But in reality I wasn't so sure.

Mariah's eyes fluttered opened again. It took a moment for her sight to adjust and for her to look around the inside of the ambulance. Finally her gaze settled back on me and she squeezed my fingers. I was instantly relieved by the strength of her grip.

"Thank you for riding to the hospital with me, Ms. Adams," Mariah's voice was thin and wispy. A worried frown appeared on her mouth and she hesitated, before saying, "Do my parents know?"

"Last thing I heard was that Sheriff Gentry was going to your farm to pick them up and take them to the hospital."

Mariah nodded weakly. "That's nice of him."

Yes, it is, I thought. I couldn't help but feel that Brody was a good man who had made some bad decisions. Did he know that three Amish kids had set fire to the barn that had killed his grandson? I suspected that he did. Why he had never acted on it was curious, but his feigned ignorance about what was going on with Asher Schwartz and his other grandson, Damon, was inexcusable. He had allowed a cancer to grow in his town, and it had spread to affect so many.

The bright street lamps and traffic lights were a welcome sight when we reached the town. "We're almost there," I told Mariah.

I held onto Mariah's hand until she was on the gurney and being rolled into the emergency room. At that point, a nurse politely asked me to go to the waiting room. I gave Mariah an encouraging smile and backed away.

The glass entrance doors opened and Brody came through them, along with Abner and Joanna Fisher in tow. Just before the doors closed, they opened again and Jotham joined them. My brows raised, but I didn't say a word about his appearance.

"How is she, Sheriff? Is my Mariah going to be all right?" Joanna asked as she rushed up to me and took my hands in a tight grip. The woman's eyes were desperate and wisps of her hair were sticking out all over the place, indicating a frantic departure from their home.

"She's talking and her vital signs are stable." I hesitated, after all I wasn't a nurse, but I decided to give my opinion and hopefully Joanna some peace of mind at the same time. "I think she's going to be fine."

Joanna hugged me and murmured into my ear, "Thank you."

I disengaged from Joanna and the bishop asked, "What happened to her?"

I exchanged an uncomfortable glance with Brody, who only sighed and looked away. Either the Poplar Springs' sheriff wasn't going to talk to them about it at all or he was going to say something that would probably upset them even more. I decided that the ball was in my court on this one.

I cleared my throat and looked at Abner and Joanna's expectant faces. "Have either of you noticed anything…different about Mariah lately? Maybe she's been moodier or more tired or a lot less social."

Joanna nodded vigorously. "Why yes, she's been very aloof lately, and always sassing back at me."

"Well, that's because she's been getting into some things that have affected her health and her mind. I'm sorry to say that your daughter has been doing drugs with a few of the other Amish kids." I said it as delicately as possible, but it still sounded so horrible.

Luckily, I only had to see Joanna's stricken face for an instant when a nurse popped up and asked if Joanna and Abner were Mariah's parents. The nurse quickly hustled them away to the counter, and I was left uncomfortably alone with Brody and Jotham.

I glanced at Jotham. As much as I tried to look neutral, I know that I failed miserably.

"How is my friend, Rowan?" He tilted his head at Brody and said, "Sheriff Gentry told me that it's pretty bad."

I nodded slowly and pursed my lips. The burning desire to confront Jotham about the barn fire nearly twenty years ago was only tempered by the obvious distress on his face. After quickly thinking it over, I decided that *that* conversation could wait a little longer.

"Honestly, I'll be surprised if he lives. His injury was substantial." I paused as a thought popped into my mind, "What about his kids—do they know?"

"I was visiting with Abner when the sheriff arrived and gave us the news. We stopped at the King's on our way here and I asked Anna to go to Rowan's and spend the night there so that the children wouldn't be alone, come morning. She'll tell them the news."

I breathed out in sudden relief that it would be Anna telling the kids about their father. The woman loved Rowan and his children and I was sure that she'd be there one hundred percent for them. But then I wondered who would be there to comfort her. I quickly let the thought go and said to Jotham, "The waiting room is over there. You're not going to be able to see Rowan until after surgery." Or maybe not at all if he dies, but I kept that to myself.

Jotham began to turn away and then suddenly stopped. "I don't understand exactly what happened tonight, but did you find out who has been setting the fires?"

I glanced at Brody who was still looking off into space, completely ignoring the conversation. "Yes I did. Right now, all you need to know is that your community doesn't have to live in fear that it will happen again. We got our man."

Jotham nodded acceptingly, but his lips were still tight. My gaze narrowed as I waited for him to speak.

Finally, he said, "And…did you discover anything else of importance?"

I stared hard at Jotham. He obviously suspected that I knew the truth about the ninety-seven fire, but was still playing cloak and dagger with me about it. And then there was the house explosion that killed Hedy Schwartz still on my mind.

"Actually I found out several new items of information tonight, but I still have a few questions unanswered. Don't worry. I'll be contacting you when it's a more appropriate time."

Jotham's eyes acknowledged that he understood. He said to Brody, "Thanks for allowing me to ride along."

I saw a wave of conflicted emotions wash over Brody's face as he watched Jotham walk away. Oh yeah, I was sure that he knew, but I still couldn't figure out why he didn't just go ahead and arrest Jotham. I was still too confused on the matter to speak up myself, and decided that the best course of action at the moment was to remain cautiously silent.

"How many men do you have looking for Asher?" I asked casually.

"I've called in the neighboring counties, probably about twenty-six officers out there right now." He seemed to be finished talking, but then he dared to look at me with moist eyes and asked, "What the hell happened?"

I had seen Brody talking to both Nathan and Cody and even Jory. He had also said a few words to Damon. And he had listened in as I had spoken to one of his deputies taking notes for the official report. He already had a pretty good idea of the way it went down, so I guessed that his question now was much more about the fire that had taken his other grandson's life.

"Asher and Julian had arranged to meet the Amish kids in the secluded hunting cabin to sell their wares. At the point that I arrived, Asher was outside arguing with Damon. The gist of the conflict was that Damon was growing concerned about the more dangerous type of drugs that were being provided to the teenagers. He was worried about the kids, especially since he was already aware that Asher's own girlfriend had overdosed on a bad batch of Hash oil." I paused and took a quick breath before continuing. "I already knew about Kristen Humphrey before I even went into the woods and had drawn the conclusion that the only reason Asher had burned down the Fisher barn was to hide the body. Damon knew that too… and so did you. But you chose to ignore it in an attempt to protect Damon from the law." Brody tensed, but remained silent. "I suspect that you feared that Damon had burned the other barns in retaliation for his brother's death, but once again, in an attempt to protect Damon, you didn't do your duty." I sighed and added, "You were afraid of Asher bringing Damon down with him, so you let him go along with his criminal activities…and now look at your town."

"You're right about most of it, except two things. I didn't have the woman's identity until this afternoon and secondly, I had no idea that Damon had set those other fires." He took a deep breath. "Now that part of the story is a little hazy from the boys' statements. Maybe you can enlighten me."

I was inwardly relieved myself. I really had hoped that Brody wasn't entirely corrupt. How the sheriff decided to handle the truth would be the ultimate judgment of his ethics, though.

"Damon was driving an old woman with Alzheimer's a few months ago and she let it slip that the fire that had killed your grandson and his girlfriend was set by a few of the Amish boys. He must have internalized the information, and decided to strike back. I knew early on that the Fisher barn fire was set by a different person than the others. I don't think that Damon intended to hurt anyone, even livestock, purposely. But there you go."

Brody was deep in thought and the silence was becoming uncomfortable when he finally spoke.

"Rowan set the fire that killed Austin?" Brody said the words slowly and carefully, never taking his gaze off me.

"We don't know that for sure. Asher's a psychopath. He might have been placing blame away from himself."

Brody's phone went off. I began to walk away to give him some privacy, but stopped when his hand touched my arm.

"Hello...what the hell...are you sure...all right...I'm coming."

Brody hung up and cupped his mouth in distress for a moment before he spoke. "That was one of my deputies. He said that Anna King had just met him on the road with her buggy. She told him that when she arrived to the Schwartz house, the littlest girl was missing."

My jaw dropped and I interrupted, "Maybe she's hiding or something."

Brody shook his head sadly and went on to say, "My deputy found blood in the house and a trail through the snow. It disappeared about halfway through the field, covered by the freshly fallen snow."

"Asher?" I dared to say.

"I would stake my life on it," Brody said steadily.

"I'm coming with you," Jotham said from behind us. He must have been listening.

I could hardly breathe, let alone argue about whether Jotham came with us or not. My only thought as we sprinted out of the hospital was that I should have shot Asher right in the head when I had had the chance.

26

I had hugged or been hugged by more women in the past few hours than I ever had in my life, I thought, as I pulled back from Anna to look at her tear streaked face. Her gray eyes were bloodshot and her usually pale skin was even whiter than normal.

"Why would he take her? I don't understand," Anna asked in between sniffs.

I put my arm around her shoulder and guided her over to the chair by the fireplace. Jotham was filling it up with wood in a fit of anxious energy as Anna sat down. I gazed around the room and noted that the two deputies were doing a good job at collecting samples of the blood on the floor and smeared on the door handle. The blood was Asher's, I was sure of it, but the evidence still needed to be collected to build a case.

The minister, Mason Gingerich, was seated at the table with Gabe and Seth, and his wife, Martha, was busily brewing coffee at the cooking stove. I knew that dozens of other men from the community were riding their hastily saddled horses through the snowy fields and along hedgerows in the darkest part of night. Again, it amazed me how quickly the Amish came together in a crisis, but the English were doing their part too, with over one hundred emergency response person-nel and neighbors already scouring the roads and fields.

I turned my attention back to Anna and said, "I think he's using Cacey to get out of town. She's a bargaining chip for him."

"He might hurt her," Anna cried out softly.

"Shhh, you don't want the boys to hear that kind of talk and you just got the girls back in their beds," I said, trying to keep the worry out of my own voice. "All you can do is keep on praying and let us do our job."

Anna nodded in agreement, but Jotham spoke up, "We aren't doing anything, Serenity, except sitting here, waiting."

The ruined part of his face twitched and, I wondered once again if he lived with constant pain from the scarring. His eyes were certainly shining with pain, but the psychological kind, not the physical kind.

I took a deep breath and told him once again what I had already told him five minutes earlier. "Everyone else is out there searching, hoping that by chance, they come across Asher and Cacey—and with the snow still falling it's going to be impossible to track them anyway. We're just going to stop, breathe and think." I spoke up louder, addressing the room, "Where do *you* think he would go with Cacey. He's a smart man and trudging through a snowstorm with a little girl is not something that he would likely rush into unthinkingly. He's also injured. Asher used to be Amish. There might be a safe place that he remembers from his childhood that he would go to hole up in until the weather breaks."

My own heart still thrummed against my chest, even though my words were spoken with calm sensibility. I knew the statistics all too well. The longer it takes to find a missing child the more likely that the child is dead. And I couldn't erase the memory of the sick smirk that Asher had directed my way, even after his brother had been shot. He was definitely deranged and I seriously worried that he'd use Cacey to take revenge on his former community. Asher was also the type of guy that would gladly go out in a blaze of glory if he thought that he had no chance of escape. I shivered thinking about it and looked up at Jotham with a pleading look that silently shouted, "Think man, think!"

It was Gabe who broke the hanging silence. "What about the schoolhouse? There are no classes this week…"

The mustached officer looked up and added, "And the schoolhouse isn't that far from Hoover Road, which goes straight to the interstate."

Bingo. I grabbed my coat and toboggan and headed for the door. Jotham was at my side and for the first time since I had first seen him at the hospital, there was hopefulness in his good eye.

"Be careful you two. After Rowan and Cacey, I don't think I could handle any more bad news," Anna called after us.

Over my shoulder, I replied, "Don't worry, we'll bring Cacey home."

It was still a long shot that Asher and Cacey were in the schoolhouse, but just in case, we parked about a quarter mile away on a side road and hiked through an open field toward the school, with the hopes of taking Asher off guard.

The snow was falling more gently now and the wind had subsided. I actually had to unzip my coat to keep from sweating too badly with the physical exertion.

"You must be exhausted," Jotham commented.

It was nearly one o'clock in the morning and this was my second hike through half a foot of snow that evening. Normally, I would have been passed out, but the adrenaline to find Cacey was keeping me going. I wouldn't be able to sleep until we found her.

"I'm all right. What about you? You've had a rough night yourself," I said, glancing at Jotham from the corner of my eye.

"God gives us the strength to keep going when we really need to."

"I hope God's with us right now, we might need Him," I said seriously.

Jotham smiled. "Oh, no worries, He's here."

His confidence made me feel a little better, but then the schoolhouse came into view and I took a measured breath. The building looked almost lonely resting on the snow covered knoll with only a large tree and a swing set as company. I didn't like the fact that if Asher was indeed in the school, he had a bird's eye view of anyone approaching. I suddenly wished that Jotham and I were both wearing white instead of black. If someone was indeed looking out of one of those darkened windows, we'd stick out against the snow for sure.

When we reached the fencing that enclosed the schoolhouse yard, I motioned for Jotham to stop. We kneeled on the ground, using the boards for a little bit of cover.

Jotham sighed and his breath was an icy puff in the air between us. "What's the plan?"

I liked that he had listened to what I said earlier in Rowan's kitchen. He was amazingly calm.

"Rowan is fighting for his life because he insisted on going into danger with me. Are you sure you want to do this? I'll be perfectly honest with you—we might not make it out alive."

A sad smile tugged at Jotham's mouth and a single tear fell from his good eye, but when he spoke, he was completely resolute.

"I was there to save Cacey's life five years ago," he swallowed, "I won't let her down now."

"All right then."

We stole silently up the softly rising hill, past the swing sets and only paused when we finally reached the trunk of the tree. I peeked around the bark and studied the building. All was eerily quiet and dark.

"There aren't any lights on," Jotham whispered.

"There wouldn't be. Asher's too smart for that," I replied, slowly running my gaze over the front of the building, stopping on the door. It had a small glass panel near the top and a silver colored knob. With the snow illuminating the scene, the red smear on the white board beside it was clearly visible—and exactly what I was looking for.

"Damn. He's in there," I said softly, pointing at the door for Jotham to take a look.

"He's injured. We have the advantage," Jotham said when he straightened back out.

"No, don't fool yourself into thinking that. Sure, he's lost a lot of blood, but I would guess that he has his hand wrapped by now…and he has Cacey. He's holding all the cards," I scolded him in a hissing whisper. "Here's what we're going to do…"

I carefully gave him instructions and then slipped away to the side of the building. I only hoped that God really was with Jotham, because I had just put the man's life in jeopardy.

27

I took a quick breath and turned the corner alone. Bending down, I passed directly below the windows at a jog, only stopping when I reached the back door that Jotham had told me entered into the school's kitchen.

Careful to not jingle the keys, I pulled them from my pocket. Since Jotham was one of the men who volunteered to do regular maintenance at the school, he had a set of keys into the building. Unfortunately, the handle was an older type that would be easy to jimmy open with the right tool. Since there weren't any broken windows, I assumed that must have been what Asher did to enter the front door.

The key turned with a quiet click that normally wouldn't have even been noticed, but with the desperate need for silence, the sound seemed to split the snowy night air. Pushing the door ever so softly, I peeked in. The room was empty, but there were a few wadded up sheets of paper towels on the counter. There was blood on them and the smell of a cleaning agent was still strong.

I closed the door quietly behind me and moved through the kitchen as if I was a ghost, listening, but careful not to make a sound. I took another steadying breath, hoping to slow down the pounding of my heart, which was blasting loudly in my ears as I pressed myself up against the wall and glanced down the hall way. The coast was clear.

As I began to step away from the wall, my back brushed against a broom that was hanging in the corner. There was a scraping sound that I stopped quickly with my hand. Holding my breath, I listened again.

It was still deathly silent. I suddenly wondered if we were too late. Asher might have already killed Cacey and taken his own life. It made no sense why he would bring the child into the equation if he was going to give up so easily, but crazy people often times did completely irrational things. I remembered a case that I had worked on in Indy where a bipolar mother had thrown her five month old baby boy into a frigid river in February and then shot herself on the bridge. Both had died and none of it made any sense at all. That was the really scary part. It couldn't even begin to be explained.

The muffled sound of movement at the end of the hall caught my attention and I quickly squeezed myself in between the counter and a trash can. It was a pretty lame hiding place, but I didn't have anywhere else to go.

I held my breath and listened. The sounds were definitely from the plastic tread of tennis shoes on linoleum.

I eased the gun from my side and forced myself to take shallow breaths. At this close range I only had one shot if Asher was armed. Poised on the ball of my foot, I prepared to go around the corner.

"Asher—where is Cacey?"

My heart immediately hit my stomach and I sagged. Dammit, Jotham was playing the hero.

There was a moment of silence, but I held my position and waited. Jumping out now could be a disaster.

"Why, Jotham. I didn't expect you to be visiting," Asher said sweetly.

I could hear Jotham slowly walking up the corridor as he answered in the soft tone of a person speaking to a child, "You don't have to do this, none of it. I know you're just punishing yourself, the same way I've done all these years. But it's over now. Rowan is probably dead and that sheriff woman has it all figured out. She knows, Asher. She knows what we did."

Sick curiosity stalled my forward motion and I continued to listen, but I also had my gun up and ready to shoot when the time came. I had a mental picture that Asher hadn't turned around yet and when he spoke, his voice was louder and clearer than Jotham's, telling me that I was right.

"Do you really think that's why I've become what I have?" Asher laughed and the jolting noise made me shiver. "I was fucked up way before we crept through the cornfield to the Gentry barn. My parents and their insistence that my only salvation was through the Amish was my downfall. They've shunned me, Jotham, ignored me, as if I didn't even exist, for nearly twenty years. But it wasn't my fault. I couldn't live that way any longer. I didn't give a fuck about Austin Gentry and his skinny little girlfriend. They meant nothing to me."

"You don't mean that," Jotham sounded appalled.

"Besides, I didn't light the match—Mr. Perfect, Rowan, did," Asher challenged.

"No, it wasn't Rowan at all. It was me. I'm the one who lit the match and tossed it into that wood pile," Jotham said with a quaking voice.

Asher's confusion was evident when he replied, "I was guarding the door, so I couldn't see you guys very well. But Rowan told me it was him. When his house blew up and Hedy died, he said that it was God's punishment. The only thing that kept him going was the kids."

"Rowan took responsibility for it because he was the oldest and he wanted to protect me. Even though he knew that Gabe was mine...he never turned his back on me."

"Well, damn. I guess that God punished you the same as He did my brother then," he mocked.

"Please, Asher, where's Cacey? She needs to go home," Jotham pleaded.

"Was it really worth getting half your face burned off visiting Hedy that night? Were you getting some action or what?" Asher growled and then paused when Jotham didn't answer him. He went on to say, "Cacey's in the coat closet in the first classroom, but you won't be taking her anywhere. She's my ticket out of here and you're going to be too dead to tell anyone anything."

At that instant, I left my cover and went around the corner. The shadow of Asher's body whirling around is all I saw when I fired. This time I did put the bullet into his head. But just as my weapon fired, another shot rang out, like a sickening echo.

My stomach clenched and I ran forward, jumping over Asher's body to reach Jotham who was also on the ground. I grabbed the flashlight from my pocket and shined it down on Jotham. The large hole in his black coat was all too obvious, but I frantically pushed the material away anyway. The blood seeping into his shirt was dark red and exactly where his heart was located. He should already be dead, I thought, as I leaned forward and smoothed the hair away from his face.

"Serenity," he said so weakly, that I had to bring my ear to his mouth quickly to hear his words, "please tell Sheriff Gentry what we did. He deserves to know." Jotham gasped for air, his mouth gaping grotesquely, but he managed to whisper, "Tell Gabe that I love him"

Jotham's head dropped to the side as he took his last breath and then he was still, except for the steady leaking of his blood.

I didn't have time to feel any remorse over a man who I barely knew. My gaze settled on the pool of blood beneath Asher's head for an instant and then I leaped up and ran down the hallway, turning into the classroom.

I flung the door to the closet open and found Cacey crouched in the corner with her wrists bound and a strip of gray tape across her mouth. I knelt down to her and as gently as I could, worked the tape away from her mouth. Once her mouth was free, I cut the thin piece of rope with my pocket knife.

Cacey leaped against me, flinging her arms around my neck. Her body bounced with her sobbing and her face was warm and wet against my neck.

As I rocked her back and forth, I finally began breathing again. My thoughts were bittersweet. I hadn't been able to save Jotham, and I didn't even know if Rowan was still alive, but I had managed to rescue two Amish girls.

28

aniel's hospital room was empty and I couldn't stop myself from inwardly cringing when I looked at the crisply made-up bed. I glanced out the window at the bright sunshine and let out a tired sigh. It must be almost noon, I absently thought.

After Brody and the rest of the deputies had arrived at the schoolhouse, Cacey was quickly taken away in an ambulance to have a thorough checkup, and then I had spent several hours being questioned about every detail of the night. I understood. There were two bodies and I was responsible for one of them.

The part that really irked me was after all that, I still had to go into the station to formalize my statements and make them all over again. Sure, Brody could hardly contain his joy at seeing Asher dead on the floor, but Jotham was another story. He genuinely seemed upset that the Amish man had lost his life, and I wondered if maybe he blamed himself for the chaos of the night. If he had arrested Asher earlier for any number of crimes, things might have turned out a lot different. But who was I to interfere at this point? Asher had a death wish and it was just a matter of time before someone killed him.

As for Jotham, he had seemed awfully sure that God was with him. And maybe He was. It was almost uncanny how really bad deeds always caught up with a person. I certainly wasn't going take the jobs of judge, jury and executioner on this one, but the whole life-for-a-life thing seemed to apply here, unfortunately.

Damon was in custody, and since Rowan had made it through surgery, there was a fair chance that he wouldn't die, after all. That meant Damon would only be charged with the barn fires and possibly attempted murder, and I had the tickling sensation that the Amish wouldn't even want to press charges. They'd chalk it up to punishment for their own cover up of the Gentry barn burning. How many of the community actually knew or suspected the truth, I had no idea, but the old woman had known, so I was willing to bet several others did as well.

On a hunch, I turned and walked out of the room and headed towards the intensive care unit. I stopped at the desk and quickly flashed my badge. It didn't matter that it wasn't my jurisdiction and that I had no legal right to be there, the shiny badge usually did the trick with nurses. When I said Rowan's name, the older blonde smiled and pointed to the room directly across from the nurse's station.

When I peeked into the room, I wasn't at all surprised to see Daniel sitting in the chair besides Rowan's hospital bed. I quickly absorbed the half dozen flower arrangements in the room and the tall cup of what I believed to be coffee on the table. Rowan's eyes were open and they widened when they saw me. A tangle of tubes stretched into his nose and both of his arms and his face were swollen. He looked terrible, but at least he was alive.

"Is that coffee, Daniel?" I asked bluntly as I walked into the room.

Daniel looked over his shoulder with a broad smile. He chuckled, nodding his head expectantly. "It's all yours. And it's warm," he said.

I picked up the cup, doing imaginary summersaults in my mind, when I took a whiff and discovered that it was strong, just the way I liked it. I took the only other chair in the room and slowly sipped the coffee. After everything that happened the night before, there wasn't an easy way to begin the conversation.

"Are you feeling all right?" I gazed at Daniel who was still smiling.

"I'm feeling a hell of a lot better now that you're here," he said with an even tone.

It embarrassed me that he would talk that way in front of Rowan, even though the man was probably so doped up that he wouldn't remember anything that was said the next day. It just bugged me a little that he presumed so much, and yet his words also sent a warm jolt to my insides.

I certainly didn't want Daniel to see my satisfaction, so I quickly turned away and asked Rowan, "What about you—are you on the road to recovery?"

Rowan was still very weak, but the whisper of a grin appeared on his mouth, and he said in a dry, cracked voice, "I thought the Lord was taking me to be with Hedy...but I guess He had other ideas."

I tried to think of something of significance to say—something clever about cosmic plans or even divine destiny. What goes around comes around? But I was just too wary to be philosophical.

"Yeah, you sure are lucky," I managed to say.

"I know about Asher...and I forgive you," Rowan said thinly.

I glanced at Daniel. "Boy, news travels fast around here."

Daniel nodded. "It is amazing that even without modern technology and cell phones, Amish gossip travels pretty quick," he motioned with his hand at the flowers and said, "Rowan's already had visitors this morning. Everyone in the community knows about it."

The suddenly serious expression on Daniel's face sobered me. He hadn't come right out and said it, but he had been worried about me. Looking into Daniel's eyes, we had a moment of connection that sent chills up my spine. I graced him with a small smile and returned my gaze back to Rowan.

The man's face was pale and drawn, but not so bad that I felt guilty about asking him a couple more important questions, if for nothing else than to wrap up the entire case in my own mind.

"Is what you said last night about the Gentry barn true...or did Jotham actually throw that match?" I asked quietly.

Rowan hesitated for only a moment and said, "Why do you ask?"

The cat and mouse crap had to stop. "Right before Jotham died, he told me that he had actually been the one to set the fire, but that you had insisted on taking the blame for it because you were the oldest of the group."

Except for the rhythmic beeping of Rowan's monitor, there was silence in the room that stretched on for such an uncomfortable amount of time that I glanced at Daniel questioningly. He only shrugged.

Finally, Rowan coughed a little and said, "Our ages weren't

the only reason that I shouldered the blame, but Jotham never understood that." Rowan sighed lightly and went on, "My father was suffering from diabetes. His medical expenses drained his own savings and he was struggling to support the family. In ninety-six he had to have his leg removed. After that, it was up to me and Asher to carry on the family construction business. I liked the job, so it wasn't too much of a burden on me, but Asher was another story altogether."

I couldn't help snorting, and Rowan paused to smile sadly at me before continuing.

"Asher was very resentful of the extra work and pressure he was handed. He was only fifteen at the time, so it's no wonder. But it's definitely what helped push him out the door for good." Rowan took another breath. His voice was becoming weaker and I was almost tempted to tell him that we'd talk later so that he could rest, but I didn't and he began speaking again. "Just before we went to the Gentry barn that night so very long ago, Michael Gentry, Austin's father had outbid us on a new housing contract. If we had gotten the contract, we would have been able to save our farm...and everyone, including Gentry knew it, but greed made him do it anyway. Others in the community helped us to buy back the house and twenty acres, but we lost one hundred and fifty acres. It nearly killed my father."

Rowan paused again to catch his breath and Daniel frowned at me. I glanced away not being able to take the accusatory look Daniel shot me. This was important. If he couldn't see that clearly, then that was his problem.

"That still didn't give three teenagers the right to set someone's barn on fire," I said simply.

"No, you're absolutely right. We were young and ignorant...and we didn't know that Austin and Kathryn were in the building. Afterwards when we heard the news, we were beyond devastated. Asher became angrier and more aloof than ever and Jotham, well Jotham felt the worst of us all because he had been the one to light the match."

A young nurse with her long brown hair pulled back in a ponytail entered the room at that very moment. The tension in the room must have been palpable. She hesitated and then said firmly, "You all are going to have to leave now. I have to check Mr. Schwartz's vitals and redo his bandages."

I accepted her words in defeat and began to rise, but Rowan put his hand out to stop me.

"Please, ma'am, just a few minutes more. This is very important," Rowan said with a steadier voice than I had heard from him yet. He was putting on a good show for the nurse.

The woman thought about it, glancing at me and Daniel and back at Rowan. Finally, she relented, saying, "All right. Five more minutes, but that's it."

Once she had disappeared through the door, Rowan quickly began speaking again. "Jotham did it for my family. He thought that if the Gentry's lost their equipment and had to rebuild their storage barn, they would have to back out of the contract. Of course, it was a horrible thing to do, but he was only sixteen at the time and he wasn't thinking clearly. None of us were."

I absorbed what he said with the conflicting prickling sensation of both pity and disgust toward Rowan. In all likelihood, Brody wouldn't be able to come up with enough evidence after all these years to charge Rowan, the only survivor of the crime, with murder, but manslaughter was still a possibility. The old woman who had originally let the cat out of the bag had Alzheimer's and wouldn't be considered a reliable witness. Basically, it was Rowan's word against Brody's.

"How many people in the community know of your involvement?" I asked slowly, hoping Rowan would get the gist of where I was going with the question, so that I wouldn't be forced to give him advice that was against every ounce of training and pledges I had taken as a law officer.

"The woman that Damon was talking about last night is Adeline Graber. Her husband, Simon, used to be our bishop. He knew, and a handful of elders, who are mostly dead now." Rowan met my gaze squarely and said, "We went to them immediately after we set the barn on fire, even before we had learned that Austin and his girlfriend were killed. Jotham and I felt so guilty about what we had done. We repented our sins to Bishop Graber."

"And he protected you by keeping your secret?" I felt my face flush in anger, but I managed to keep my tone soft.

"Don't be so upset with him, Serenity. He had a very difficult situation to deal with. On one hand, a barn had been burned down and two people had been inadvertently killed. On the other, Asher and I were needed to provide for our parents and family. There was no way to bring Austin and Kathryn back and it was a terrible accident. The bishop decided to leave it in God's hands."

I looked at Daniel with a raised brow, and he returned the same type of, 'Are you serious,' expression.

I knew the five minutes were ticking down and I wanted to take full advantage of Rowan's sudden openness before he decided to be Mr. Secretive again.

"I hate to be the one to tell you this, but there's no statute of limitations for murder in this state. And even though you didn't pull the trigger, so to speak, you were there and you let it happen. I'm sure that Brody will do everything he can to prosecute you to the fullest extent of the law."

Rowan nodded weakly.

"And it's the right thing for him to do. I will take full blame for my actions and tell Sheriff Gentry everything that I've told you," Rowan said with a stronger voice of determination.

It made me feel a little better that he was finally accepting responsibility. And Brody would get his closure too. Still, the idea of Rowan spending time in jail made me squirm inside. His kids needed him more than ever.

"The sheriff might try, but he's not going to be able to get you on murder charges. You will probably be convicted of a lesser crime and serve, maybe three to five years tops. Good behavior might get you out in two." I took a breath and added, "It's not the end of the world and definitely worth getting the ugly truth out in the open once and for all. Maybe Anna will stay with the kids if such a thing happened," I offered tentatively.

It might have been my imagination, but Rowan's drained face seemed to flush a little bit. He said, "That might be a possibility. And I'm sure my parents would help in any way they could."

I scooted to the end of my seat and looked deeply into Rowan's eyes. I had one more question to ask and I was really afraid of the answer.

"Was the explosion of your house an accident, or is there more to that story too?" I whispered.

I held my breath and waited.

A tear slipped from Rowan's eye and he said, "It was an accident, but my fault just the same. I should have taken the gas problem more seriously. But then again, I've always wondered if perhaps God was punishing me for my sins."

I sighed with relief. "Jotham thought that he was the one

being punished..." I stopped in mid-sentence. Jotham was dead. Hedy was dead. Even if Rowan had suspected all along that Gabe was really Jotham's son, what good would that knowledge do now? It would probably mess up Gabe to know the truth, and then he'd have to grieve over losing a biological father. Rowan would have enough on his plate in the upcoming months to work through. I certainly didn't need to add more trouble to his life. Maybe someday I would come back and tell him the truth, but not now.

I abruptly stood and said, "You need your rest and any second that uptight nurse is going to be back in here."

Rowan sluggishly lifted his arm, pulling the tubes with him, to offer me his hand.

I felt a little awkward taking it, but I got out of my comfort zone and did just that.

"Thank you for everything that you have done for me, my family and the community. Aaron was right about you."

"What did he say?" I ventured.

"That you were one hell of a woman."

29

I was surprised to see Mariah and Brandy waiting in the hallway for me when I left Rowan's room. They quickly walked over together and stopped in front of me while Daniel hung back at a discreet distance.

My gaze passed between the two girls, the most unlikely of friends. Mariah's skin was still a little pale, but much of the youthful pink complexion had returned to her face, and although her eyes were bloodshot, they were bright and alert. She was wearing a fresh, sky blue dress that matched her eyes perfectly. The cap on her head was crisp and white and concealed all of her brown hair, except for a little bit right above her forehead. She looked tired, but the girl was definitely going to be okay.

Brandy was Mariah's polar opposite. She wore a fitted jean jacket and tan suede boots. Her red hair hung wildly around her shoulders and her brown-eyed gaze sparked with energy. I briefly wondered how the two girls had become friends in the first place when Mariah began speaking.

"My parents are waiting for me in the van, but they allowed me to come looking for you."

I raised a questioning brow at Brandy and she smiled. "I came in to see Mariah. She's one of my buddies," she said as she reached over and put her arm around Mariah's shoulders and gave a squeeze.

"You're lucky to have a friend like Brandy. If it wasn't for her calling me, you might not have gotten to the hospital in time," I told Mariah.

Mariah nodded vigorously. "I know. I'm so thankful for both of you." She blinked, trying to hold back the tears. "I'll never do anything like that again."

I searched her eyes for a moment and decided that she was sincere. I still wondered what drove her to play around with drugs in the first place and said, "It's not as easy as just having the desire to straighten out your life, Mariah. There's always another reason for that kind of behavior. And I know with you being Amish and all, it's even more complicated."

Mariah's face sobered and she swallowed. She understood me perfectly.

"Mother is going with me next week to a special home for Amish kids who have…issues…like me. She's going to stay there with me until I'm all better."

"And don't forget, I'm going to visit you every weekend until you get out," Brandy promised.

I looked between the girls, feeling comfortable with Abner and Joanna Fisher's course of action for their daughter. I was sure that it would be difficult for the picture perfect Amish couple to accept that their child needed more help than they could give her, but they were doing the right thing. Mariah had the real opportunity of a happy future, especially with the support of a friend such as Brandy, unlike poor Naomi.

For the very first time since I had walked up to Naomi's body lying in the cornfield, I was able to think about her without a pounding sense of regret that I wasn't able to save her.

Somehow, helping Mariah and little Cacey erased all the anxieties about my first Blood Rock Amish case. I smiled. It was nice to feel a little bit lighter for a change.

Mariah and Brandy said their goodbyes, but before they'd gone more than a few feet, Mariah raced back and threw her arms around me. The hug was very quick, but also very strong.

When she pulled back, I assured her, "I'll get the information about that home you're going to from your mom before I leave. Maybe I'll pay you a visit myself."

Mariah's eyes rounded, "Oh that would be wonderful!" Mariah glanced at Daniel behind me and then with a quiet voice asked, "When are you leaving?"

I thought for a moment and answered, "I desperately need some sleep. I'm heading back to the Schwartz's to take a nap and then we'll be on our way, I believe."

"I'll see you soon then," Mariah smiled deeply and then hurried away with Brandy.

I thought back to the first time I had met the Amish girl and how distant and cool she'd appeared. It turned out that she was a bubbly teenager, after all. Just proved how messed up drugs could make a person.

"That was nice," Daniel said simply.

I grinned up at him and admitted, "Yeah, it was."

The sun was shining brightly when we exited the hospital and I was thinking how grateful I was that the snow from the night before had been cleared out of the parking lot when I heard my name called out.

I turned to see Brody striding purposely towards me.

"Can I have a word with you?" Brody asked, looking straight at me.

"Sure," I said, kind of wishing that we had left a few minutes earlier.

"You did some good police work," Brody said, surprising me. He quickly added, "Of course you broke about every rule of investigative etiquette imaginable, but you kept a level head, and that's saying a lot in this town."

"Thanks...I think," I replied.

"Asher's violent death was bound to happen sometime, but I wish Jotham hadn't died in the process." He took a breath and paused for a moment, thinking, and went on to say, "I remember the day I responded to the Schwartz's house explosion. If Jotham hadn't protected that little Amish girl with his own body, she would have died for sure, just like her momma."

I stared at Brody for a second wondering if he'd still feel bad about Jotham's death when Rowan told him the whole truth about the fire that took his grandson's life, but I highly doubted it. Human nature kept even a decent man from taking pity in a situation like that. I was hoping that I was wrong though.

Deciding to leave the details to Rowan, I said, "Are you going in to talk to Rowan now?"

Brody's mouth tightened, "Yeah, along with getting a statement from Julian West. He was too out of it to say anything coherent last night."

"You might have to wait on your conversation with Rowan. He was with the nurse, the last I saw," I offered.

Brody's brows rose high. "Did you already speak to him?"

"Just to tell him that Anna King was taking care of his kids," I lied easily.

"I take it you'll be heading home soon," Brody said it in a nice way, but it was more of a command than a question.

"If there isn't anything else you need from me, we're heading out later today," I said casually.

Brody nodded, "If I think of something, I know where to find you." He shook Daniel's hand and then mine, and was about to walk away when he paused, and said, "When you see him, tell Tony, I said hello. He needs to come up for a visit and a poker game."

I sighed with irritation, "Sure thing."

This time we'd just about made it to the car when Brody called after me once again.

"I know that you have a pretty snug arrangement in Blood Rock, but if you're ever in need of a change of scenery, I'd be honored to have you in my department." Brody tipped his hat and turned, finally leaving us for good.

"Did he just offer me a job?" I asked Daniel incredulously.

Daniel laughed. "He sure did."

Driving up to Rowan's house felt kind of surreal. The day was very much like the first one I had spent at the farm. The sun was shining and all the snow that had fallen the night before was melting quickly in a frenzy of drips from the corral boards and sheds we passed by. The black cows were separated into groups of four or five munching on round bales of hay, and several calves were laid out in the snow, enjoying the sudden warm up.

But what really caught and held my gaze was the pile of barn rubble. It was pushed into a giant, yet neat pile, and where the barn originally stood was a stack of brand new boards. Several men were marking out the dimensions of the new structure with stakes and strings and a few others were unloading more boards from the bed of a trailer. Once again, I was amazed by the Amish generosity and work ethic.

"That was quick," I commented to Daniel as I slowly drove by the workers to park in front of the guest house.

"You've got to take advantage of good weather in the winter." Daniel grinned.

I wondered why he was so damn happy. Had he secretly won the lottery or something?

"I'm going to check in on Anna and the kids and say goodbye. I only need about five hours of sleep. We can head out just after dark if it works for you," I told Daniel.

He was wearing a brown and black flannel shirt beneath his unzipped, stockman coat. The stubble on his jaw was almost a short beard and his eyes were tired, but otherwise he looked amazingly good for someone who had been shot and bitten by a dog the day before. Almost too good, I thought as I experienced the usual butterflies in my belly when I gazed at him.

"I'd like to catch a little more shut eye myself, but I think I'll go see what the new barn plan is first," Daniel said in a silky tone that was completely different than his usual tough-guy voice.

Our eyes stayed locked. I couldn't turn away, yet. I could almost smell the primitive scent of mutual desire in the air. My heart actually began racing. It was so uncomfortable that I broke contact and stepped out of the car. My knees were a little weak, which irritated me even more.

Not looking back, I went to the house. After knocking lightly, I heard Anna call for me to come in. When I opened the door, the delicious aroma of cinnamon, spices and baking dough assaulted my senses. I took a deep breath as I closed the door behind me, holding it in and savoring it fully before finally exhaling again.

I was surprised that Anna was alone with the girls. I had expected there to be a woman helping in the kitchen for every man working in the barnyard. But I had to admit, I was happy to have a few moments alone with them.

Cacey was covered in flour, but she dropped her ball of dough and jumped off the chair. She crashed into me with a hug. The flour that was all over her was transferred to me, but I didn't care. I squeezed her back and patted her on the head.

"You're a hero, Ms. Serenity!" Lucinda cried.

Lucinda had her fair share of flour on her too, but it was mostly concentrated on her apron. She was busily cutting up apples when she paused from her work to make her declaration.

"Not really. It's just my job," I tried to convince her.

"Oh, don't you dare make light of what you did for Cacey and Mariah and the boys," Anna scolded me.

I shrugged.

Mareena left the stove and put her arms around my middle and murmured, "Thank you for bringing Cacey back to us." She was only a few inches shorter than me, but she still had to lift her chin to look me in the eye. "I know Mamma would have been happy to hold her again, but we weren't ready to let her go yet."

Wetness threatened to fill my eyes at Mareena's words. I sniffed and stepped out of her embrace. I was way too sleep deprived for that kind of emotional sentiment.

"Are you going home today?" Lucinda asked with a disappointed frown.

"Yeah, I'm afraid so." I turned to Anna and added, "I'm going to try to get a few hours of sleep before I leave."

Anna nodded tightly and then turned to the girls. "Let's bring these mini apple pies out to the men to fill their bellies while they're working." When Mareena began to protest, Anna raised her voice and said, "Say your goodbyes, girls, and get going."

Cacey was the first one to move. She picked up several of the hand-sized pastries and placed them in a basket. She stopped in front of me and handed me one.

"Bye, Ms. Serenity," she said. Showing what a resilient spirit she had, she smiled up at me and then went out the door with a marching stride of determination to do what Anna had told her to.

Mareena and Lucinda filled their baskets more sluggishly and I caught a glimpse of Anna rolling her eyes. She had adapted to the role of their mother easily.

"Will you ever come back to visit us?" Lucinda asked after she hugged me for a long time.

I didn't hesitate. "Sure I will, maybe even this summer."

"That would be lovely," Mareena said. Her eyes were wet, too, and she hurriedly turned away and left with Lucinda.

When the door was shut and we were alone, I glanced at Anna before sitting at the kitchen table and taking a bite of the pie. It tasted as good as it smelled.

After I swallowed, I said, "I take it you want to speak to me alone?"

Anna took the seat across from me and let out a nervous sigh. "Did you see Rowan in the hospital?"

"I did. He's doing all right, all things considered," I told her.

Anna breathed and smiled a little with a nod of her head.

The poor thing had been strong for the kids, but inside she was a mess. I reached over and touched her hand.

The physical contact caused her emotions to rush out. "Is it true what everyone is saying—that Rowan took responsibility for burning the Gentry barn all those years ago?"

I didn't want to get into the whole Jotham part of the equation with her. It was too confusing and ultimately, I trusted Rowan to tell his story to the authorities and then to his people. It wasn't my place to bring it up.

I nodded. "That's what he said." When I saw her face drop, I hurriedly added, "but it's not the end of the world, Anna. Even if it somehow goes to trial and he's convicted, he won't have to serve too long, maybe a few years, tops."

Her eyes widened and then she sighed heavily. "Rowan was always distracted. I thought that it was losing his wife, but maybe it was the barn fire all along." She stopped and stared into my eyes with her own sharp ones. "Do you think he is a bad man?"

I had already asked myself the same question a dozen times, so I was prepared to answer her quickly. "No. Rowan is a good man who did something very wrong and reckless when he was a stupid teenager. We've all done things when we were young that could have turned out badly, but we were lucky. Rowan wasn't."

My statement seemed to be just what Anna needed to hear. She stood up and came around the table. When she reached me, she picked up my hands and squeezed. "That's what I thought. I just needed to hear it from someone else."

I rose and said, "Rowan is in for a rough time, both healing physically and dealing with the fallout from his confession. The kids are going to need you."

Anna smiled. "I know and I'm here for them, don't you worry about that."

By the time I stepped out of the warm kitchen and into the crisp air, I was wearier than ever. Saying goodbye was never my strong suit, and here I'd been forced to say it a half dozen times in less than an hour.

I lifted my face to the breeze and closed my eyes for a moment. In the short time that I had been in the house, clouds had moved in, blocking the sunshine and dropping the temperature several degrees. But it still felt nice. The cold wind was like a gentle shake to my shoulders, bringing me out of the moody depression that had fallen over me while I had listened to Rowan tell his story.

I stopped at the shed and patted both Dakota and Midnight before heading to the guest house. It was hard to believe that it had only been a few days since I'd shot the mamma cow. The really disturbing thing was accepting the fact that it had been more traumatic for me to put a cow of her misery than to kill Asher Schwartz. When it had happened, I almost took perverse pleasure in ending his wretched life. The only thing that had sobered me was Jotham bleeding out at the same time. Once again, I couldn't help but wonder if God really had a plan for everyone or if we were all just flying by the seat of our pants.

It was all so depressing, really. Several Amish kids buying illegal narcotics, revenge burnings, overdoses, secrets, lies, kidnapping…and several shootings—and all in one northern touristy Amish community. Who would have thought this trip would be so mind blowing. And the really crazy thing was that I still had a week left of vacation.

"Serenity, wait up."

I stopped and turned around. It was Gabe. Seth waved and went to the house, but Gabe walked up and met me at the door of the cabin. Looking into his blue eyes, a shiver crawled up the skin on my arms. It was as if I was seeing Jotham's good eye right before he died. There was no mistaking this boy's identity, but maybe now that Jotham was gone, everyone would forget his exact features. The Amish didn't keep portraits of themselves, so people had only their memories to guide them. In this case, that was probably a good thing.

"What's up?" I asked.

"Daniel said you're leaving tonight. Do you have to go so soon? I mean, you didn't really get to have any fun while you were here."

His words touched me deeper than any of the goodbyes or even shooting the cow. I quickly wiped the stray tear away and cleared my throat. "I would love to stay, but I have my own town to take care of. I came here to do a job…and that job is finished."

Gabe nodded slowly. "I understand, but I hope you'll come back someday." He hesitated and I knitted my brow together waiting curiously. "You didn't get to see our community in its best light. It's not always so…exciting around here."

I laughed and patted Gabe on the shoulder. "I know that. And I already told your sisters I'm coming back for a proper touristy vacation this summer."

Gabe grinned and was beginning to leave when I remembered something.

"Wait. There's something else," I took a breath, "Jotham wanted me to tell you that he loves you."

The words hung on the winter air as if they were shirts on a clothes line. I watched confusion play across his face for a moment, and then came understanding. He took a cautious breath and nodded. When he walked away, he stood straight and tall and his stride was long and relaxed.

He was going to be all right.

The one room cabin was bathed in soft afternoon light that made me instantly sleepy. I dropped my keys on the table and forced myself to meet Daniel's dark gaze. He rose from the bed and stood looking at me. I can only describe the look in his eyes as needing. I felt the same way, so I understood perfectly. All the violence and death of the last couple of days had left a coating of lonely despair all over me, and Daniel was feeling it also.

Without a word, he closed the distance. He grabbed my arms and pulled me against him. And then he kissed me. His lips were firm and fit perfectly against mine. He tasted so good, that I couldn't believe that I had not surrendered to him long ago.

When he nuzzled my neck, I made a hoarse noise that I never heard come from my throat before. The sound made Daniel groan in return. He pushed the coat off my shoulders in a single movement and I was only half aware of him helping me pull my shirt up over my head.

He stopped just long enough to gaze down at me for a moment and smile. His eyes told me that everything would be all right, his hands told me that he would never let go of me unless I forced him too. I had waited too long for this moment and now that it was really happening, I couldn't make it happen fast enough.

Daniel's breath was warm and minty against my ear, his fingers kneaded my hips and his tongue traced the corner of my mouth. Somehow, his shirt was off and my hands were rubbing into his back, forcing him even closer.

Then we were in the bed and our clothes were off. Our bodies were finally completely skin to skin and I marveled at how well we fit together, almost as if we were created only for each other. He kissed me again, deeper and harder than before. His fingers moved from my hips over my belly. Desperate chills raced through me and I couldn't stop myself from wantonly arching against him. But Daniel wasn't in as big of a hurry as I was. He leisurely traced a path between my breasts. His fingers moved over a nipple, causing me to cry out again. I couldn't have formed a coherent word if I'd wanted to. Daniel was relentless with the exploration of my body and I writhed beneath him as if I was a total slut. But for the first time ever, I didn't even care. I was being moved completely by instinct, and that was all.

Just when I thought I was going to faint dead away, he was inside of me. At first his rhythm was controlled and smooth as silk, but soon his pace quickened and I was the one in control. With a deep groan, he came just an instant after I did.

I was panting as if I'd run a mile and shivering at the same time. Daniel rolled over and pulled me up under his arm. His breathing was as erratic as mine and our sweat mixed together as we continued to stay tightly pressed against each other.

After a few quiet moments, my breathing returned to normal and I finally looked up at Daniel. He was already staring at me with glowing eyes that made me shiver all over again. The look on his face was so intense that it scared me a little. I had spent my entire romantic life since Denton trying to avoid such strong emotions towards a man, but here I was, completely lost to them. And it seemed that Daniel was, too.

"You are the most precious thing in the world to me," Daniel whispered.

Sure, it wasn't an, "I love you," but it was damn close. I almost opened my mouth to tell him how deep my feelings were for him as well, but instead, I swallowed a knot in my throat. Why was it so damn difficult for me to let Daniel completely in?

Daniel was waiting and I began to form the words in my mind, almost ready to push them out when my cell rang.

"Don't answer that," Daniel ordered.

It was perfect timing, so I wouldn't ignore it. I struggled away, inch by inch, and then stretched to reach my coat lying on the floor. I managed to answer the phone on the last ring. Daniel rolled onto his back and growled.

"Hey, Todd—what's up?"

"I was going to ask you that. How did my intel work out?"

"Uhm, well, it was right on. It's a pretty long and crazy story, perfect for a retelling at lunch time on Friday at Nancy's Diner. Make sure Bobby joins us, too. He'll love this one."

"Glad to hear that you're coming home, especially now," Todd said flatly.

I laid back into the pillow with the feeling of apprehension crawling all over me. "What now?"

"It's Aaron Esch—remember him—our cult leader? Well, he's in a tizzy about a new Amish family that's moved into town."

"That doesn't have anything to do with the sheriff's department," I stated flatly.

"I don't know—something about strange healing practices. It sounded like voodoo shit."

I really wanted to say, "That's impossible," but I'd been down that road before. Anything was possible with the Amish.

Instead, I said, "Get as much information as you can and we'll meet in my office on Friday morning."

"But it's only Monday," Todd complained.

I cut him off. "If you haven't forgotten, I'm still on vacation," I reminded him and then I hung up. I turned the phone off and tossed it onto my pile of clothes on the floor.

When I rolled back over into Daniel, he was already facing me with a broad smile on his mouth. "You're not rushing back to Blood Rock after all?"

I lifted my hands up and cupped his face, bringing his mouth back to mine. This time the kiss was less urgent, sweeter, and I savored it in the same drawn out way that I had the delicious apple pie. Only Daniel tasted even better.

When we finally came up for air, I whispered, "This rustic little cabin is beginning to grow on me. Maybe we should stick around here for a few days and do the tourist thing. I always wanted to shop for crafts," I teased.

"There won't be any time for shopping…I promise you that," Daniel breathed and then his mouth was on my breast again and I couldn't think at all.

Look for the next chapters in Serenity's story, UNHOLY GROUND & BLOODY TIES, to hit the shelves in 2020. You might also enjoy the romantic companion books, FORBIDDEN WAYS & SWEET REGRETS.

Thank you for reading!

You can find Karen Ann Hopkins and all her books at https://www.karenannhopkinsfiction.com Karen Ann Hopkins, Serenity Series, at Amazon

CPSIA information can be obtained
at www.ICGtesting.com
Printed in the USA
LVHW080604240620
658856LV00011B/700